RENEGADE JUSTICE

"What should I do?" Touch the Sky asked Arrow Keeper. "I am a *Shaiyena*. But my white parents are the soul of my medicine bag. How can I let these things happen?"

"Do you realize what the rest will say if you desert your tribe now? And, little brother, have you considered Honey Eater? She loves you. But Black Elk loves her. When her father dies, she will need you more than ever. She will be alone. A Cheyenne who is alone is a dead Cheyenne. Do you go to help the whites who raised you, knowing it may turn your tribe against you forever and cost you Honey Eater?" Arrow Keeper asked. "Or do you stay?"

VISION QUEST

Wolf Who Hunts Smiling lunged. Touch the Sky pivoted hard to his right and felt his enemy's blade nick the leather band around his left wrist as it passed harmlessly by. Touch the Sky leaped on top of the powerful Cheyenne and wrestled him to the ground.

"Stop!" Arrow Keeper shouted. "I forbid this fighting."

"But Father," Wolf Who Hunts Smiling said, "he—"

"Silence! Return to your clan circle."

After Wolf Who Hunts Smiling had departed, his face a mask of hatred for his enemy, Touch the Sky started to leave. But Arrow Keeper called his name.

"Yes, Father?"

"I have had a medicine dream. The vision tells me you will die soon."

The *Cheyenne* Series:

JUDD COLE

CHEYENNE

RENEGADE JUSTICE / VISION QUEST

LEISURE BOOKS   NEW YORK CITY

A LEISURE BOOK®

September 1997

Published by

Dorchester Publishing Co., Inc.
276 Fifth Avenue
New York, NY 10001

Printed in the United States of America.

RENEGADE
JUSTICE

Prologue

When the short white days of the cold moons had ended, Running Antelope of the Northern Cheyennes and his party of 30 braves were ambushed near the North Platte by Bluecoat pony soldiers.

Running Antelope was a peace leader, not a war chief, and his band flew a white truce flag. His wife Lotus Petal and their infant son accompanied him in order to visit her Southern clan. Badly outnumbered, the Cheyennes sang their battle song and fought bravely with their bows, lances, clubs, and single-shot muzzle-loaders. But they were no match for the Bluecoats' thundering wagon guns and percussion-cap carbines. The lone survivor of the bloody assault was the squalling Cheyenne orphan.

The child was taken back to the river-bend settlement of Bighorn Falls near Fort Bates in the

Wyoming Territory. Raised by John and Sarah Hanchon, owners of the town's mercantile store, he was named Matthew. Despite occasional hostile glances and remarks from some whites, he grew up feeling accepted in his narrow world.

Then came 1856, his sixteenth year, and tragedy: Matthew's forbidden love for Kristen Steele, daughter of the wealthiest rancher in Bighorn Falls. A jealous young officer from Fort Bates, Seth Carlson, eager to win Kristen's hand in marriage, threatened to ruin John Hanchon's contract with the fort unless Matthew cleared out for good.

The saddened youth left his white parents and rode north into the upcountry of the Powder River, hostile Cheyenne country, determined to find a place where he fit in. Captured by Cheyenne braves from Chief Yellow Bear's camp, he was accused of being a double-tongued spy for the whites. He was sentenced to death by torture.

Only the intervention of old Arrow Keeper, the tribal medicine man, spared him. The shaman recognized the birthmark, buried past the youth's hairline, from a recent and powerful medicine vision: a mulberry-colored arrowhead, the mark of the warrior. Arrow Keeper hoped it was not a false vision placed over his eyes by his enemies. If true, this young buck was destined to lead his people in a great, victorious battle against their enemies.

Renamed Touch the Sky by Arrow Keeper, the tall youth was hated by the rest of the tribe, especially a stern warrior named Black Elk and his bitter young cousin, Wolf Who Hunts Smiling. Black Elk was stung by jealousy when he realized that Chief Yellow Bear's daughter, Honey

Eater, loved Touch the Sky instead of him. And Wolf Who Hunts Smiling openly walked between Touch the Sky and the campfire—the Cheyenne way of announcing his intention to kill the suspected spy.

Touch the Sky bravely and cunningly employed his white friend Corey Robinson in a bold plan to save the Cheyenne village from annihilation by Pawnees. He was honored in a special council, and Honey Eater secretly declared her love for him. But he was still far from full acceptance as a warrior.

Then whiskey traders invaded Indian country. Once again Touch the Sky was suspected of spying for the long knives—the traders tricked him into getting drunk with them, convincing his angry friend Little Horse that he was one of them. The traders, led by the ruthless Henri Lagace, threatened to rapidly destroy the Indian way of life with their strong water.

But Lagace didn't stop at peddling devil water. He and his men were also fond of getting Indians and other white traders drunk, then slaughtering them in their sleep and robbing them—and making the massacres look like Cheyenne handiwork. The panicked Territorial Commission declared a bounty on the scalp of any and all Cheyennes.

The peace-loving Chief Yellow Bear knew his warriors had to paint their faces for war against Lagace if the Cheyennes were to survive. But Lagace kidnapped Yellow Bear's daughter. He threatened to kill Honey Eater if the war was not called off.

Yellow Bear could not sacrifice the tribe to spare Honey Eater. The only hope was to send a small Cheyenne war party, led by Black Elk, into the heavily fortified white stronghold. Touch the Sky was told, in a medicine vision, that he must defy Black Elk or Honey Eater would die. He deserted the war party and infiltrated the white camp on his own.

Taken prisoner, he was brutally tortured. But his courage in defying the whites rallied the other Cheyennes to mount an heroic surprise assault. They scattered the whites and freed Honey Eater. Touch the Sky then pursued his enemy Lagace across the plains until he killed him, ending the scalps-for-bounty decree and the immediate threat to the Cheyennes.

But much of his valor went unwitnessed. Many of his enemies within the tribe were still unconvinced of his loyalty. He was still trapped between the white man's hatred and the red man's mistrust.

Chapter One

"Shorten the reins, Wade!" shouted John Hanchon. "You want to control his head!"

Hanchon was perched on the top pole of a corral so new it still reeked of fresh pine. He was a thickset, middle-aged man wearing a broadbrimmed plainsman's hat, sturdy linsey trousers, and calfskin boots.

He watched his foreman expertly snub the reins so the mean roan bronco couldn't get its head down for some serious bucking.

"Some horses hate the saddle, others save it for the rider," he explained to the two men flanking him on the corral pole. "Each horse bucks to its own pattern. You don't try to power a strong pattern bucker. You learn to feel it coming and ride with the motion."

The three men watched the roan futilely sidejump a few more times before it finally gave up and stood defeated, its bit flecked with foam. A cheer rose from the rest of the hands scattered around the corral. This was the spring's first "Sunday ronnyvoo" at John and Sarah Hanchon's new mustang spread, and a festive spirit hung in the air.

"You got a fine spread here, Mr. Hanchon," said Corey Robinson, a freckle-faced redhead with a gap-tooth grin. He was 16, the youngest of the trio seated on the corral pole. "I wish to Jesus my pa would get out of the preaching business so we could start us a spread. It ain't just Fort Bates that needs remounts. Seems as how every keelboat crew that comes past Bighorn Falls is looking for good horses and mules to take out west with them."

"Sure, there's good money in it," said the third man, Corey's friend Tom Riley. He was a brevet officer, an enlisted man temporarily promoted from the ranks until more commissioned lieutenants arrived at nearby Fort Bates. He was 20, a rangy, clean-cut towhead whose face was sunburned where the black brim of his officer's hat turned up on one side. "But it's damn hard work breaking green horses to leather."

"Speak the truth, lad, and shame the devil," said Hanchon. "And it takes money to make money. Sure, my herds are grazing the new grass now. But I had to hay them all winter long. It took everything I made from selling the mercantile just to weather the cold."

"It ain't fair," said Corey. His freckles stood out even more as he flushed with anger. "It's bad enough that Hiram Steele drove Matthew off like he was a killer coyote hanging around the henhouse. There was no call for running you out of business."

At the mention of his adopted Cheyenne son, the seams in Hanchon's face deepened. He still didn't know exactly what had passed, nearly one year ago now, between Matthew and the wealthy rancher Hiram Steele. Whatever it was, it somehow involved Steele's daughter. And it had been serious enough to send Matthew packing for good in the middle of the night. Though his good-bye note made it clear he was leaving to protect his adopted white parents, his departure still hadn't been enough for Hiram Steele—he and friends at Fort Bates had conspired to turn the once-friendly fort sutler against Hanchon. When orders from the fort began going to the mercantile at Red Shale, Hanchon's mercantile in Bighorn Falls was doomed.

" 'Fair' don't mean spit to a man like Steele," said Hanchon bitterly. "I was doing tolerable well until he ruined me. But I'm plumb bullheaded when I get my dander up. That's why I started this mustang spread. Oh, I knew there'd be trouble. I knew Steele wouldn't set still for this. He's the kind that always figures there's too many pigs for the tits. Still, I never marked him down for a common criminal. My hand to God, I thought he'd get used to the notion of another spread in this valley. So far I'm wrong."

Hanchon pointed toward one corner of the house, where the wood was badly charred.

"A while back, riders came in the night and tried to burn us out. All winter long, I found mustangs in my herds that'd been shot dead. My hands have been dry-gulched and beaten. It's gettin' to be the devil's own work just to keep enough help around here."

It was the spring of 1857. Up in the higher

country the golden aspens were coming to leaf, and the winter ice no longer had the valleys locked. Hanchon and his men had recently moved the mustang herds out from their nearby winter range to an outlying summer range dotted with new hayricks.

The Hanchon spread was located in a fertile piece of bottom land where the Tongue River oxbowed just south of Bighorn Falls in the Wyoming Territory. The split-log house was surrounded by a raw plank bunkhouse and outbuildings, two huge pole corrals, a stone well, and a long stone watering trough.

"Good lands!" said a cheerful female voice behind them. "Men surely do love to raise the dust!"

All three men turned around to a pleasant sight: Sarah Hanchon, her copper hair pulled into a tight bun, looked gay and lively in a bright yellow gingham dress. The young beauty at her side, Kristen Steele, smiled shyly when Corey and Tom hastily jumped down off the fence and touched the brims of their hats. She wore a dark calico skirt and a white shirtwaist. China-blue eyes were offset by a golden waterfall of hair tumbling down over her shoulders.

"Miss Steele," said John Hanchon, smiling with obvious pleasure at seeing her. In his book, Hiram's daughter was as pleasant and decent as her father was mean and low-down. No wonder that Matthew had fallen in love with her—what healthy young sprout wouldn't?

"I can't stay long," she said apologetically. "Pa would have a conniption if he knew I was here. But I wanted to see your new place."

A horse whickered loudly, capturing everyone's

attention. They all turned to watch a hired hand rope a white mustang and lead it into the horse-breaking pen. First the hand carefully checked his saddle, cinches, latigos, and stirrups. Then he examined the halter and rein. The horse had already been choked and water-starved until it could be saddled and harnessed. Finally the hand cinched on the bronc saddle and swung up into leather.

Cheers and shouts rose from the rest of the hands as the rider put spurs to his mount and rode it with his rowels until the bucking mustang rolled its eyes in fury, showing the whites.

A moment later a rifle spoke its piece, and the mustang collapsed as a scarlet rope of blood erupted from its flank.

"God-in-whirlwinds!" said Corey.

Suddenly the air was alive with more gun-shots, the hollow thunder of hooves. From a long, sloping rise behind the house, a group of six marauders bore down on the gathering. Their faces were hidden behind bandanas.

A claybank horse crumpled, whickering pit-eously, as a bullet caught it in the hindquarters. More slugs thwacked into the corral poles, raised plumes of dust, flew past their ears with a sound like angry hornets.

"You two!" Hanchon shouted to his wife and Kristen as he scrambled down from the corral pole. "Into the house!"

It was Sunday, and the only man carrying a weapon was Riley. He unsnapped his stiff leather holster and drew the silver-gripped Colt service revolver.

Some of the hands were already running toward the bunkhouse for their weapons. But the attackers, anticipating this, laid down a withering field of fire between the corral and the bunkhouse. Two hands went down, wounded, before Wade McKenna shouted out the order to take cover instead.

Hanchon had fled into the house with the women. Now he burst back out through the leather-hinged door, a .33-caliber breechloader in one hand, a lever-action Henry in the other.

"Corey! Heads up, boy!"

Hanchon tossed the breechloader to the youth. Riley had already taken cover behind the stone watering trough, taking aim. He was reserving his ammunition until the attackers were within short-arms range.

A yellow cloud of dust boiled up behind the riders. Wood chips flew from the corral poles and outbuildings; another horse whickered in pain and went down. The other horses had panicked, and now their shrill nickering added to the din of shouts and gunshots.

Hanchon, standing in the open, fired the long-barreled Henry. One of the attackers slumped in his saddle but hung on, one hand covering the wound in his thigh.

"Cover down!" shouted Riley to Hanchon, jumping up and dragging the older man behind the trough with him and Corey. Now the attackers were within easy range, and all three men returned fire in earnest.

Another marauder slumped, then slipped from his mount. One foot caught in the stirrup so that his dead body bumped and leaped over the uneven ground. This broke the momentum of the attack. Another rider caught the dead man's horse, dismounted, and tossed their fallen comrade across his saddle. Abruptly, the group veered west toward the Bighorn Mountains.

The raid had been sudden and fast, but took a grim toll: two hands wounded, one seriously, and three horses dead or dying. The men carried the gut-shot hand into the house and the women tended to him while another hand, a rifle poking from his saddle scabbard, rode out to Widow Johnson's place on Sweetwater Creek. She was the closest thing to a doctor in the territory.

"Who in tarnal hell was it?" said Riley after the rest of the men had armed themselves and formed a perimeter guard in case of a second attempt.

Hanchon, staring at the dead claybank he had just put out of its misery, shook his head. Another hand had just quit on the spot and demanded his wages, claiming only a soft-brained fool would risk his life like this for beans and sowbelly. Hanchon knew he was right: This wasn't their fight.

"I didn't recognize any of 'em. But I'll wager Hiram Steele knows who they are."

"Steele's a rich man," said Riley. "And he's been selling remounts to the fort for a long time. I don't have much authority, but if he's behind this, I swear he *won't* get away with it."

"I expected trouble, but I never figured Steele had the stomach for this kind of business," said Hanchon bitterly. "He knows I can't go to law against him. The nearest U.S. marshal is in Laramie. That's two days' hard ride from here. 'Sides, what proof do I have?"

"The Army is the law out here," said Riley. "I'm going to my superiors about this. I'll take Corey as a witness."

Hanchon slowly nodded. "Give it a try, lad. But Steele is thick as thieves with that bunch at the fort. I got a feeling I'm in for six sorts of hell."

"The U. S. Army has no jurisdiction in civilian legal conflicts," said Lieutenant Seth Carlson. "We protect the settlers from Indians, yes, but *not* from each other."

Carlson was close to Tom Riley's age. But he held a permanent commission, and currently served as the adjutant to the commanding officer of the 7th Cavalry.

He was also, thought Corey, an arrogant, sneering bastard. Corey felt a warm glow of satisfaction as he recalled what Old Knobby at the feed stable in Bighorn Falls had told him—how Matthew had set the officer on his duff with two good punches.

"But sir—"

"Keep your 'buts' in your pocket, mister! You don't speak until I'm finished. I want to know why you took Kristen Steele out to the Hanchon spread with you?"

Riley's jaw slacked open in surprise at the unexpected question.

"We didn't take her. She came on her own, far as I could tell."

It was Carlson's turn to look surprised. He rose from behind his desk at Regimental Headquarters and paced nervously back and forth in front of a huge wall map of the Wyoming Territory. His hand rested on the hilt of his saber, nervously working it.

"She came on her own," he repeated woodenly, as if storing the fact away for later. Corey was not as baffled as Riley—he knew Carlson was trying to stake a claim to Kristen Steele. In fact, the jealous officer had jumped Matthew after learning about his secret visits to her.

"Yes, sir, on her own. But she's not the point here."

"Stow it, mister! The *point* is, from now on you best make sure she stays away from the Hanchon spread. Is that clear?"

"She's a civilian. What law says she can't visit where she's a mind to?"

"The same law that says my permanent silver bar outranks your temporary gold one. Is *that* clear?"

"Yes, sir."

Riley was visibly angry. But Corey realized he was also powerless.

"Are you saying," said Corey, "that you don't plan to do *nothing* about this?"

Carlson's lips curled in a sneer. "Clean the wax outta your ears, boy. That's exactly what I said."

"This ain't fair! John Hanchon done honest business with this fort for years."

"He *done* business with this fort," said Carlson, cutting him off. "You got that part right. But that's all behind us now."

Hot blood crept up the back of Corey's neck. "You got no right to let the Hanchons be drove out just on account of you had a fight with their boy Matthew."

"Stow it!"

"I ain't in no damn Army," said Corey. "You don't push me around."

But Riley gripped Corey's arm above the elbow, silencing him.

"Permission to leave, sir," he said to his superior.

Carlson glanced at Corey for a full ten seconds. "Dismissed," he finally said curtly.

Riley took two steps backwards, saluted smartly, then did an about-face and left, Corey in tow.

"We did what we could," said the young officer as Corey prepared to mount and leave the fort. "I'll keep my eyes peeled. But Hanchon was right as rain. There's no help to be had here."

Corey was silent for a long time, thinking. He knew that Matthew's tribe—Yellow Bear's Northern Cheyennes—had established their winter camp just north of the Bighorns halfway between the Powder and the Rosebud Rivers. But by now they would have returned to their summer camp at the fork where the Little Powder joined the Powder. It was perhaps three days' hard ride from here.

Corey slipped three fingers into the fob pocket of his vest, touching the specially notched and dyed blue feather which he always kept there. It had been given to him by Chief Yellow Bear himself after Corey had helped to save Yellow Bear's tribe from a Pawnee raid. It also guaranteed safe passage through Plains Indian country: Show it to any tribe, Yellow Bear explained, no matter if they were Sioux or Arapahoe or Shoshone, and they would treat him as a brave and honored friend of the red man.

Right there on the spot, Corey made up his mind.

"You're right," he said to Riley. "There's no help to be had here."

Corey knew Matthew was still his good friend, even though he was now called Touch the Sky and rejected the white man's ways. And he would never forgive him if Corey sat idly by while Matthew's adopted parents were ruined and driven out—maybe even killed.

Soon all hell's gonna be a-poppin', thought Corey. *But tomorrow I ride north into Cheyenne country.*

Chapter Two

Touch the Sky lifted aside the elkskin flap covering the entrance to his tipi and stepped out into the cool morning mist.

His sister the sun was just beginning her journey across the sky. The short white days of the cold moons were over. It was now the Moon When the Green Grass Is Up, and the Cheyenne pony herds had been turned loose from their rope corrals to graze in the lush meadows bordering the Powder River.

Touch the Sky had 17 winters behind him. The young Cheyenne was lean and straight and tall, with a strong hawk nose and keen black eyes. His black hair hung in loose locks except where it had been cropped close above his brows to keep his vision clear. He wore beaded leggings, a breechclout of soft kid leather, elkskin moccasins.

He paused outside his tipi and listened to the strong, deep voice of an old squaw as she sang the Song to the Sun Rising. Then he glanced across the camp clearing toward a lone tipi reigning by itself on a low hummock between the river and the rest of camp: Chief Yellow Bear's tipi.

White plumes curled from the smokehole at the top. But Touch the Sky knew it was not smoke from a cooking fire. The old chief lay near death. Now the tribal medicine man, Arrow Keeper, kept incense burning day and night while members of the tribe took turns sitting beside the chief's sleeping robes, singing the ancient cure songs.

Most of the tipis were erected in circles by clans. The center of camp was reserved for the council lodge—a huge willow-branch frame covered with buffalo hides. In front of the council lodge, a pole had been carved with the magic totems of the tribe. The enemy scalps dangling from it looked like tufts of coarse hair clipped from horse tails.

A cooking fire blazed in front of Arrow Keeper's tipi. Touch the Sky felt his stomach churning in hunger when he smelled elk steaks sizzling over the tripod. He had started to cross the clearing toward Arrow Keeper's tipi when a mocking voice behind him stopped Touch the Sky in his tracks.

"Woman Face!"

Angry blood pulsing in his temples, he turned to face the speaker.

"You are walking in the wrong direction," said Wolf Who Hunts Smiling. "The women's sewing lodge is at the other end of camp."

The speaker had a wily face befitting his name, with swift, furtive eyes that missed nothing. Wolf

Who Hunts Smiling had been present when Bluecoat pony soldiers killed his father. Now he despised all whites with a hatred unmatched by anyone else in the tribe. He had accused Touch the Sky of being a spy for the whites ever since the wandering outcast had been captured still wearing his white man's clothing. The mocking name "Woman Face" was a reference to Touch the Sky's former habit of letting his emotions show in his face—a white man's habit despised by Cheyennes as unmanly.

Touch the Sky saw Wolf Who Hunts Smiling carefully eye the knife in his sheath. The obsidian blade was small but honed on one side to a lethal edge that could shave the callus off a pony's hoof.

"Call me Woman Face again," said Touch the Sky, his features stony, "and you will humiliate your clan when this *woman* feeds your liver to the dogs."

Wolf Who Hunts Smiling was accompanied by another of Touch the Sky's sworn enemies in the tribe, Swift Canoe of the Wolverine Clan. Swift Canoe blamed him for the death of his twin brother, True Son, during a raid against the lice-eating Pawnees. But Touch the Sky alone knew it was Wolf Who Hunts Smiling's disobedience which had alerted the Pawnees and resulted in True Son's death.

Both of his enemies stared at him, their eyes revealing the hatred their faces refused to show. But wisely, neither of them tested his boast. They had witnessed his courage under torture and strength in battle.

"He talks the he-bear talk now," said Wolf Who Hunts Smiling. "He knows he is safe here in the middle of camp. Perhaps he has forgotten that I have walked between him and the fire."

"I have not forgotten this thing," said Touch the Sky. "What? Forgotten it? I am weary of hearing you repeat it like the camp crier. Words are nothing, things of smoke. Let your battle axe speak for you. For my part, I have no desire to kill either of you. Have you listened to the counsel of Arrow Keeper and Yellow Bear and the elders? We have enough enemies. It is foolish to kill each other."

For a moment, his unexpected words softened the hatred in the eyes of his enemies. Then, perhaps recalling the sight as Bluecoat canister shot turned his unarmed father into stewmeat, Wolf Who Hunts Smiling said bitterly, "A dog who sleeps in manure stinks like manure. You may dress like a Cheyenne, talk like a Cheyenne. But you have the white man's stink on you for life!"

Touch the Sky abruptly turned his back on both of them and joined Arrow Keeper. The old shaman had squatted near the tripod to collect the tasty fat dripping from the steaks, catching it on a broad leaf.

"Good morning, Father. How is Yellow Bear?" the youth greeted him. Wolf Who Hunts Smiling's parting remark had left angry veins pulsing over his temples. Perhaps it was true and Touch the Sky didn't have the courage to accept it. Perhaps he *did* have the white man's stink all over him.

Arrow Keeper, whose medicine bundle was the owl, drew his blanket around him tighter and slowly shook his head. The old medicine man's long gray hair was shot through with parched white streaks. His ancient face was still hatchet-sharp in profile, but as wrinkled as an old apple core.

He made the cut-off sign in answer to Touch the Sky's question. It was bad luck to use the word death directly.

"He will soon be called to the Land of Ghosts. I fear greatly for the tribe. The loss of a chief is strong bad medicine for his people. Our enemies, hearing of it, may well choose such a time to attack."

These words troubled Touch the Sky. He had already witnessed the awful death and destruction Pawnees had inflicted in a surprise raid on Yellow Bear's tribe.

Arrow Keeper read these thoughts in the young buck's troubled eyes. It was the old shaman's important mission to protect the tribe's four sacred Medicine Arrows with his very life. The fate of the arrows, always kept clean in their coyote fur pouch, was the fate of the tribe. If the Medicine Arrows were lost, the tribe was lost.

"Yellow Bear has served his ten winters as chief," said Touch the Sky. "Cannot the Headmen appoint a new leader?"

Arrow Keeper shook his head. "The chief-renewal ceremony should be held now that the snows have melted. But the Sun Dance, and the required feasting, cannot take place while our chief lies ill."

Touch the Sky glanced again toward Yellow Bear's tipi. "And Honey Eater? How is she?"

Worry smoldered deep in Arrow Keeper's dark eyes as he thought about Yellow Bear's daughter. "She is like a beautiful lark that has forgotten how to sing. Her father's death will leave her alone. You must be strong. She loves you straight and true, little brother. But as you know well,

Black Elk has already sent her the gift of horses. True, she returned them. But her father was well then. The Cheyenne way will not permit her to remain unmarried for long once her father leaves this world."

Touch the Sky nodded, deeply troubled. Only a battle-tested warrior could court and undergo the squaw-taking ceremony. He was now a blooded warrior. And Honey Eater had declared her love for him. But besides two fine ponies, what riches could he bring to the marriage? And her refusal of Black Elk's bride-price had led that fiercely jealous young war chief to declare to Touch the Sky: *Know this. There must come a time when Honey Eater either accepts my horses or you and I must fight to the death!*

Touch the Sky saw the entrance flap of Yellow Bear's tipi lifted aside; then Honey Eater stepped outside.

She was distracted with worry and did not notice him. Again Touch the Sky admired the frail beauty of her high, finely sculpted cheekbones. Her long black hair was braided with white petals of mountain columbine. Her buckskin dress was ornamented with elk teeth and eagle tails, with gold coins serving as buttons.

She joined a group of girls who were headed toward the women's lodge. Some were already, as they walked, stripping bark from willow stems with their teeth. They would use the stems to weave baskets for gathering berries, which would be dried and stored for the cold moons.

Suddenly, the camp crier burst into view over the rise south of camp. "The hunting party has returned early!" he shouted, riding up and down through the village. "Firetop rides with them!"

Immediately, excited voices buzzed throughout the camp. Touch the Sky couldn't believe his ears. Firetop was the name the tribe had bestowed upon his friend Corey Robinson when they honored the redhead as a savior of the tribe. He had faced down great danger when, pretending to be insane, he had frightened the superstitious Pawnees away before they could launch their bloody second raid on Yellow Bear's camp.

Now the hunting party, led by a young brave named River of Winds, topped the rise. By now the central camp clearing was crowded with braves, elders wrapped in their bright Hudson's Bay blankets, naked children dashing around like the excited dogs. When the redhead broke into view on his big blood gelding, a warrior honored him by raising the Cheyenne war cry.

"Hiya hi-i-i-ya!"

It was repeated by all the warriors, Touch the Sky included. By the time the party reached the clan circles, Corey's horse was forced to a standstill by the knot of Cheyennes trying to touch and greet him. Corey smiled sheepishly as hands groped for him, squaws attempted to hand him food, gifts were showered on him.

Finally Touch the Sky worked his way closer and Corey spotted him. His gap-toothed grin widened.

"Matthew!" he shouted, offering his hand from force of habit. Then, quickly, he withdrew it, remembering that his friend could no longer follow the white man's customs.

"Touch the Sky!" he corrected himself. "God-in-whirlwinds, am I glad to see you!"

Momentarily moved at seeing his good friend again, Touch the Sky permitted himself a rare smile. But the English words felt stiff and heavy in his mouth when he said, "Good to see you too, Corey."

Despite his joy, Touch the Sky was worried. He knew that Corey would not have made the long, dangerous ride across Plains Indian country just to pay a social call. His special blue feather was no protection from enemies of the Cheyenne. But it was almost mid-morning before the two friends finally found themselves alone in Touch the Sky's tipi.

" 'Fraid I got bad news," Corey said bluntly as soon as they had settled in among the elkskins and buffalo robes.

Carefully, leaving nothing out, he told all of it: how Hiram Steele had driven the Hanchons out of the mercantile business; how someone, most likely Steele, had harassed the Hanchons all winter, attacking hands and killing horses and even trying to burn the homesteaders out; how Seth Carlson and his superiors at the fort were deliberately ignoring the dangerous situation.

Touch the Sky struggled to keep the emotions from his face as Corey spoke. But anger at Steele boiled up inside him like a tight bubble escaping. It was tempered only by fear and concern for the only parents he had ever known—good, loving parents who had bucked all criticism by raising a Cheyenne boy among whites. After all, it was to protect them that he had left in the first place.

"Come with me," said Touch the Sky when Corey was finished.

The two youths sought out old Arrow Keeper at his tipi. Touch the Sky explained everything Corey had told him. When he was finished, he said, "Father, what should I do? I am a Shaiyena.

But these two whites are the soul of my medicine bag. How can I let these things happen to them? Am I not a warrior? Is their battle not mine?"

Arrow Keeper was silent a long time, his seamed face impassive.

"Only three sleeps ago I had a troubling medicine dream," he said finally, almost to himself. "This thing was foretold."

Now he looked at the young Cheyenne.

"Do you realize what the rest will think and say if you desert your tribe now? Now, when your chief will soon rest on his burial scaffold and leave the tribe vulnerable to attack?"

Unable to keep all the misery from showing in his face, Touch the Sky nodded.

"And, little brother, have you also considered Honey Eater? She loves you. But Black Elk loves her. When Yellow Bear leaves us—and soon he must—she will need you more than ever. She will be alone. A Cheyenne who is alone is a dead Cheyenne. Do you have ears for my meaning?"

Again Touch the Sky nodded. His heart felt heavy as a stone. Arrow Keeper was telling him that she would almost surely have to marry Black Elk if Touch the Sky were gone too long.

"Tell me," said the old shaman, "do you love these white people? Were they good to you?"

Touch the Sky nodded. "They were good to me. I would die for them as I would for the tribe."

Another long silence. Then Arrow Keeper repeated to himself, "It was all foretold."

He seemed to reach some decision. He met the young Cheyenne's eyes.

"Place these words in your sash and carry them with you always. Your place is with your tribe. You know I speak only one way, straight-arrow.

My heart is a stone toward most whites. But some there are"—here he looked at Corey with fondness in his red-rimmed eyes—"who are friends to the red man. A Cheyenne who forsakes his father and mother, no matter what color their skin, is no Cheyenne."

His last words surprised Touch the Sky.

"You are a blooded warrior now," Arrow Keeper said. "I have spoken. Now let your heart decide. I have seen the mark of the warrior buried in your hair, and I have spoken to you of the great vision I experienced at Medicine Lake. It told me that a great destiny is in store for you as a war chief of the Cheyennes. I trust in this medicine dream, though indeed, it may have been a false vision placed over my eyes by enemy magic.

"Now make your decision, Cheyenne brave. Do you go to help these whites who raised you, knowing it may turn your tribe against you forever and cost you Honey Eater? Or do you stay?"

It felt like a hot knife was being twisted deep in his guts. But Touch the Sky's mouth was a determined slit—he knew what he had to do.

"I go to my parents. Their battle is my battle."

Old Arrow Keeper held his face impassive. But a brief twinkle in his eyes told the youth that he was proud of this decision.

"Then go," he said simply, turning his back in dismissal.

Chapter Three

"No need to get ice in your boots," said Hiram Steele. "Hanchon can't prove nothing. You just keep following the plan, and I'll make you a rich man."

Seth Carlson was impatient to broach the subject of Kristen's visits to the Hanchon spread. But Steele got blood in his eyes quick when anyone pushed into his personal life.

"I ain't getting icy boots," Carlson said. "I'm just telling you, he's filed a homestead at the Territorial Office. He aims to prove up the land and stay."

"Where you been grazing? That's old news. Well, maybe he filed a homestead, but I'll wager he won't be roosting there. John Hanchon's got no spine for fighting."

Steele was a big, heavy-jowled, flint-eyed man in homespun shirt and trousers and a rawhide vest. He stood in front of a fieldstone fireplace in the parlor of his spacious, notched-log house. The room's sole reminder of his dead wife was a cherry spinet against the back wall. Bearskin rugs were scattered across the plank floor.

" 'Pears to me," said the young lieutenant, "he's got more starch in his collar than you credit him with. He stood up to that raid good enough last Sunday."

"He's small potatoes," insisted Steele. "Besides, it takes plenty of help to run a mustang spread. Even if Hanchon does have enough sand in him to stick it out, it's getting hard for him to feed and pay help. Ain't too many men want to put their bacon in the fire for three hots and a cot. This new bunch I hired on, they ain't wranglers. These are hard-bitten men who'd rather risk getting shot to doing honest work. One man killed won't stop them."

"That shines right," agreed Carlson. "But Tom Riley worries me. He's thick with the Hanchons and that freckle-faced sprout that was friends with their Injun boy."

"Has this Riley got friends at the fort?"

"Nobody that counts. But he can be mule-headed and he's often on maneuvers with the new recruits. He could easy poke around enough to find out it's your men that's been raiding the Hanchon spread."

Steele shrugged. "Then let him. Finding out something ain't the same as proving it. Just keep an eye on him. He starts causing us any trouble, we'll make him regret it. Won't be the first green officer that got knocked out from under his hat by a bullet out here on the frontier."

Carlson sensed that the moment was right to

bring up the topic he was aching to mention.

"And I'm just the man to do it," he said. "I don't like the way he looks at Kristen."

Steele's brows rose at the mention of his daughter. "Kristen? Where the hell does he know her from?"

"Why, from the Hanchons, I reckon."

"The Hanchons? She's got orders from me to have nothing to do with them. I made sure of that when I drove their redskin buck off."

Carlson's habitual sneer twisted into a frown. "I was just coming to that. It's none of my mix, you being her father and all. But I was going to mention to you that she shouldn't be visiting their spread. She was out there when your men raided."

Steele's eyes turned smoky with rage. His voice was dangerously quiet when he said, "She was out there? You know that?"

"Riley and the Robinson boy both told me. Besides being dangerous for her, it doesn't look good for me. Career officers don't hitch up with women who hobnob with Injun lovers. Not if they want to keep their commission."

Carlson didn't bother to add the fact that much of the resentment smoldering in his words now was because of the sound thrashing Matthew Hanchon had given him a year ago—when Carlson had threatened to ruin Hanchon's contract with Fort Bates if the Cheyenne didn't clear out for good.

"You say you got your C.O. believing there's Injun trouble?"

Carlson nodded.

"I'm thinking," said Steele, "that the U.S. Army ought to maybe post a sentry, just as a courtesy to the Hanchons. Maybe on top Thompson's Bluff."

Carlson thought about it and nodded again. "I could authorize that on my own." He knew full well that Steele too had Kristen in mind, not renegade Indians.

Steele paced once around the room, his hobnail boots echoing on the planks. Then, without a word, he went out front of the house and banged the triangle three times—the signal for summoning Kristen to the house.

She was daydreaming in a sheltered copse south of the house when Kristen heard her father's signal. For a moment she was tempted to pretend she hadn't heard it. The morning's chores were finished and she just wanted to go on listening to the sweet song of the meadowlarks, to the angry jay scolding her from a coarse-barked cottonwood nearby.

But reluctantly she decided to obey her father's summons. Slowly she emerged from the copse, the secret spot where she and Matthew used to meet. At the same moment, she watched a doe with a fawn break from a thicket down near the river. It had been a hard winter in the high country, and deer had come down into the lower valleys to escape the snow. How, she wondered, had the winter been for Matthew? Was he even still alive?

She was halfway back to the house when she saw a quick-darting prairie falcon swoop down on an unsuspecting squirrel. Kristen shivered when the squirrel suddenly chittered in fright that quickly turned to pain. It made her again recall that awful day when her father and the hired hand Boone Wilson had likewise pounced on her and Matthew in the copse. Never would she forget how she had been forced to lie to save Matthew's life—how she had looked him right in the eye and told him she never wanted to see him again. Something had died inside of him on that day; soon after, he had left to join the Cheyenne Indians.

Corey had told her a little bit about Matthew's new life since then. And though Corey had said nothing about what happened to Boone Wilson, she couldn't help wondering—could it have been Matthew who left the bullying, murderous Indian-hater dead and scalped in the road?

As she neared the house, she noted a hired hand repairing the broken tongue of a wagon. Another was splitting stove lengths with a wedge; still others worked green horses in the pole corral. Her gentle piebald, too lazy to require picketing, drank from the rain barrel at one corner of the house. There was nothing out of the ordinary to explain her father's summons.

Again, for a moment, she thought of the new men her father had recently hired. These were not the usual types who showed up willing to "earn their breakfast," as her father put it. They were mean, dirty, lazy men who looked out at the world from lidded eyes and surly faces. What good were they on a mustang spread?

Then she lost that thought when she spotted Seth Carlson's handsome cavalry black, reins looped over the tie-rail. Her pulse quickened in nervous anticipation.

A moment later the officer himself emerged from the house and mounted.

Kristen ducked behind the corner of an outbuilding so he wouldn't spot her. Ever since Matthew had been run off, Carlson had been coming around more and more. Why he spent so much time secretly conferring with her father, she didn't know. But the arrogant young officer had made it clear he wanted to marry her. Kristen had already decided she would run away before she would let that happen.

She lifted the latch string and opened the door. A moment later she cried out in surprise and pain as her father met her at the door with a vicious slap to the face.

"The hell you mean by defying me, girl?"

The stinging blow left her ears ringing and brought tears leaping to her eyelashes. "What do you mean?"

Another hard slap left her dizzy. Moments later he had her pressed against the back of the door, her arms pinioned.

"Don't play the larks with me, girl, I'm warning you! I'm talking about you sneaking around behind my back to visit the Hanchons."

"I only wanted to see their new place."

"I don't care *what* you wanted! I won't brook defiance, you hear me?"

"But Father! I—"

She cried out in fright when he snarled like a rabid animal and threw her hard to the floor.

"Shut your cake-hole, girl, and listen to me! Don't have *nothing* more to do with the Hanchons or their redskin boy. No daughter of mine gives the time of day to Injun-lovers. You hear me?"

He towered over her, frightening in his rage. Kristen wanted to tell him he was all wrong about the Hanchons and Matthew. She wanted to tell him that this was wrong, unfair. But she knew protest was useless. When he was in a rage like this, all she could do was humor him.

"Yes, Father."

"I mean it. You don't have anything more to do with any of that bunch. It's bad enough my men saw my own daughter kissing that redskin pup of theirs. Your mother and I raised you decent."

Kristen wished she had the courage to ask if his "decency" had included that Sunday raid on the Hanchon spread. But wisely, she bit back her retort.

"Yes, Father," she repeated. But suddenly, even as she spoke, Kristen knew she would have to defy her father. For one thing, she would have to warn the Hanchons. Whatever Seth Carlson and her father were up to, it meant that John and Sarah Hanchon were in for a world of grief.

And, if he was fooli-h enough to return again, so was Matthew.

At 0700 hours sharp, Brevet Officer Tom Riley conducted morning roll call and inspection of his platoon of new recruits. His hat in one hand, he was about to knock smartly on the door of the Regimental Headquarters Office to make his morning report.

The door was not quite closed. He hesitated, recognizing the voice which easily carried through the one-inch gap between the jamb and the door. Seth Carlson.

"We have evidence, sir, that it was renegade Cheyennes who attacked the Hanchon spread. They first robbed a mining camp near the Crazy Woman Fork of the Sweetwater, stealing white men's clothing, weapons, and shod horses. Then they attacked the Hanchons dressed as white men, apparently planning to steal horses."

Riley's jaw dropped open in astonishment. He

leaned closer and pressed one eye to the gap.

"Renegade Cheyennes?" said Major Bruce Harding, regimental commander. "According to the last scouting report, all the Cheyennes in the territory are camped up near the Powder."

"Yes, sir, they were. But we think this is a small band of warriors in the Dog Soldier Society. That's one of the Cheyennes' military societies, led by a younger warrior who's rebelled against their peace leader."

Riley watched Major Harding lean back in his chair. He was a small, neat, worried-looking man who constantly rubbed one knuckle across his mustache, smoothing it. He did so now as he stared at the huge territorial map covering one wall.

"How do you know," said Harding, "that the redskins who robbed the miners also attacked the Hanchons?"

"One of the Injuns was shot and dropped his rifle. It was an old Kentucky over-and-under, carved with the initials of one of the miners."

Riley couldn't believe his ears! Carlson had shown absolutely no interest in investigating the attack when he and Corey reported it. Now he was making up a pack of lies about it. Carlson knew damn good and well that the Cheyenne Dog Soldier Society had not been active anywhere north of the Platte River for at least two years. But he also knew that Harding was ignorant and incompetent, a West Point graduate who had never commanded a garrison before Fort Bates.

Riley, his face flushing warm with angry blood, was about to push the door open and storm into the C.O.'s office.

Then he realized: If he did that, Carlson would

know that someone had spotted his hand before he played it. *Why warn him now*, thought Riley, *when I can wait and see exactly what he's up to?* Besides, Major Harding was a staunch Indian-hater. Why should he believe a temporary recruit-platoon commander over his own adjutant?

"I expected this kind of trouble," said Harding. "I say the government must either fish or cut bait. Either give this damn territory to the sav-ages, and make sure they *stay* here, or take it for the white man. But Washington and the Indian-lovers in Congress have tied my hands. We are technically at peace with the red nations, so any type of organized offensive campaign is out of the question."

"Yes, sir," said Carlson. "But we are authorized to mount small troop movements. It might be a good idea to keep Tom Riley's trainees camped further north of here, closer to the Indian hunt-ing grounds. That way they can observe the Cheyennes and establish a military presence as a reminder. We can also step up patrols closer to the fort."

Harding, smoothing his mustache, approved this with a nod. "This new trouble will also put some teeth into my request to Washington for more troops."

Harding thought of something else. "If we step up patrols, we'll need more remounts. Can Steele provide them?"

Carlson nodded. "Yes, sir. I spoke with him recently, and he informed me that he has a corral full of fresh-broke mustangs. Top-notch horse-flesh."

So that's *the gait*, thought Riley. Carlson and Steele were feeding at the same trough! That explained the "Indian menace." This way, Carlson got Riley out of the picture so Steele's men could freely raid the Hanchon spread. And not only did that story allow Steele to secretly ruin John Hanchon. False reports about "Indian scares" were common because they stirred up settlers. Stirred-up settlers meant more soldiers, and thus, more lucrative contracts to opportunists like Steele for supplying them. Major Harding was perfect for their scheme. He considered Indians heathens without morality, an obstacle to Puritan progress.

Besides, Harding had a brother in the St. Louis settlements, a master gunsmith who was making a small fortune by arming the spirit of Westward expansion.

Riley made up his mind right then and there— he was sending a letter by guardmail to the territorial commander at Fort Laramie. The lieutenant colonel in charge of that garrison had a reputation, scorned by many of his fellow soldiers, for negotiating with red men rather than simply hunting them down.

"Sir," said Carlson, "I agree that we should either fish or cut bait. It won't do much good to increase patrols if the men are still restricted from returning fire."

His meaning was clear to Harding. The C.O. debated for a long moment, one knuckle worrying his mustache.

"As a purely practical matter," said Harding, "it's safe to assume that any Cheyennes caught in this area are up to no good, right?"

Carlson nodded. "They're either killing or thieving, sir. There's no other reason for them to be this far south."

Harding nodded again. Then he said, "Send the company clerk in when you leave, Lieutenant. Until these attacks subside, I'm authorizing an emergency shoot-to-kill order against the Cheyenne tribe."

Chapter Four

At last the tall grass finally gave way to the shortgrass prairie. Now Touch the Sky and Corey turned due south toward the Tongue River valley and the river-bend settlement of Bighorn Falls.

Touch the Sky had left two magnificent ponies back with the Cheyenne herds—a beautiful spotted gray, the prize for counting first coup on a Crow brave, and a swift, powerful cavalry sorrel. This last was his by right of killing the white whiskey trader, Henri Lagace, in fair combat. But Touch the Sky was saving both of these ponies as part of the bride-price he hoped to offer for Honey Eater. Instead, he now rode the pony he trusted most, the spirited dun Arrow Keeper had given him.

They avoided wagon tracks and the new forts with their loopholed gun towers and squared-off walls of cottonwood logs. Only the discipline of a blooded warrior kept Touch the Sky from thinking of this familiar route as a journey "home"— home to big trouble with his old enemy Hiram Steele. Nor did he allow himself to worry about what they must be saying about him back at Yellow Bear's camp.

Instead, he obeyed the teachings of Arrow Keeper and Black Elk. He tried to keep his mind free of any worry or thoughts except awareness of the present. He kept his attention focused on the helpful language of nature.

Thus, he immediately worried about it when a startled sparrowhawk suddenly flew off from a tangled deadfall well ahead, where the sloping wall of the valley crowded the game trail they were following.

Touch the Sky gave the high sign to Corey, halting him. The young Cheyenne only needed to pat his pony's neck once and she stopped—already troubled by whatever sense of danger had alerted Touch the Sky. She laid her ears back, snorting something to Corey's big gelding.

Touch the Sky warned Corey with his eyes not to move. Then he slid to the ground silently and hobbled his pony. Unsheathing his obsidian knife, he clutched it at the ready in his teeth. He had recently fashioned a strong new bow from oak and shaped and feathered a quiverful of arrows. He slid one of the arrows out and strung it. The shaft was made from dead pine, the point hardened in fire.

His moccasined feet moved silently as he neared the deadfall. His heart throbbed in his palms, but he concentrated, watching for the slightest movement.

His arm drew the arrow back a few inches, tightening the buffalo-sinew bowstring.

A few heartbeats later, the sharp stone tip of a streamered lance thrust forth out of the deadfall and stopped just short of skewering the hollow of his throat.

"You just died without singing the death song, careless Cheyenne warrior!"

Recognizing the voice before he saw a face, Touch the Sky lowered his bow and took the knife from his teeth so he could speak.

"Little Horse!"

His friend, permitting himself a grin of triumph, emerged from the tangle of brush.

"Good thing for you and Firetop I only counted coup, brother. If I were a lice-eating Pawnee, your scalps would be dangling from my clout."

"Good thing that few lice-eaters strike as silently as you. But what are you doing this far from camp?"

Little Horse was small but his compact body was powerful and sure in its movements. Like Touch the Sky he wore a leather band around his left wrist for protection from the slap of his bowstring. He circled around behind the deadfall and retrieved his pony.

"I am going with you and Firetop," he said. "I asked Arrow Keeper why you rode off. He explained this thing with your white parents. I told him you and Firetop should not face these paleface dogs alone. He agreed and gave me permission to join you. I caught up with you this morning, then passed you by riding hard above the rim of the valley."

"You have already saved my life once from white dogs. This is my battle and you owe me nothing. Ride back to our people, brother."

Little Horse stubbornly shook his head. "True it is, I saved your life in the paleface camp. But who saved Honey Eater from them? Who stood up to a night of torture that would have killed or broken a lesser brave? Who courageously sang the death song and prepared to ram an arrow down his own throat rather than help an enemy? And when the scar-face who sold devil water and slaughtered our people escaped, who trailed him across the plains and killed him?

"You are a true Cheyenne warrior, and your medicine is strong! We are brothers. Our blood is one. Therefore, our battles are one. And if we fall, we will fall as one. Not on the ground, brother, but on the bones of our enemies!"

A tight lump rose in Touch the Sky's throat, and he was silent for a long moment. He knew well that Little Horse was paying dearly for this loyalty. Even with Arrow Keeper's blessing, the Headmen would be furious that a strong young buck, a blooded warrior and one of Black Elk's favorites, had left the tribe to fight a battle for whites.

"Then let us ride," said Touch the Sky. He knew it would insult Little Horse to thank him more directly. "We are still two full sleeps from our destination."

Corey, who knew only a few words in Cheyenne, said, "What did Little Horse and you talk about?"

"Little Horse is fighting beside us against Steele."

They rode hard for the rest of that day, subsisting on cold river water and the dried venison the Cheyennes carried in their legging sashes. Several times they dismounted at game trails to search for moccasin prints. They were relieved that there was no sign of the distinctive cross-weave stitching of the Pawnees.

Besides the Bluecoats, the many enemies of the Cheyennes and their nearby cousins, the Lakota Sioux, included the Absaraka or Crow tribe and the turncoat Utes who lived in the high country. But among their Indian enemies, all Cheyennes most feared and hated the bloodthirsty Pawnees.

Nearly thirty winters ago, Pawnees had captured the Cheyennes' sacred Medicine Arrows. Though the Cheyennes had gotten them back in a revenge strike, the two tribes had been mortal enemies ever since. The lice-eaters had proven themselves eager mercenaries for the strong water and trinkets of the long knives, razing many Indian villages for them. The fierce Lakotas had at one time driven all Pawnees from the Powder River country. But they had begun drifting back. And Touch the Sky feared they would again attack Yellow Bear's camp—while warriors were in short supply and he and Little Horse were gone.

On the first night after Little Horse joined them, the trio slept in a cold camp near the game trail. Touch the Sky had spotted a spruce grove near a good patch of graze. They tethered their horses with long strips of rawhide. Then they pushed the drooping spruce branches aside and disappeared inside. They spread their robes on the deep mat of needles and slept in a hidden lodge of silence, safe from all eyes.

"Brother," whispered Little Horse after Corey's deep, even breathing signaled that he was asleep. "I would speak with you."

"I have ears for your words. Speak them."

Little Horse waited for a moment, listening to make sure Corey was still asleep.

"I mean no disrespect toward Firetop," Little Horse assured him. "His medicine is strong, and by right of courage he is one of us. But we will soon be among other whites. I must ask that you not say my name in front of them. Introduce me as War Eagle, but avoid even that false name."

It wasn't necessary to explain his meaning. Indians believed their names lost power if spoken by other Indians in front of whites.

Touch the Sky had learned this from Arrow Keeper but forgotten. Now he thought about it, then nodded.

"Of course, brother. In front of whites, I will not call you by any name but brother."

"Nor I you. Do not be offended. I will honor your parents as my own."

On the second night they sheltered in an old bear den in the cliffs overlooking the Tongue River. Earlier that day they had killed a deer and butchered out the loin and kidneys. Now, safe within the well-hidden den, they built a small cooking fire to roast the meat.

Later, before he drifted off in bone-weary sleep, Touch the Sky heard the ferocious kill-cry of a badger. It shot chills through him, reminding him of the Cheyenne's own shrill war cry—and reminding him that death and danger lurked nearby constantly on the frontier. Nor was it only animals and red men who must fight constantly for survival. Were his white parents not locked in a struggle for their very existence? Black Elk was a harsh man tempered more by battle than by love.

But he was right. Life meant always being a warrior.

And perhaps, after all, that kill-cry had been an omen: The next morning they rode into trouble.

They were making the most dangerous leg of the journey, crossing the vast, open stretch of sage flats surrounding Bighorn Falls. It was a level range pockmarked by prairie-dog towns, making footing dangerous for the tired ponies. Halfway across the flats, their path crossed that of a squad of Bluecoat pony soldiers from the soldiertown of Fort Bates.

The three held a hasty council as the squad drew closer. Touch the Sky translated when necessary.

"We should try to outrun them," said Little Horse.

"I think not, brother," said Touch the Sky. "I know it is foolish to trust Bluecoats. But our ponies are tired, and truly, where would we run? Recall that talking papers have been signed, papers which say there is no war between red men and white."

Little Horse considered these things, then nodded. "The talking papers are nothing. The white man speaks two ways always. Still, I have ears for your words. We are with Firetop. Surely they will not fire upon a white man."

Touch the Sky repeated all this for Corey.

"Sure, Little Horse is using his head! I ain' heard of no trouble lately between Indians and the cavalry at Fort Bates. Besides, plenty of th soldiers know me. It might even be Tom Riley though that's not his paint this officer is ridin If they challenge us, I'll tell 'em I got lost arour the upcountry of the river and you two bru me back on account of my blue feather requiring you to."

Touch the Sky explained this plan to Little Horse and he nodded his approval. They rode on, the two Cheyennes folding their arms in the symbol of peace.

"What in tarnal hell?" said Corey nervously when, still several hundred yards away, the squad suddenly formed into a skirmish line. The officer leading them raised his saber, then lowered it sharply in the signal to attack.

"Ride like the wind!" shouted Touch the Sky to Little Horse in Cheyenne. To Corey he said, "You just stay here! If you don't run, they won't hurt you. It's us they plan to kill!"

"Then, by God, they'll have to kill three of us! Gee-up!" Corey urged his mount.

A moment later, startling both of his companions, Corey unleashed a ferocious Cheyenne battle cry: *"Hiya hi-i-i-ya!"*

The trio drove their exhausted mounts mercilessly, racing far too quickly across the uneven, pockmarked terrain. Their destination was the river valley with its protective thickets. But Touch the Sky knew they'd never reach it in time. Already the first bullets were whining past their ears, raising dust plumes all around them.

The two Cheyennes instinctively flattened themselves low against their ponies' necks to make a smaller target. Corey made do with hunkering low over the saddle horn. They had only one firearm between them, the old breechloader protruding from Corey's saddle scabbard. He pulled it out and laid it across the saddle at the ready. Touch the Sky and Little Horse, having practiced this so many times the movements came without thought, strung their bows at a full gallop.

"Brother!" shouted Touch the Sky to Little Horse above the hollow thunder of their horses' hooves. "They are closing too quickly! Remember what Black Elk taught us. When all seems lost, we must turn the fox into the rabbit!"

Little Horse nodded, understanding that it was their only chance. It was an ancient Cheyenne fighting trick to split up during a retreat and divide the enemy force. A brave would then suddenly turn in mid-flight and attack his surprised enemy.

The two Cheyennes veered sharply to either flank while Corey continued straight toward the river valley. As Touch the Sky had hoped, the pony soldiers ignored the white youth and divided up to pursue him and Little Horse.

One of the Bluecoats, a young corporal on a powerful bay, surged ahead of the others pursuing Touch the Sky. The Cheyenne waited until the NCO had closed to within perhaps 50 yards. Abruptly, Touch the Sky jerked back hard on the dun's buffalo-hair bridle. The battle-trained pony responded magnificently, whirling to reverse herself seemingly without breaking stride.

The corporal's jaw dropped in astonished disbelief when he realized he was suddenly under attack. In a heartbeat Touch the Sky was upon him, streamered battle lance pointing before him. His eyes met the soldier's, and he saw that his enemy was barely older than he was. He read fear in those eyes, but also the determination to fight and die like a man.

At the last moment Touch the Sky diverted his lance, cracking it down harmlessly on the bay's hindquarters.

"I have counted first coup, Bluecoat!" he shouted in English as both of them halted and turned their mounts. "I would let you live, that forever you will speak of Cheyenne bravery! Now make your choice."

The soldier started to lift his carbine. Then he lowered it. His face showed confusion at this spectacle of an English-speaking Indian who had just spared his life.

"I'll be damned if my weapon didn't just hang-fire on me!" he said. "But get the hell clear of here *now* and stay out! We got orders to shoot all Cheyennes on sight!"

Touch the Sky had already touched heels to his pony. He was just in time to watch Little Horse turn on his surprised pursuer. The Bluecoat got off just one shot, missing the brave, before Little Horse knocked him from the saddle with a deft sideways sweep of his lance.

But now the officer leading the charge on his powerful black was bearing down on Touch the Sky, saber raised for the kill. Again Touch the Sky whirled around to face the attack, an arrow strung in his bow.

When the officer had closed to about 20 yards, Touch the Sky recognized Lieutenant Seth Carlson.

For a long moment their eyes held in mutual recognition and hatred. Then, as quick as a blink, one of the black's forelegs sank deep into a prairie-dog hole. The bone snapped with a loud sound like green wood splitting. Carlson flew head over heels from the saddle and hit the ground hard.

At the sound of the injured horse's scream of pain, another cavalry mount balked, snorting bloody foam. With two men down, including their badly shaken lieutenant, the momentum of the charge was broken.

There was no one in pursuit as Touch the Sky and Little Horse raced to join Corey. But even as he felt the swelling elation of victory, Touch the Sky recalled the hatred smoldering in Carlson's eyes. And again he heard the corporal's ominous warning: *We got orders to shoot all Cheyennes on sight!*

Chapter Five

"I shan't stay long, Mrs. Hanchon," said Kristen. "Pa will skin me alive if he finds out I've been here again since that trouble last Sunday. He thinks I'm at Holly Miller's house in town, being fit for a dress."

The two women were walking back from the small, windowless shed John Hanchon had constructed over a spring to keep food cold. Kristen wore a split buckskin skirt and a leather jerkin. She and Sarah had met before they reached the yard. Now Kristen led her lazy piebald by the reins. Sarah carried a wooden pail of milk.

Sarah halted and used her free hand to sweep the golden curls away from Kristen's left cheek. There were still faint, puffy blue traces of a bruise.

"Oh, my land, child! You poor thing! You know we love having you here. But not at *this* kind of expense. You'd best do as your pa says and stay clear of here."

Kristen nodded. "I know. But I have to talk to you and Mr. Hanchon. I'll only stay a few minutes."

"Well anyway, you came at a good time. John's in the kitchen hungry as a field hand, waiting on his supper. Come along, dear heart, and at least have a cup of cool milk. Seems to me you're losing weight."

The kitchen was spacious and airy and smelled of sourdough mash and strong ash soap. John Hanchon, perched on a sturdy three-legged stool over a deal table, was entering figures in an account ledger by the light of a coal-oil lamp. His long-barreled Henry was propped against the nearest wall.

He closed the ledger when the two women entered. For just a moment the worried frown was not etched quite so deeply into his face.

"Talk about your sight for sore eyes! I swan, there's none prettier than you two anywhere in Paris."

His temporary good mood soured quickly, however, when Kristen explained the purpose of her visit.

"I don't know exactly what Pa's up to," she said. "He was always a private man. But when my mother died, he just ducked inside himself and hasn't come back out once. I don't like to believe that he's breaking the law. But he and Lieutenant Seth Carlson are in on something together, and it involves you. They've been meeting together often lately. They almost always quit talking or change the subject when I'm within hearing.

"I feel awful saying this against my own father,

Mr. Hanchon. But he's taken on plenty of extra hands lately, and I don't see many of them working horses. And after the way Pa carried on about my being here on Sunday, I'm afraid he had something to do with that raid."

"Seth Carlson, huh?" Hanchon nodded, his big, blunt features now lost in thought. "So *that's* what's on the spit. I wondered exactly who Hiram was in cahoots with at the fort. No offense, pretty lady, but I already guessed your pa is mixed up in all this trouble lately. I got no hand-to-God proof, mind you. But he's been on the scrap something fierce ever since I started this spread."

"It's no say-so of his," said Kristen indignantly, "if another man legally trains and sells horses in this territory. Pa can't keep up with the need as it is, and more's wanted every day."

A startled gasp from Sarah interrupted the conversation. "Great day in the morning!"

Kristen glanced in the direction Sarah was staring. For a moment she simply refused to believe what she saw.

Then she screamed.

John Hanchon too glanced toward the door, which had been quietly lifted off its latch. But this wasn't anything like the trouble he'd been expecting, and for a long moment he simply sat there. Then his eyes widened in fear and he lunged for his rifle.

"No, John, you big, handsome fool!" said Sarah. "Don't you know your own son? It's Matthew, or one of them is anyway!"

Corey, his face sheepish at being present at such a time, stepped into the kitchen behind Touch the Sky and Little Horse.

"I figured he had a right to know what's been going on around here," said Corey. "And now Touch—I mean, Matthew, has made up his mind to help you."

"Matthew! It's really you, isn't it, son?"

Sarah moved quickly forward and embraced the youth she had raised as her own, unable to say more. At first, overcome with love for his adopted mother, Touch the Sky forgot his new dignity and restraint as a blooded Cheyenne warrior. He returned his mother's embrace, tears momentarily blurring the room.

Then he remembered himself and glanced quickly toward Little Horse. But this was the smaller Cheyenne's first time inside one of the lodges whites called houses. He was too awed by the novelty of his surroundings to notice his friend's reversion to former ways—or that his parents called him by his paleface name, the name Arrow Keeper had buried in a hole.

"Matthew," said John Hanchon, finally clearing the tight lump from his throat. "It's damn good to see you alive, son."

Only then did Touch the Sky notice, in his bone-numb nervousness, the pretty blonde. He suddenly felt as if the wind had been knocked out of him.

"Kristen?"

"Matthew?"

Their eyes held for a long moment, though he was seeing a familiar memory while she saw a shocking transformation. Like the Hanchons, she couldn't stop gaping at this spectacle: two fierce, young Indians, their bodies muscular and sun-bronzed, the fringes of their leggings spotted with the stiff, black blood of old hunts, old battles.

That was certainly Matthew's face, his distinctive nose and deep-set, perceptive eyes.

But there was also a new confidence and strength about him, places where muscle had hardened, and a distant, wary look in his eyes that Kristen had seen in older men—and wild animals in unfamiliar surroundings. And those scars! Like Sarah, she bit back an exclamation of pity when she noticed the gnarled lines of burn scar on his stomach, the ragged ridge of knife scar high on his chest.

For his part, Touch the Sky felt like he was trying to stand up in a dugout on a raging river. How many times, his heart suffering sharp pangs of loss, had he thought of Kristen? But then, slowly, thoughts of Honey Eater had filled the empty place in his heart. Now, so near again to Kristen, it was as if he had never stopped loving her for even one moment. Was he *not* a Cheyenne then, after all his suffering to earn the name?

"I must go," Kristen said suddenly.

She added, before she could stop herself, "And you, Matthew. It's not safe for you around here! You shouldn't've come back. Please leave before my pa hears about it!"

She muttered a hasty good-bye and was gone before Touch the Sky could reply. Corey left too, saying his pa must be on the warpath by now.

As they had agreed, Touch the Sky introduced Little Horse as War Eagle, avoiding his real name. Little Horse kept his eyes cast down at the floor when spoken to by John or Sarah—not out of disrespect, but because he believed an Indian's soul could be stolen if he made eye contact with whites.

For nearly two hours, the Hanchons kept their

son busy with eager questions. But despite their obvious joy at seeing him again, they were clearly troubled by Kristen's parting warning.

"Kristen was right, son," said Sarah after she had fed everyone fried potatoes and side meat and cornbread. "I'm so happy to see you I could just burst! But it isn't safe for you around here. Seems like trouble's been happening ten ways a second lately. You and your friend risked enough just by riding here."

"Your mother's giving it to you straight," said Hanchon. "There's no real law out here and scarcely any gum'ment except the Army. And I reckon you already know how much the Army will help us. Hiram Steele is mean and low and spiteful, the brooding kind that holds a grudge until it hollers mama. And he grudges me every honest dollar I earn. You should clear out tonight, under cover of darkness."

Dutifully, Touch the Sky translated these warnings to Little Horse. His friend was still devouring hot slabs of cornbread as quick as Sarah pulled them from the oven. He listened with an impassive face as Touch the Sky explained the danger in remaining there.

Then Little Horse shrugged.

"Brother, when have we *not* faced danger? We are Indians and we live like the buffalo, always hunted, killed for sport. Only, tell me this one thing. This paleface girl with hair like morning sunshine, I saw how you two looked at each other. Have you held her in your blanket and made love talk?"

Touch the Sky's troubled face answered the question clearly enough.

"Brother," said Little Horse sternly, "we are

warriors and we have come to grease our enemy's bones with war paint! *That* is our mission and we must hold our purpose close to our hearts. This golden-haired squaw, I sense danger if you let her into your thoughts. You are a Cheyenne, and Honey Eater waits for you back at Yellow Bear's camp!"

"What did War Eagle say?" asked Sarah when Little Horse quit speaking.

Touch the Sky felt thoroughly miserable. But at least Little Horse's impassive face and tone made the lie easy.

"He said that he's never tasted anything so good as your cornbread!"

All through the day Honey Eater had listened to the hypnotic rhythm of chanting, to the rustling rattle of snake teeth in dried gourds.

He was slipping away, ravaged by the red-speckled cough, but Chief Yellow Bear was still alive. Honey Eater had fresh cause for worry: The only nourishment her father could hold down now was hot yarrow tea with wild bee honey. But he was still alive, and for this Honey Eater gave thanks to the sun and sky and the four directions of the wind.

She stepped past the flap of the tipi she shared with her father. The evening air felt cool and fresh after the thick smoke of the interior, where dogwood incense was kept burning day and night. The days were gradually growing warmer and longer. Soon they would enter The Moon When the Ponies Shed.

Today, as usual, she picked fresh columbine and pressed it between wet leaves. Then she returned to the tipi and placed it near her robes. In the morning she would braid her hair with it.

Despite the sad vigil for Yellow Bear, daily life in camp went on as always. The young men wrestled and ran foot and pony races, sometimes all night until dawn; the children threw stones at birds and staged mock battles; the women talked and cooked. In the still, quiet hours of darkness, the old grandmothers and new widows mourned their dead with sad songs and chants.

Things went on as usual, even though Touch the Sky had coolly ridden out of her life! Now she could still hear the harsh calls of willets and grebes and hawks, the softer warblings of orioles and thrushes and purple finches. But since he had left her alone in this terrible time, none of it was anything but noise.

Arrow Keeper had told her little about why Touch the Sky left. Whatever trouble called him away, could his former life be more important than his life now as a Cheyenne? Did he not realize how vulnerable she would be if Yellow Bear crossed over to the Land of Ghosts? Surely he knew the decree of tribal law, that no young woman could live on her own but only with a father, a brother, or a husband. She had no brother, and soon she would have no father. If Black Elk again sent her the gift of horses, how could she refuse?

These thoughts skittered around inside her head like frenzied rodents. Now, as she stoked the embers to life under the cooking tripod, she noticed several of the clan Headmen walking toward the council lodge. Other males, all warriors or elders, also drifted across camp toward the lodge. She knew they must be meeting in formal council—they wore their best ornamental clothing, decorated with porcupine quills, stones, feathers, hair from enemy scalps.

"Honey Eater."

The sudden words startled her. She turned around to confront a fierce-eyed young warrior dressed in battle finery, complete with feathered war bonnet.

"I would speak with you before the council begins."

"I always have ears for your words, Black Elk."

"But *do* you? When I speak, do you truly place my words next to your heart? Or are they like pesky gnats, which bother you a moment until you slap them away from your ears and then forget them?"

Black Elk's bonnet was full of the eagle feathers of bravery. There was a dead flap of leathery skin where one ear had been torn off in battle, then later sewn back onto his skull with buckskin thread.

"What does Black Elk mean by this odd question?"

"You play the fox well, little one! You know I speak of Touch the Sky. The entire tribe knows that you have declared your love for this stranger who rides among us reeking of the white man's stink! But you must turn stone ears to his love talk. Even now, despite Arrow Keeper's objections, the Headmen are meeting to discuss his and Little Horse's desertion."

"He has not deserted his tribe!" said Honey Eater. "He is a brave and strong warrior."

"Would you tell this thing to me, who trained him? I will not speak in a wolf bark against him. He *is* brave and strong. With a handful of bucks like him, what battles I could win! He spoke brave love talk to you when the paleface dogs held you prisoner and tortured him in their camp. And yes, he has respectfully cut short his hair to mourn our dead. But a dog that walks on two legs is still a dog, not a Cheyenne.

"Bravery and strength are good things, but they are not enough. Looking like a Cheyenne is not enough. There is also loyalty to the tribe, duty, discipline. He was not raised a Cheyenne. In his heart he is white. This is why he so easily deserts us now to join them. In his heart he is still our enemy!"

The next moment Black Elk turned his back on her protests and headed toward the council lodge.

The lodge fell silent for a moment when Black Elk lifted the flap aside and stepped inside. This silence was a mark of respect for the young brave Yellow Bear had named as their battle chief.

Arrow Keeper sat in the center of the lodge, wrapped in his blanket. The voting Headmen filled nearly one half of the lodge. The younger warriors, who could speak but were not yet permitted to vote with the stones, occupied the other half.

Arrow Keeper, their acting peace chief, lit the common clay pipe and passed it on. After all who wished to had smoked, Arrow Keeper began the council.

"Brothers! The cold moons were harsh. Now what game can be found is lean and snow-starved. The meat is stringy, with no juice or tasty fat.

"Cheyennes, today these old hands carry no weapons. But I fought Utes beside Yellow Bear and buried my wife and children after the Pawnee raid at Wolf Creek. I have smoked the common pipe with you, and duty instructs me to speak only things that matter. So I say only this, that when game is short, tempers grow short. When there is hunger in the belly for meat, there is hunger in the spirit for blood! Do not punish Touch the Sky and Little Horse simply because of your hunger and bloodlust."

"But Father!" said Wolf Who Hunts Smiling. "You are brave and wise, but you speak in riddles. Think what they have done. Our chief is about to enter the Land of Ghosts. Even a hen will remain at the nest to fight for her chicks! Yet will these two 'warriors' fight for Cheyenne children?"

Wolf Who Hunts Smiling was a warrior now, one of the youngest in the tribe. He wore scalps dangling from his clout and practiced the fierce dignity and restraint he had learned from his older cousin, Black Elk.

Arrow Keeper folded his arms until the lodge had quieted. Now Black Elk rose.

"Fathers! Brothers! I do not question the manly courage of Little Horse or Touch the Sky. However, both are weak in judgment. And perhaps we were too hasty in presenting the blue feather to Firetop. Has he not abused our token of friendship? Has he not used his special place among us to entice away two of our best warriors to fight white men's battles. True it is, he showed bravery in helping us fight the lice-eaters. But is it not also true that the Indian can *never* trust the paleface?"

"Our war chief speaks the straight word," said Swift Canoe, who, as always, sat beside Wolf Who Hunts Smiling. "I have heard much about Touch the Sky's bravery after he was captured in the paleface camp. But did he not willfully disobey Black Elk's orders, which led to his capture *and* the death of our brother, High Forehead?"

"These words ring clear," said Wolf Who Hunts Smiling. "And who has actually seen most of the brave deeds Touch the Sky claims to have performed? Just because he fought the white sellers of strong water, this is no proof he is not a spy for the Bluecoats. The palefaces too war among themselves just as the red men do. I still believe he is a spy!"

Again old Arrow Keeper was forced to fold his arms to quiet the excited buzzing in the lodge. He longed to answer the young Cheyenne's unjust accusations. Arrow Keeper and Honey Eater were the only witnesses when Touch the Sky killed the Pawnee leader War Thunder, saving Yellow Bear's life. But they were both forced to remain silent—the rest of the tribe knew they favored the new arrival. Any support from them would only harden the others against him even more.

The medicine man sensed what was coming next. The younger warriors would demand a vote to permanently ostracize Touch the Sky, and perhaps even Little Horse, from the tribe. But a stroke of recent good fortune had suggested an alternative plan to Arrow Keeper: For the duration of the next moon, Chief Sun Dance of the Lakota Sioux had moved his clan circles just across the river from their Cheyenne cousins. This was only a temporary move while they hunted elk in the foothills of the Bighorns. But the presence of so many fierce Sioux warriors made attack from any Cheyenne enemies unlikely.

This meant that some braves could now be spared. Now, before Touch the Sky's enemies could move to expel him forever, Arrow Keeper spoke up.

"Brothers! The wildcat fights, or it flees. It is time to either expose Touch the Sky for a spy or lay these charges behind him forever. I suggest a plan.

"Our number is now swollen by Lakotas. Therefore, let us send two capable young bucks to report on Touch the Sky's activities. If he is a spy, surely we can find this thing out now. If so, his enemies may kill him as tribal law decrees! If not, his enemies must cease forever to speak in a wolf bark toward him."

Arrow Keeper's plan was practical, yet just, and met with strong voice approval. Both Swift Canoe and Wolf Who Hunts Smiling volunteered to go. But Arrow Keeper stubbornly shook his head. He reminded the others that Wolf Who Hunts Smiling had walked between Touch the Sky and the fire. And Swift Canoe still blamed the death of his brother on Touch the Sky.

To avoid rebellion from the young warriors, Arrow Keeper knew at least one of Touch the Sky's enemies would have to go. But he insisted that the other must be someone neutral toward Touch the Sky. Finally it was decided that River of Winds, whose medicine bundle was the rattlesnake, would accompany Swift Canoe.

Now, thought Arrow Keeper, *I have done my best*. The rest was up to Maiyun, the Supernatural. Arrow Keeper still believed in the powerful vision at sacred Medicine Lake, which foretold a warrior's glory for Touch the Sky.

But it was a terrible place Touch the Sky was now trapped in, caught between the sap and the bark. Had he cut all ties to the white man only to be savagely murdered by the red man?

Chapter Six

Two sleeps after the Cheyenne council voted to send spies to the south, John Hanchon showed Touch the Sky and Little Horse the lay of his mustang spread.

Before they left, Wade McKenna had been called up to the house. The tough old Irish foreman had lived in the territory for ten years. He recognized the tall, broad-shouldered redskin buck as the quiet kid who used to work for his adopted white parents at Hanchon's mercantile. McKenna never even batted an eye when he was asked to pass the word to all the hands: If you come across Cheyenne Indians on or near Hanchon land, don't pull down on them. They're flying our colors.

It was well after sunset, but a full moon painted the grass silver and made riding easy. The three stayed abreast except when forced to ride single file through narrow defiles. They were close enough to the river to hear the steady chuckle of the current, made more lively by spring runoff. Before them, the lush bottomland rose gradually into gentle hills dotted with stands of juniper and scrub pine.

John Hanchon reined in his roan cutting horse. He sat his saddle, gazing out toward the vast summer pasture.

"So help me Hannah, son, it's just now sinking in. First the store, now this place. A man doesn't bust his hump just for the love of sweat. I was hoping to put by against the future, mainly for your ma's sake after I'm gone. Now I see how close I am to losing everything. I've worked until I'm mule-tired, but I still go to bed scared every night. Scared your ma will be taking in washing after I'm planted."

Hanchon shook off his pensive mood and became all business.

"This is where the summer pasture starts," he said, pointing with a vast sweep of his arm. "Most of the mustangs are grazing out of sight behind the line shack on top that shoulder. See it? You could maybe sleep there except that Woody Monroe, the line rider, isn't too partial to Indians. You sure you won't stay up at the house with us?"

Touch the Sky shook his head. The rest of the hands were not all as likely as Wade to accept the presence of Indians so close to the bunkhouse. And no point in mentioning that Little Horse would never sleep in any paleface lodge.

"If word gets out," he said, "that Cheyennes are anywhere near the house, they'll be sure to burn it to the ground this time. From up here we can watch the horses and the approaches to the house."

There was no denying this. Hanchon nodded. "Well, since that last raid I got a guard set up for the yard and main corrals. We'll be safe enough. But if you two got your minds set on mixing into this, you'll need rifles. Ride back to the house with me and I'll loan you a couple."

Later, Touch the Sky thought, perhaps he would tell his father what happened to the rifle he took when he first left Bighorn Falls a year ago—how it had been given to Wolf Who Hunts Smiling when the intruder named Matthew Hanchon was declared a spy.

"I wonder," said Hanchon, mostly to himself as he glanced toward the dark line shack again, "why Woody hasn't lit his lamp and stove yet? Prob'ly still grouping the herd for the night. Sometimes they'll scatter to hell 'n' gone up into the high country."

They held their horses to a long trot and quickly returned to the house. Hanchon waited until Sarah left to tend to the wounded man staying in the lean-to bedroom built off the rear of the house. Then he unlocked a sturdy oak gun cabinet in the front parlor.

"I kept these when the mercantile went bust," he said. "Take your pick. Wade will set you up with powder and ball and percussion caps. You can fire them tomorrow when it's light, get your wind and elevation."

Touch the Sky hefted a percussion-action Sharps, then a .44-caliber North and Savage revolving-cylinder rifle.

"The trigger guard is combined with the lever," explained Hanchon. "When you move it, you revolve the cylinder and cock the hammer."

Touch the Sky liked the balance of the Sharps better. Little Horse owned a scattergun, acquired when he defended himself against the miner Enis McGillycuddy. But the tribe had no skins to trade for shells and ammunition, and he had left it behind. Now he chose a four-barrel flintlock shotgun. The barrels, each equipped with its own pan and frizzen, were rotated by hand. Little Horse smiled at the sharp, precise clicks as each barrel snapped into place.

"Tell your friend," said Hanchon to his son, "that a man could toss a biscuit farther than that piece shoots. But close up, one shot will strip the clothes off three men standing shoulder to shoulder."

As the two Cheyennes rode back out through the moonlit yard, the hired hand riding sentry by the horse-breaking pen stared at them as if they were a rare circus act. The warriors proudly ignored him.

"You boys want to buy a saddle?" the hand called out behind them. "Sell it to you heap cheap. Then you can ride in style without gettin' blisters on your sitter."

"Brother," said Little Horse after Touch the Sky had translated the hand's remark, "look at this thing."

They halted at one corner of the horse-breaking pen and Little Horse pointed inside. Touch the Sky spotted a small white mustang. Its muscular flanks were bloody from being viciously roweled, its eyes wild from a day of being choked to break it to the harness.

"Why," said Little Horse, "must the white man break a horse's spirit when he trains it? The red man cannot understand this. Because we do not break their spirit, our ponies are superior in battle. I have seen our elders lead a vicious horse miles away to deep sand, where it cannot buck its rider, rather than beat the animal into submission."

"It is as Arrow Keeper told me," said Touch the Sky. "I saw it myself growing up among them. It is not the paleface way to respect nature. They must always defeat her and her creatures, just as they must always defeat each other. See how this man Steele works to destroy my father?"

As the two Cheyennes pointed their mounts toward the summer graze, Touch the Sky again felt John Hanchon's words gnawing at him like a chancre: *I've worked until I'm mule-tired, but I still go to bed scared every night.*

They made camp just beneath a thickly forested ridge overlooking the summer pasture and the outlying line shack. They chose a thick stand of wind-twisted juniper which formed a windbreak near a cold seep spring. This site would permit a small fire and provide a natural bulwark against attack if they were surprised.

Then, while Little Horse slipped off into the forest to set a few snares for rabbits, Touch the Sky gathered wood. He removed a piece of flint from his legging sash and struck fire from it with his knife. He made the campfire Indian style by burning the logs from the ends, not the middle, to avoid wasting wood.

The location of the Grandmother Star to the north told them night was well advanced by the time they had tethered their ponies and let the fire burn down for the night. By the flickering light of the dying flames, Little Horse sharpened his knife against a flat stone. Touch the Sky used a bone awl and split-sinew thread to mend his extra moccasins. The sinew was a little tough at first, but he softened it in his mouth with saliva.

Twice he pricked his fingers deep, distracted by constant thoughts of Kristen—thoughts he had once believed were smoke behind him. But after seeing her again today, he couldn't help contrasting her golden, nimbus-haired looks to Honey Eater's dusky beauty.

Nor could he help wondering to which race he owed his heart and his life. Old Knobby, the hostler in Bighorn Falls, had insisted the red man and white man could never live together in peace. But why? Why must he choose one group and turn his back on the other?

Suddenly a horse whickered, cutting into his thoughts. The sound did not come from the herd behind them but from the line shack below.

"Brother!" said Little Horse in a tense whisper. "A rider approaches our camp!"

Quick as a blink they were both out of their robes and had backed into the surrounding brush, abandoning the circle of remaining light around the fire. Touch the Sky eased back the hammer of the Sharps and felt to make sure a primer cap was centered in the loading gate.

A moment later a saddled but riderless horse walked into the camp clearing. The girth had been uncinched under its belly, and the saddle had slipped halfway toward the ground, one stirrup dragging.

The horse, clearly hungry for human company, nuzzled Touch the Sky's shoulder when he stepped out from hiding.

"The owner was jumped while saddling or unsaddling," said Little Horse. "But who is it?"

At the same moment, both Cheyennes glanced downridge toward the dark line shack. Still no sign of fire or light.

"I think," said Touch the Sky, "it is time to check on this paleface who does not like Indians."

He quickly unsaddled the horse and pointed it toward the main corrals below, slapping it hard on the flank to send it running. He knew that, unsaddled, it would return on its own to the barn it was used to. Its arrival should alert the hands to send help.

Their uncle the moon still shone brightly, making secret progress difficult across the open expanse. As Black Elk had taught them, they rubbed their bodies with saliva, then smeared their wet skin with sand to cut reflection. Rifles would slow them down, so they chose their knives instead. Then, relying on isolated trees and bushes, they made their way on foot to the shack.

The door, caught in a steady breeze, repeatedly banged open and shut as they sneaked up from the rear. Touch the Sky eased around one corner, Little Horse the other. They saw him at the same time—a man lying spread-eagle in front of the shack, jaw slacked open as if he were drunk.

But the paleface wasn't drunk. His right temple was a raw, pulpy mess, as if he'd been struck hard with a rifle butt.

Touch the Sky gently shook him. The line rider groaned but remained unconscious.

"The blood is dark and crusting," said Little Horse. "He was attacked earlier. Much earlier."

Touch the Sky nodded. He squatted to examine the matted grass in front of the shack. It had been well trampled within the past few hours by many well-shod horses, as many as six or seven. But where were the riders now, and why had they come?

Perhaps thinking the same thing, Little Horse lowered his voice even more and said, "Brother, think on this thing. These men may have come even as your white father first showed us this lodge and wondered why it was so dark. They may have ridden on up to gather horses, only waiting for the moon to hide his bright face a bit so they may drive them out of the valley."

"Which means," said Touch the Sky, "they may have seen us make camp. They may know we are here."

Both youths were disheartened at this prospect. Only dead Cheyennes, Black Elk had insisted over and over, lost the advantage of surprise.

"It also means," said Little Horse, "that they may be very near, right now. Watching us."

"The wind is from the sun's resting place," said Touch the Sky.

Little Horse nodded, understanding. They stepped away from the shack, faced into the wind blowing from the pasture to the west. For several minutes they stood stone silent, stone still, simply smelling the wind.

At first Touch the Sky smelled only the sweet grass, the clean, woman smell of mountain laurel, faint cooking odors lingering in the shack. Then, gradually, he became aware of something else: the musty stink of leather-shod horses and white men.

Little Horse met his eyes and nodded. He smelled it too.

No words were exchanged. It was nighttime,

and they both understood that no Cheyenne who expected to live ever attacked a foe at night. Now they needed to observe while this fat moon aided them.

They stuck close to bushes and trees and ducked behind hummocks, crossing open expanses on their elbows and knees. They leapfrogged, one dashing ahead to cover and then waiting for the other to join him before moving on. Steadily they worked their way along the ridge and around the shoulder of the hill.

Little Horse was about to scramble into a coulee when he suddenly froze in his tracks and lifted his hand to halt Touch the Sky.

Touch the Sky edged up beside him. Little Horse pointed further into the dry gulch. A half-dozen men waited there, their horses picketed nearby. One man squatted on his rowels, smoking. Several others shared a bottle of whiskey. They looked bored and impatient.

Below them, on the other side of the wide coulee, hundreds of mustangs were bunched together in the moonlight. Steep-sloping hills formed a natural pen on three sides. The only way out was through the coulee.

"By hell, I'm tired of waiting," said the man smoking the cigarette. He flipped his butt away in a wide arc and rose to his feet, spurs jingling. "I say let's point 'em out of here now, moon or no. We got 'em bunched good now, but they won't stay that way forever."

"Winslow, you work us too damn hard," said one of the men passing the whiskey bottle around. "You hadn't spooked that wrangler's horse, we wouldn't be in such a damned all-fire hurry, would we?"

"Last I checked, that hoss was just wandering the ridge," said another man. "With the saddle on, it'll stick close."

"Maybe so. But I ain't heisting skittish mustangs in full moonlight."

"Anyhow," said Winslow, pointing north, "there's clouds boiling up over yonder, heading straight for the moon. Just a little longer and we can push 'em out of here."

The man called Winslow was tall and stringbean thin with shaggy hair the color of wet sand. Something about his voice alerted Touch the Sky. He strained his eyes in the clear moonlight, watching as Winslow turned in profile.

The man's face was badly pockmarked from smallpox. A moment later Touch the Sky remembered him, and a cold, numbing hatred iced his limbs. He glanced at several others and recognized two of them.

Touch the Sky and Little Horse had fought these hardcases before, further north in Plains Indian country. They were former members of the private "army" paid by the whiskey trader Henri Lagace! But the army had disbanded after the Cheyenne raid on their camp which led to Touch the Sky's killing Lagace.

Clearly, Hiram Steele had found good use for unemployed cutthroats.

Little Horse jabbed his shoulder excitedly, and Touch the Sky realized that his friend too had recognized their former enemies.

They backed slowly away from the rim of the coulee and held quick council behind a huge boulder.

"Brother," said Little Horse, glancing over his shoulder into the sky, "soon the moon goes into hiding. Under cover of darkness, the white dogs will easily drive the ponies. Without our ponies, we cannot run for help in time."

"These are the white-livered cowards who killed High Forehead and the rest of our brothers," said Touch the Sky. "They invaded our camp and killed children and elders. Now they land like carrion birds to destroy my white parents! We cannot let them succeed."

"I have ears for your words and courage to back them. But we cannot anger Maiyun by raising our battle axes after dark! We must play the fox, not the lion."

Touch the Sky nodded. Both youths knew full well what had to be done and the best way of doing it. They circled wide around the mustang-filled clearing, hugging the steep slopes. At some places they were forced to cling to scrub pine to avoid sliding down the slope. But they made good time, unobserved, and were soon behind the mustang herd.

Little Horse nudged him as they crouched low, trying not to spook the herd too soon with their human scent now that the wind was behind them.

"I am quicker on my feet than you," he said. "And you make the noise better. Let me get closer. I will scatter them while you make the call."

A heartbeat later Little Horse was gone, already blending into the herd and slapping flanks left and right.

All horses everywhere, Black Elk had assured his warriors many times, are frightened sense-less by bears. Now Touch the Sky swallowed a huge breath and brought it back out from deep in his guts, making a noise that was half bark, half growl—the deep, menacing woof of the grizzly.

Instantly, scores of horses reared in panic, then bolted for the coulee. The ground thundered and vibrated, divots of soil flew everywhere.

Touch the Sky again loosed his guttural imitation of a prowling grizzly. Now and again he caught a momentary glimpse of Little Horse, still smacking mustangs. Only the small Cheyenne's quick, sure movements saved him from being trampled as he leaped first left, then right, twirling just out of harm's way.

Above the thundering din, Touch the Sky heard the white men shouting and cursing. They wisely decided to flee rather than attempt to halt the panicked herd as it squeezed itself into the gulch, threatening to crush them.

He found Little Horse covered with dirt but unharmed. The two grinned in triumph. They knew the herd would scatter once it cleared the coulee on the other side, drifting back eventually to the lusher pastures of the high country. A light burned at the line shack, where someone was tending to the injured Woody Monroe. And shouts from further down the valley announced that wranglers at the Hanchon spread had been alerted to the rustlers. Winslow and his friends would count themselves lucky if they cleared the valley alive.

But as they returned to their camp, the two Cheyennes sobered quickly. The shock of once again meeting their hated enemies filled them with grim determination to triumph.

"Brother," said Little Horse later, before Touch the Sky drifted down a long tunnel into sleep, "I recall well how those paleface devils piled hot rocks on you and laughed as you were about to swallow the Sioux arrow. I recall well the suffering they caused our tribe. This is no longer a white man's battle I am helping you fight. And I swear this: Either we defeat them, or we will die the glorious death trying!"

Chapter Seven

"Damn it all, man!" said Hiram Steele, snapping his watch shut and returning it to the fob pocket of his vest. "Couldn't you get here sooner with the news? It's too late to warn Winslow and the rest."

"Get here sooner? I'm damn lucky to even be alive," said Seth Carlson. "Before I could leave the post, I had to file a report on the skirmish. And there was clerical work to do on the wounded trooper. He broke an arm when one of the bucks knocked him off his horse. Not to mention that I had to get medical care myself and requisition a new horse."

Steele barely wasted a glance on the patch, the size of a silver dollar, where skin had been scraped off Carlson's face in the prairie-dog-hole mishap. The rancher paced before the fieldstone fireplace, his heavy boots thudding on the bare planks. The flint-gray eyes focused on nothing, lost in worry.

"You're sure it was him?" said Steele. "All Injuns look alike."

"It was the Hanchon boy, all right. I didn't recognize the buck with him."

"So it was just the two?"

Carlson nodded. "And Corey Robinson, though he wasn't fool enough to fight against us. All he did was rabbit."

"Hell, two pissant redskins and a freckle-faced sprout don't put snow in *my* boots."

"Maybe, but I don't like the turn this trail is taking," said Carlson. "This is more than I bargained on. Today that red bastard humiliated me in front of my men. And because of him I had to shoot the best horse I've owned since I drew orders to this hellhole!"

"I'll give you a better horse. After this raid tonight, you can have your pick. As for that buck humiliating you, don't forget the shoot-to-kill order. He'll get his comeuppance soon enough."

If all went as planned, thought Steele, a good portion of Hanchon's best horseflesh would soon be scattered among the herds grazing Steele property. No brands were used until the horses were broken and ready to sell, so Hanchon would have no legal claim against him.

"Just a warning," said Carlson. "Harding checked up in his orders manual, said something about having to maybe appoint a military board of inquiry to look into this Indian problem. If Hanchon reports this raid, there might be someone from the fort nosing around, asking you and your men questions."

Steele shrugged his beefy shoulders. "Anybody asks any of my wranglers, they were all in the bunkhouse tonight playing dominoes and checkers."

"That's just fine for you and your men," said the young lieutenant, irritation clear in his voice. "But who covers *my* back-trail? I've been submitting false reconnaissance reports. If Harding ever gets wind of it, I'm headed for the stockade. Harding is no Indian-lover, and brains are not his strong suit. But he lives by the book."

Steele had a hair-trigger temper and did not usually tolerate ill temper from others. For a moment, the resentment in Seth Carlson's tone made angry blood throb in his temples. But then he reconsidered. He needed Carlson's influence at the fort.

"Look here," he said reasonably, "no need to get on the peck. Harding doesn't know sic-'em about what we're up to."

"I'll grant that. Harding wouldn't notice his own reflection in a hall of mirrors."

"All right, then. We'll just keep Major Harding flummoxed like we been doing all along. You been blaming all this ruckus lately on renegade Cheyennes, right? And didn't two just ride into the territory today raising hell and wounding soldiers?"

Carlson had already told himself all this. What really pricked at him like a burr in his boot was the fact that the Hanchon boy was back—and that Kristen had evidently known he was coming and gone to meet him.

"Do you remember," he said, "when we talked about posting a sentry on Thompson's Bluff overlooking the Hanchon spread?"

Steele nodded.

"I checked with him before I rode out here. The two Injun bucks and Corey Robinson rode to the Hanchon place, all right. But just before they arrived, Kristen showed up there too."

For a moment Steele simply stared in disbelief, as if Carlson had just announced that pigs could fly. Then, all of an instant, his broad, bluff face flushed purple with rage. But his voice was deadly calm when he finally spoke.

"You're not seriously telling me that my daughter went out to the Hanchon spread *today*?"

"Unless there's another pretty blonde hereabouts who rides a swayback piebald."

"Did she meet with the Indian?"

"The sentry can't see their place from the bluff, not the yard. Just the wagon road leading out to it. But she had to see him. She was still there when he rode in."

Steele was struck dumb with disbelief. He stopped pacing for a moment as he fought down the urge to rush back to Kristen's bedroom and drag her out by the hair. Hadn't he already warned the girl—twice, by God!—to steer clear of that place?

Obviously, trying to keep a woman on the straight and narrow was like trying to train a cat. Threats were useless with Kristen, she was too bullheaded. But nobody bucked Hiram Steele, not even his own daughter.

He glanced at Carlson. The officer's injured face was still twisted in a petulant frown. Maybe it was time to throw the dog a bone, and at the same time punish Kristen.

"They say," said Steele, thinking out loud, "that if you're on the plains and you have no tree for hanging a man, you can always drag-hang him."

Carlson's frown turned from anger to puzzlement. "Could you spell that out clearer?"

"Just wait here," said Steele, heading back toward Kristen's bedroom. "You'll soon catch my drift."

Kristen lifted the chimney from the coal-oil lamp and lit the wick with a sulphur match.

Light splashed the rose-patterned carpet and pushed shadows back into the corners of her room. She opened the top drawer of a sturdy pine dresser and tugged aside a neatly folded calico skirt. Then she removed a packet of letters tied with a bit of red silk ribbon—letters from Matthew Hanchon. Letters he used to leave, in their secret meeting place, on those awful days when he delivered supplies and she couldn't manage to meet him.

She knew Seth Carlson had just arrived. That's why she had feigned sleepiness and slipped back to her room earlier than usual. Now, as she again read some of the letters, she could faintly hear her father and Carlson's voices, like sounds carried on the wind.

Her thoughts and feelings had been a confused riot ever since unexpectedly seeing Matthew earlier today. Before, when he'd lived his former life in Bighorn Falls, she had always known, of course, that Matthew was different. But seeing him this way—today—made that difference so stark and real.

The way he was dressed, those awful scars, that new glint of hard mettle in his eyes—and the strange language he spoke with that other Cheyenne! All of it made her realize how impossible was this love she still felt. He couldn't live in her world, nor she in his, any more than a hawk could nest with a falcon.

And yet, despite his fearsome, savage aspect today, she couldn't help thinking about how magnificent he had looked. Stronger, more confident, with that heightened sense of alertness which characterized frontier survivors.

While her fancy coined these ideas, three quick taps on her door startled her.

"Kristen?"

Her heart leaped into her throat. Her father never visited her room unless it was something serious.

"Yes, Pa?"

"You dressed?"

"No," she lied.

"Well, put some clothes on. Then come out front. I got something to say to you."

Kristen's brow furrowed in a frown of confusion. Her father's voice was low, composed, calm—frighteningly so.

·She put the letters away and waited a few minutes until her breathing was under control. But her pulse quickened again when she found that Carlson too was waiting in the front parlor, seated in a ladderback chair. He rose smartly when she entered, trying to keep the injured side of his face out of her sight.

"Miss Hanchon. I hope you're well?"

"As well as a body can be when she's tugged out of bed."

Despite her bravado, Kristen was so scared her limbs trembled. Her father was being oddly polite and formal with her. Some disaster loomed, and she knew by now that it had something to do with her forbidden visit to the Hanchons. But despite being prepared, she felt his next words with the force of hard slaps.

"Did you have a good time with your friend Matthew Hanchon today?"

"I—I don't—"

Warm blood rushed into her face and she blushed deep to the roots of her hair. What her father was suggesting was a lie, but the shock of the confrontation made her feel guilty.

Steele read his daughter's blush as a confession. Rage sparked in his eyes for a moment. Then they went dull and flat and calculating.

Carlson too read her blush as a confession. Indignant anger welled up inside him. Wasn't she always high-hatting him and looking down her nose like she was quality goods? Yet here she was, admitting to consorting with a savage redskin!

"It crosses my mind more and more lately," said Hiram, "how easy a young girl can go astray out here in the wilderness. Especially a young girl without a mother or older sisters to guide her."

When her father actually smiled, Kristen knew she faced a crisis.

"Lieutenant Carlson has requested the honor of your hand in marriage. I've given my blessing to the union."

Carlson started and moved to the edge of his chair, then settled back again and assumed a poker face. Steele winked at him, then turned to his daughter again.

"Wha'd'you say to that, girl? Think you'll be a good Army wife?"

Kristen's mouth felt dry and stuffed with cotton. She swallowed hard.

"I've never given it any thought."

She was staring at Carlson as she said this. Some of his former servility returned to his tone as he said, "Your pa's not trying to sell you a bill of goods tonight, of course. You'll want time to think on it."

Her icy tone strained her father's smile, but he only widened it before he said, "Well, you best *start* thinking about it. The day's coming quick when you're gonna have to choose. Life as an officer's wife on the frontier, or moving back to Providence to stay with my sister Thelma."

A shudder moved up Kristen's spine like a cold finger. She recalled her spinster Aunt Thelma's talcumed face and stale-as-dust old-lady smell.

"It'll have to be one or the other," said Steele. "A white girl that hobnobs with murdering redskins is wanting looking after."

"Murdering! Matthew Hanchon is no murderer!"

"Who do you think killed Boone Wilson, the Queen of England?"

"If he did, it was self-defense, not murder."

"When a daughter of mine," said Steele, "takes up with Indians against her own people, that's the day I wish I'd died as a child. You're going to make up your mind and make it up quick. Either you marry Seth Carlson or you move to your Aunt Thelma's. And you better write this on your pillowcase. If I hear of you visiting the Hanchon spread or meeting with that redskin bastard of theirs again, you'll *have* to get married because you sure's hell won't have a home here!"

Chapter Eight

His eyelids eased open from deep sleep. At first, before the last cobwebs of slumber were swept from his eyes, Touch the Sky didn't recognize where he was.

He saw a wall of wind-bent juniper trees slightly below him on the sloping ground, felt the dew in the grass where his arms lay outside of his buffalo robe. The weak light and warmth of the sun told him it was still early. Then he suddenly remembered everything and rolled over to wake Little Horse. But his friend's robe was empty.

And less than a pace from Touch the Sky stood a Bluecoat officer!

He recalled the warning the corporal had given him yesterday: *We got orders to shoot all Cheyennes on sight!*

Instinctively one of Touch the Sky's hands patted the doeskin pouch on his breechclout. It held the badger claws Arrow Keeper told him were the magic totem of his clan.

His medicine bundle was safe. The very same moment, remembering not to signal his intention in his eyes, he kicked his robe aside and rolled hard into the Bluecoat intruder's legs.

The officer fell heavily, cursing, then rolled free with amazing quickness and strength. Touch the Sky leaped after him and wrestled him down again. They grappled, rolling through the wet grass, crashing through small bushes.

The Cheyenne finally slipped a powerful choke-hold on his adversary. The next moment he felt an explosion of fiery pain as the pony soldier brought a short but accurate knee thrust up into his groin. This loosened his choke, but he refused to let the soldier squirm out from under him.

For a moment they were locked eyeball to eyeball, both gasping for breath as they struggled for dominance. The Cheyenne's face was an impassive mask except for the determined slit of his mouth. The Bluecoat's face, in contrast, twisted into a fierce scowl.

The soldier slumped under him for a moment, and Touch the Sky managed to slip the obsidian knife from its sheath. Despite the shoot-to-kill order, however, he couldn't bring himself to plunge the blade home. The Bluecoat wore a sidearm but had not once tried to draw it. A Cheyenne was honor-bound to keep the sacred Medicine Arrows forever sweet and clean by killing only those who tried to kill him.

When Touch the Sky suddenly raised the knife, the Bluecoat's eyes mirrored fear.

The Cheyenne hurled the knife, point first, into the ground just beside the officer's head.

"Christ on a mule! Get off him, Matthew, you tarnal fool! That's Tom Riley!"

In his excitement, Corey forgot to use his friend's Cheyenne name. Now he burst out from the trees above them, still tucking in his shirttail after relieving himself.

At the same moment, Little Horse stepped out past the tree line carrying a pair of dead rabbits. He saw the Bluecoat and Touch the Sky, still apparently engaged in combat, before he spotted Corey. He dropped the game and raced toward them, unsheathing his knife.

"No, brother!" said Touch the Sky in Cheyenne. "He is Firetop's friend!"

Little Horse managed to avert his knife. But he had too much momentum going to avoid colliding with the two on the ground. Moments later all three rose from the tangled confusion of arms and legs.

Corey swooped double in sudden laughter.

"Ain't you three a fine pack of scrappers! You look like a bug with too many legs!"

"I told you to wake him up first," said Riley. He picked up his bent-brim hat and slapped the dust off it. His sunburned face turned even redder as he flushed with sheepishness. "I tried to tell you," he said to Touch the Sky, "but you wouldn't let me catch my wind."

"Touch the Sky, this is Tom Riley. Though I reckon you two've already met. Tom, this here is Touch the Sky's friend Little Horse. He don't speak English."

Riley knew enough about Plains Indians customs not to be offended when neither man looked him square in the eye. He caught himself before he offered his hand.

"Your pa told us where you planned to camp," Corey said to Touch the Sky. "Tom's got some news. Bad news."

While Little Horse dressed out the rabbits and roasted them on a green stick, Riley explained what he had overheard at the fort when Corey was riding north to Yellow Bear's camp. It was no surprise, of course, that Hiram Steele was involved in the treachery against the Hanchons. And John Hanchon had already told his adopted son that Seth Carlson was involved. But now, Riley made it clear, the commanding officer of the powerful 7th Cavalry had accepted their "Indian menace" tale—meaning it was not just Steele and his hardcase gunmen they had to fight, but the U.S. Army as well.

"I'm trying to prize out what information I can," said Riley. "I like your ma and pa. They've worked hard to make a good living and to make this valley a decent place to live. It puts blood in my eyes to see the big nabobs like Hiram Steele doing dirt on them. Corey told me all about what Steele and Carlson did to you. Tell you the truth, you had every right to stick that knife in me a few minutes ago. Though I'm damn glad you didn't!"

"Tom's got an idea," said Corey. "He's off duty today, but his superiors have got him on maneuvers in the field all around this area and further north. It's hard for him to get word to me quick when he learns something at the fort. So he says we should rig up a way for him to leave messages nearby."

Touch the Sky nodded, then briefly translated for Little Horse.

"These men we're fighting," said Touch the Sky to Corey and Riley, "aren't Steele's usual wranglers. They blacked their faces for war against my people before they ever rode into this valley."

He explained about the whiskey seller Henri Lagace and his crew of mercenaries, who had scattered after the Cheyenne raid on their mountain stronghold. Riley nodded, recognizing the name.

"That bunch is wanted for a series of murders and robberies up in the Northern Territory. Crimes they tried to pin on the Cheyennes. So some of 'em are working for Steele? That means they're safe from any law around here."

"Any white man's law," said Touch the Sky grimly. "They have killed my people. My battle axe is raised against them until death."

"Maybe," said Riley, "but you and your friend will be damn lucky to keep your hide, let alone skin anybody else. It's not just Steele's riffraff you're up against. I heard all about how Carlson made a fool of himself yesterday in front of his men, trying to put you under. As sure as hell's afire he'll be looking behind every stone and bush for you two."

He again mentioned the need for a system to leave messages. When Touch the Sky translated to Little Horse, he nodded and signaled everyone to follow him. They moved up into the trees and followed a deer run, skirting wide at one point to avoid a patch of trees which had been obliterated by a rock slide. Little Horse stopped at a leather-leaved cottonwood with a fork split deep by lightning.

"That's the gait," said Riley to Touch the Sky. "Check that fork daily for messages. And be careful 'cause Carlson's got sentries posted night and day up on Thompson's Bluff, watching the road into your pa's spread."

Touch the Sky nodded. In fact he and Little Horse had already spotted the sentries. Which meant, Touch the Sky reminded himself, that there was a good chance Hiram Steele knew his daughter had been with the Hanchons and their "savage" boy.

"I've got to make tracks now," said Riley. "But I'll be in contact."

Now Touch the Sky permitted himself to meet the young brevet officer's gaze. "Why do you risk trouble for yourself helping us?"

Riley shrugged. "Maybe it'll be turnabout someday. I got kin back East want to come out here. First we need more settlers like your ma and pa, not like Hiram Steele."

Riley and Corey returned to the camp for their horses. Touch the Sky and Little Horse worked their way cautiously down to the river, staying out of sight. The two Cheyennes stripped and bathed in the ice-cold water, then lay in the warming sun to dry. Sandpipers waded along the shore, magpies screamed, woodpeckers kept up a steady rat-a-tat from the trees overhead.

At one point, hearing the distant heave-ho cadence of boatmen, the two scrambled up the bank and hid in the thickets while a keelboat floated by. A blunderbuss was mounted on a swivel in the prow, and the deck was crowded with crates of whiskey and rifles. Though the river was full, they were traveling against the current and there was no favoring wind. Six men lined each side of the flat-bottomed boat, using long wooden poles to propel it.

"More trouble for the red man," said Little Horse.

His remark reminded both of them, again, that they were up against a ruthless enemy.

"Brother," said Little Horse, "I would speak with you."

"You know that I have ears for it."

"Just now, as you were grappling with the Bluecoat? He pushed your hair far back off your forehead and I noticed the mark. Why have you not spoken of this thing?"

Touch the Sky was silent at first, though he knew well what mark Little Horse meant: In the hair just above his left temple, buried past the hairline, was a mulberry-colored birthmark shaped like an arrowhead—the traditional mark of the Cheyenne warrior.

"Brother," insisted Little Horse, "what does this thing mean?"

Again Touch the Sky held his silence, unsure how to speak or even what to say. Would Little Horse believe him if he repeated what Arrow Keeper insisted: that Touch the Sky was the long-lost son of Running Antelope, a great young chief of the Northern Cheyennes who was killed in a Bluecoat ambush?

When Touch the Sky said nothing, Little Horse only shook his head. "The hand of Maiyun is in this thing," he said quietly. "That mark means we will face many battles. If we must die, brother, let it be after we kill these paleface devils who attacked our tribe and now attack your white clan!"

Wolf Who Hunts Smiling had always claimed that Touch the Sky was secretly a spy for the Bluecoats. And although he pretended to agree, in fact Swift Canoe had always doubted this.

He had cause enough to hate this white man's "Cheyenne." Had he not caused the death of Swift Canoe's twin brother, True Son?

So it shocked him now as, hidden with River of Winds, they watched Touch the Sky and Little Horse making medicine with a Bluecoat!

The two Cheyenne spies had missed the earlier struggle, still searching for the camp after locating Little Horse and Touch the Sky's tethered ponies. Now all they saw was an earnest discussion between Touch the Sky and the officer.

Touch the Sky translated for Little Horse, and Swift Canoe said, "Did you hear, brother? They are talking about leaving messages for each other! Touch the Sky and this murdering white dog! Wolf Who Hunts Smiling spoke the straight word all along! He is a spy!"

River of Winds, who was several winters older than Swift Canoe and far less fiery-tempered, frowned. Keeping his voice low like Swift Canoe, he said, "Do not wade in before you look, Cheyenne. We do not know what this meeting means. Firetop knows this long knife—would you deny that Firetop saved our tribe? And it was Touch the Sky who rode for him when he saved us. Why would our enemy do this thing for us? Why not let the Pawnee destroy us?"

Swift Canoe stubbornly shook his head. "Perhaps he has become their spy since then. Perhaps Firetop now works for Bluecoat gold and has turned his heart to stone toward us."

They followed as the two Indians and two whites went upridge to select the lightning-split cottonwood. Then Firetop and the Bluecoat returned to camp and rode off. The spies from Yellow Bear's camp followed their fellow Cheyennes as they cautiously worked their way down toward the river.

They hid in a deep swale while Touch the Sky and Little Horse bathed.

"Brother," said Swift Canoe, "I ask only this. Once you have seen enough to convince you Touch the Sky is a double-tongued spy, let me kill him then and there."

"What, and would you kill Little Horse too? You will not kill one without killing the other. Even if, as you claim, Touch the Sky has stained the Sacred Arrows by causing True Son's death, you have no right to punish Little Horse. He must then go before the councillors."

Swift Canoe was silent at this rebuke, resenting it but knowing the older warrior was right.

Still, there would surely come a moment when Little Horse and Touch the Sky were separated, thought Swift Canoe. The warrior wanted once and for all to end the taunts and sly remarks of other Cheyenne bucks, who had begun to mock both him and Wolf Who Hunts Smiling as empty boasters. Once his enemy was proven a spy, the tribe would honor him for killing Touch the Sky.

"As you say, brother," he said. "We will wait and watch."

Chapter Nine

The Powder always ran swift and cold early in the warm moons. Shivering, her naked, coltish body dappled with gooseflesh, Honey Eater stepped up onto the grassy bank and dried off with handfuls of willow leaves.

The biting cold of the river, and a cool sting in the early morning air, had left her teeth chattering. But she welcomed the slap to her senses after another sleepless night's vigil with her ailing father.

Well hidden behind the wall of tall rushes which marked off the women's bathing area, she slipped into her moccasins and a dress made of soft kid leather. Her wet hair was unbraided now and hung in long black tresses.

Then she lingered for a long moment, her pretty, finely sculpted face sad with the weight of her problems. Touch the Sky was gone, and her father was about to leave her too! Honey Eater could not muster the usual happiness of the snow-melting season. Instead, she felt only the haunting, hollow sadness of loss that she always felt in the Moon When the Geese Fly South when the trees were shaking off their leaves.

The first thing she noticed, when she stepped past the wall of rushes, was the Lakota camp. It was well downstream on the opposite bank. Already, as in the Cheyenne camp, smoke curled from the top-holes of the tipis. They were constructed almost exactly like those of their Cheyenne cousins. But the more modest Cheyennes included a flap over the entrance to ensure privacy.

Honey Eater welcomed the presence of Chief Sun Dance and his Lakotas. Their warriors were fierce, their ponies swift. Several Lakotas had married into Yellow Bear's tribe, and Honey Eater knew of Cheyennes living with Sun Dance's people. The two tribes would fight to the death for each other.

True, the Lakotas were here only temporarily, until their hunt began. But such reassurance was welcome now, with her father fighting for each breath. The loss of any member of the tribe brought bad medicine, of course. But a chief's passing left a tribe at its most vulnerable.

As she crossed the camp, she saw some of the old grandmothers gathering with their willow-stem baskets. They were going out this morning to gather acorns and wild peas.

She kept her eyes downcast, but she was aware that Black Elk was already awake and stirring. He sat before his tipi, plaiting a bridle out of rawhide and horsehair.

Though he too avoided glancing in her direction, she knew he saw her. And she could not help wondering: Is that new bridle for one of the horses he plans to offer as the bride-price for my love?

She lifted the flap of her tipi and saw Arrow Keeper sitting cross-legged beside her father's robes.

"Come in, little daughter," he said. "I dismissed the grandmother so that we might talk."

"I always place your words close to my heart."

"Yes, you do. And therefore I always select them carefully. Come, little Honey Eater—come look at your father."

She did. Little had changed since she left to bathe. His craggy, nut-brown face was emaciated, the flesh drawn knuckle-tight on the prominent cheekbones. His silver-white hair lay fanned out like a mane. It reminded her of the days when he wore a magnificent crow-feather war bonnet and led braves into battle shouting the war cry.

"Look at him, daughter, and remember him well. Soon, very soon now, he makes his final journey."

Arrow Keeper made the cut-off sign.

"You must be strong, little one. You have suffered terribly and will suffer more. But you must not hold this bitterness in your heart toward Touch the Sky. He has not deserted you or his tribe."

"Father, I hear your words, but how can they be true? Is he here now? Did he not ride out before the Lakota made their camp near ours?"

"He did, daughter. But love fought with duty in his heart, and he did not make his decision lightly. He rode into great danger, faces danger at this moment, to help the only mother and father he has known.

"Honey Eater, are you a Cheyenne maiden? Or are you like the cold Comanches below the Platte, who scorn clan loyalties and leave their old parents to starve in the short white days?"

Tears filmed her eyes, one lone crystal drop dripping from a lash. "You are right, Father. It is good that Touch the Sky loves his white parents enough to fight for them. But I am afraid. Afraid for him, and afraid for myself."

She didn't need to say more. It would be unseemly to speak of such things now, over the dying chief. But Honey Eater was hinting about the tribal law which declared that a marriageable maiden must live with either her father, her brother, or her husband.

Arrow Keeper nodded, his seamed face troubled. It was true that he now believed firmly in the medicine vision which had foretold Touch the Sky's greatness. But nothing in that vision told him that Touch the Sky and Honey Eater, despite their powerful love, would eventually celebrate the squaw-taking ceremony. Black Elk was a fierce warrior, older than Touch the Sky and far richer in the spoils of battle. He was also the tribe's war chief.

"I understand your fear, daughter," Arrow Keeper finally said. "But you must be prepared to do your duty. You cannot defy the will of the tribe. A chief's daughter has a special obligation."

She was about to reply when old Yellow Bear abruptly sat up, eyes wide open and blazing, and called her name!

The shock of it froze both Honey Eater and Arrow Keeper. The chief, clearly in a trance though his eyes were wide open, stared only at his daughter. He seemed unaware of Arrow Keeper's presence.

"Honey Eater," said his gravelly, tired voice, "the tall young stranger is meant to be a chief. But his path will be hard and his enemies many. Love him, my little daughter, but hold these words close to your heart.

"Happiness is a short, warm moment, and suffering is a long, cold night. The red nations have tasted their greatest glory. From now on the red man runs from death alongside his brother the buffalo. This tall young stranger will be the last of the great Cheyenne war chiefs. Behind him the Shaiyena people will raise their battle cry in one last, great victory.

"I love you, Honey Eater. You have always been the soul of this old warrior's medicine bag. Now I go to join your mother. Do not weep for me, daughter. Bring children into this world, and sing to them about their grandfather and the old ways."

Yellow Bear collapsed, sucked in a long, rattling breath, then sang the death song in a weak but clear voice:

Nothing lives long,
Only the earth and the mountains.

The next moment the chief died, his face weary but at peace.

Despite his request, Honey Eater burst into sobs, a knife point of grief twisting deep inside her.

Arrow Keeper still sat motionless, profoundly moved. Hovering near death, Yellow Bear too had experienced the vision of Touch the Sky's greatness. But now Honey Eater's father was gone, and Touch the Sky had few in the tribe to speak up for him. His present battle with the palefaces was not his only problem. If the hapless youth did not return soon, he would lose the happiness of his life to Black Elk.

And even if he did return in time, Black Elk would never surrender her without a fight to the death.

But for now ancient custom took over. Arrow Keeper stepped outside and sent a young boy running to fetch the camp crier. His face solemn at the news of Yellow Bear's death, the brave swung onto his pony. He raced up and down the camp, crying at the top of his lungs:

"Our chief has crossed over! Our chief has crossed over!"

The keening wail of the mourners soon filled the camp. Downriver, the overheard cry was likewise being spread by the Lakotas, for whom this was also a terrible and solemn occasion. But Honey Eater dried her eyes and touched her father's dead face in a gesture of farewell.

Now the call of tribal duty was strong in her. There would be many things to do. Of course, at a time like this, it was usual for one of the honored grandmothers to prepare a chief for his final journey. But now she must take charge and show she was strong—was she not the proud daughter of a great chief?

His body must be washed and dressed, and he would need new moccasins for his long journey to the Land of Ghosts. She hurried outside, knowing she must greet the mourners as they visited their dead chief.

Black Elk was among the first who were heading toward the tipi. *Hurry, Touch the Sky,* she thought. *Hurry! I am alone now!*

Wolf Who Hunts Smiling was a warrior now. Despite his youth, he was entrusted with the important task of training the young bucks in the arts of Cheyenne warfare.

Nonetheless, a certain story had made the rounds at Yellow Bear's camp. It was well known that, at the very moment they were both needed to protect their war chief from white bullets, Wolf Who Hunts Smiling and Touch the Sky had instead fought each other for the honor of the first kill. None of the bucks was foolish enough to mention this in front of Wolf Who Hunts Smiling. But his ears, like his furtive eyes, missed nothing—he had heard them speak of this thing, scorn in their voices.

Now, as he led a party of six young bucks on a hunting trip near the Little Bighorn River, his mind raced for ways to unite the warriors in training behind him. Wolf Who Hunts Smiling admired his cousin Black Elk greatly. But Black Elk's heart was too soft and womanly toward this white man's dog who dared take the Cheyenne name Touch the Sky. Wolf Who Hunts Smiling had watched the Bluecoats turn his own father into raw, shredded meat when his body absorbed the full impact of a canister shell. Black Elk was indeed strong and brave. But his head and heart were soft toward the white dogs who must be driven from the red man's land!

They were hunting with bows only. Only now was the tribe starting to accumulate new beaver pelts for trade. The hunters and warriors were without ammunition and gun patches and black powder. So Wolf Who Hunts Smiling ordered his subordinates to remain silent and downwind when they spotted a black bear ahead beside the game trail. Arrows would only enrage it for the kill. They let it roll aside a log to get at the beetles beneath it before they rode on.

Good meat was scarce and the racks back at Yellow Bear's camp almost empty. There were some stringy elk in the foothills, and the Arapahoes reported small buffalo herds between the Black Hills and the Niobrara River. But most of the big herds were running well to the north, far north of the Marias River. Already they sensed that the old runs to the south had become trails of senseless slaughter, thanks to the white men and their .53-caliber buffalo balls.

"Little brothers!" said Wolf Who Hunts Smiling when they stopped to water their ponies. "The tribe needs meat. Keep your eyes sharp for a fat mule deer or antelope! He who sinks first arrow eats the liver!"

That night they camped in a cedar brake near the Little Bighorn. All day long Wolf Who Hunts Smiling had been plagued by thoughts of Touch the Sky. Every day longer that he was alive added fresh humiliation and torment to the shame Wolf Who Hunts Smiling already felt. He had vowed to kill this capable young warrior when Touch the Sky was still untrained in the killing ways. Now his boast was proving difficult to carry out.

"Cheyenne bucks," said Wolf Who Hunts Smiling while the embers still glowed bright, "there is nothing more dangerous to a tribe than an Indian turncoat!

"You know already that River of Winds and Swift Canoe have been sent into long-knife territory. They have gone for the purpose of finally proving that Touch the Sky is a double-tongued spy. Perhaps Little Horse too plays the fox with his own people. More than one red man has killed a brother in his sleep for white man's gold or strong water."

Wolf Who Hunts Smiling paused, savoring the taste of power over these young bucks who would become the tribe's future warriors. He must be careful. Though their lives were remote from those of Yellow Bear, Arrow Keeper, and the other elders with 60 and more winters behind them, they respected young warriors like Black Elk, their war chief.

"Little brothers, I do not speak in a wolf bark against any of the Headmen. But when you ask among yourselves why has this dangerous spy been permitted to live among us, look to the councillors and your medicine man and your chief. This thing has not happened because they do not love their tribe. It is because they are soft and sentimental with old age, like old women who recall their dead children and openly weep.

"A warrior must be a tree covered with hard bark! Do you not observe how the red men live who lie down like dogs for the long knives? The paleface is our sworn enemy, and we must scatter his bones across the plains and prairies, throughout the mountains and the valleys! We can trust no one who would make medicine with the white men, no one who would desert his red tribe and ride to fight battles for those who take our land

and kill our people! A Cheyenne cannot place anything before his duty to his tribe. I tell you now this Touch the Sky is not one of us, and even now he is lending strength to our enemies!"

Chapter Ten

Two sleeps passed without trouble after the horse-scattering incident. While their sister the sun made her journey through the sky, Touch the Sky and Little Horse moved with ease around the perimeter of the Hanchon spread. Several times they spotted Steele's riders on Hanchon land, apparently checking on the location of the mustang herds. The two Cheyennes stuck to the trees and thickets, made quick time through the many cutbanks and coulees. Their experience in concealment served them well now.

When their uncle the moon owned the sky, they built a small cedar and willow fire, smothering it frequently to produce smoke for scenting their clothing and moccasins. Winds changed unpredictably near the river, and mustangs unused to the smell of Indians might well stampede when they didn't want them to, giving them away.

Under cover of darkness they also visited the house. Sarah Hanchon insisted on serving them hot food, and to Touch the Sky's astonishment Little Horse devoured everything with intense pleasure. Once, when she heaped a third helping of biscuits and honey on Little Horse's plate, Touch the Sky saw his friend briefly glance at Sarah Hanchon and meet her eyes with respectful gratitude. Around John Hanchon too Little Horse was at ease. Only when Wade McKenna was present did Little Horse withdraw into himself and cast his eyes down at one unvarying spot on the floor.

"All the mustangs you two scattered are back in the summer meadow," said John Hanchon. He was cleaning the Henry, and it was broken open before him on the oilcloth-covered deal table in the kitchen. "They never left our land, so it was no trouble pointing them. Woody won't be on his feet for days yet, and it's no good to me when he is because he quit. He's the second one in as many days. Hell, the next man that demands his wages in full will have to take it in hay and grass."

Despite the forced jocularity of his remark, Hanchon showed his concern in the deepening network of lines around his eyes and mouth. He was now left with only five wranglers and Wade McKenna. Not only was defending his property a problem—soon he might not even be able to work it.

Luckily he had recently come into some hard cash providing 30 saddle-broke horses for a keel-boat company, and they needed 30 more again in a month. Still, he was unable to seek new business so long as he was tied up in fighting for his very survival.

Touch the Sky read the worry in his parents' faces, and again felt hatred for Steele and every other greedy white man who thought the green earth and all her creatures belonged to them to buy and sell. Thinking of the sentry, he asked his mother if she'd heard any more from Kristen Steele. But Sarah only bit her lower lip and frowned, answering that she'd heard nothing. She was worried about the same question that troubled Touch the Sky: Did Hiram know she'd come out here again against his orders?

On that second night, at Sarah's insistence, the two Cheyennes filled their legging sashes with cold biscuits and dried fruit and jerked beef. Early the next morning, while Little Horse went to check on their ponies, Touch the Sky went upridge and into the trees. He followed the deer run until he reached the lightning-split cottonwood. He had checked it every morning since he and Riley agreed to use it for messages.

This time, when his hand groped deep into the charred opening, his fingers encountered a folded scrap of paper.

Move your camp out of this area, Riley had written. *Carlson due through this area soon searching for you. Suggest you camp closer to Steele's property. But keep checking this spot for messages.*

They took the Bluecoat's advice. That night, aided by a moonless, cloudy sky, they rode due west until they reached a hogback ridge which bordered Steele's spread. From there they could keep an eye on his riders yet be within a short ride of the Hanchon property.

They camped well below the steep crest of the hogback, selecting a thickly wooded hollow. They built a crude brush lean-to for protection from rain. Unfortunately, there wasn't much forage available for the ponies, and it was necessary to occasionally move them about to new patches of graze, risking exposure from the main yard below.

Despite all the precaution of this move, however, the two Cheyennes very nearly rode square into death.

It was the second day after their move to the new camp. Avoiding the trail and riding high along the ridge, Touch the Sky and Little Horse rode back to their old campsite to check for messages in the cottonwood. The fork was empty. They had just swung onto their ponies and pointed them back toward Steele's property when they saw a Bluecoat pony squad advancing toward their position from below the ridge.

The arrogant Seth Carlson led them! Touch the Sky realized this was the patrol Riley had warned them about—the patrol sent to search them out like holed-up rats.

"Brother!" said Touch the Sky. "It is useless to try outrunning the pony soldiers. The trees on this ridge are our only cover, but they grow too close together for hard, fast riding."

Little Horse nodded. "And they would hear the sounds of hard riding. We must take cover."

Concealing their ponies presented the immediate problem. By now the Bluecoats were almost within hailing distance of the tree line. At a command from Carlson they formed up at close intervals, only a few yards between each trooper.

"Brother," said Little Horse, "this is a search party, not just a patrol riding through. These pale-faces mean to turn over every leaf!"

Touch the Sky's mouth was a grim, determined slit. He nodded.

"We must hide well or be prepared to sing the death song," he said. "Quickly, strip the bridle and blanket from your pony! We must turn her loose on the far side of the trees. If the soldiers spot her, we can only hope they do not recognize her. Perhaps they will mistake her for a stray mustang from one of the spreads."

Little Horse stripped the powerful little chestnut. They hoped the Bluecoats would not ride close enough to spot the handprint he had made with claybank war paint on the pony's left front forequarter, the Cheyenne way of marking a pony's owner.

Little Horse led the chestnut further up the ridge and turned her loose to graze on the opposite side of the tree line. Touch the Sky knew this ruse was too risky for his own dun. Carlson had gotten too long and close a look at her when he charged Touch the Sky. But this pony had been especially trained by Arrow Keeper.

Quickly, Touch the Sky led her to a patch of open ground which appeared worthless for hiding. He hoped the patrol would bypass it in favor of denser undergrowth.

Touch the Sky made a snorting noise like a horse drinking. Immediately, the dun lay down flat on her side, head down.

The Bluecoat patrol was only about 30 yards from the tree line, and closing steadily, by the time Touch the Sky and Little Horse finished covering the dun with fallen leaves and branches. From a short distance off there appeared to be only a small hummock rising from the ridge.

"Quickly!" said Little Horse. "There is a stream

close by. I saw a place where we might hide when I was leading my pony out. But it means we must risk leaving the rifles here with your pony."

"Stay at close intervals!" they heard Carlson shout behind them. "Dismount at the tree line and tether your horses. Then fix bayonets. We'll move through the trees on foot. Search thoroughly, and probe your steel into that brush! These are dangerous bucks, so shoot on sight!"

The two Cheyennes reached the stream and waded through it, crossing on the opposite bank toward a huge tree. Its huge, shaggy network of roots had been exposed where the stream had eaten away the dirt beneath it. This left a slight hollow tucked up under the bank of the stream.

The chilly water was dark with spring soil runoff. They ducked under and, one at a time, helping each other, squeezed through the narrow opening beneath the tree roots. They were barely able to secrete their heads and shoulders into the slight opening, the rest of their bodies hidden by the murky water.

At first they could hear nothing but the steady rush of the water all around them. But their keen ears soon detected the sounds of the thorough search as they grew steadily louder. Heavy leather boots stomped through the undergrowth, bayonets sliced into the bushes and brambles and deadfalls.

"Brother," said Little Horse, speaking directly into his friend's ear in a voice just above a whisper, "our enemy is upon us! My knife is in my hand, and I see yours is ready also. If we are meant to die, let it be like *warriors*, right here, right now, with the death song on our lips and our blades seeking warm vitals! I swear to you I will fall on my own knife before I let them take me prisoner!"

"I swear this thing to you too. By the four directions, I swear they will never lock you in the soldier house while I have breath in me."

They fell silent as the sounds of searching grew closer. Heavy, uneven splashes told them soldiers had entered the stream nearby.

"You, Davis!" shouted Carlson's voice, so close that Touch the Sky jerked in surprise. "Afraid to get your feet wet, soldier? Check up under that tree. They might have a cache there."

More splashing, much nearer now. Touch the Sky tried to pull as much of his body as possible up under the bank. After what seemed an unbearably long time, the splashing ceased as the Bluecoat left the water. Touch the Sky expelled a long sigh of relief.

The next moment, a sharp bayonet with a blood gutter tooled into it just missed his left eye by inches when it probed through the thin layer of dirt above them.

Another thrust, another, each further away from his face.

The soldier added a fourth and final jab, this one slicing deep through Little Horse's right shoulder on its way back out.

Little Horse hissed at the sudden, fiery pain which took him by surprise, but otherwise made no sound or movement to give them away. A minute later they heard the searching noises grow dimmer again as the squad advanced toward the other side of the tree line.

They knew they must wait for the Bluecoats to return and remount, moving further downridge. Little Horse ducked lower in the cold water, slowing the loss of blood from his wound.

After the patrol had finally moved further east, the fugitives gratefully escaped from the cramped hiding place. Touch the Sky retrieved their weapons and the obedient dun and quickly hobbled her before he led Little Horse's pony back into the trees. Then he gouged out balsam sap and packed it into his friend's wound before binding it with soft strips of red willow bark.

"The Bluecoat officer is more determined than I thought," said Touch the Sky. "This wound is clean, though it has sliced deep. Your arm will be stiff."

"I can still hold this weapon," Little Horse said, hoisting the scattergun to prove his words. "And good thing. After this thing today, I see that battles are coming."

A sharp lance of guilt passed through Touch the Sky. He had not told his friend exactly why the Bluecoat officer was so determined. He had not explained that Carlson was not just tracking down two renegade Cheyennes—that in fact he was after one particular Cheyenne who'd had the gall to kiss a white woman. Was it fair that he place his friend's life in danger over such a personal battle?

As they cautiously rode back to their camp, Touch the Sky tried briefly to speak of this. But Little Horse silenced him.

"Brother, if a snake crawls into my tipi, I do not ask whether it is seeking food or warmth. I know only that a snake is in my tipi. It does not matter to me why this Bluecoat seeks to put you under. All these things you tell me lead to one truth which you may place in your sash: Your greatest crime is being a Cheyenne!"

He spoke straight-arrow, and Touch the Sky fell silent. Their enemies surrounded them, and now it was time to forget words and listen to the language of nature. They had fooled the Bluecoats today, true. But neither Cheyenne felt like boasting or celebrating their great skill, as warriors often do after a victory.

The Bluecoats would be back. And even now, with each step their ponies took, they grew closer to Hiram Steele's property and a second enemy even more ruthless than the Bluecoats.

Chapter Eleven

"Truth to tell," said Abe Winslow, "I ain't seed hide nor hair of these red varmints that got you all consternated."

"They're out there," said Hiram Steele. "Sure as gumption, they're out there. That was no bear that spooked those mustangs the other night."

"By hell, it sounded pure-dee bear, and this hoss has let daylight into more than one. You yourself say that shavetail lieutenant and his men have combed this area and can't find sign of them."

"There's only two," said Steele. "That makes it easier to hide."

Winslow absently scratched at his pockmarked face. He stood just inside the door of Steele's house, slouched beaver in his hand. Removing his hat was not a mark of respect toward Steele. It was nervousness—the only solid buildings the former mountain man turned outlaw had been inside in 20 years were trading posts and jail-houses.

"Two," said Winslow. "And what tribe did you say they was?"

"I didn't, but it's Cheyenne."

This news did not set well with Winslow. Frowning, he said, "You didn't say nothing about no Cheyennes when we talked terms."

"They weren't around then."

"Well, they are now. And I'll tell you straight from the shoulder, me and my men have already had our bellyful of fighting Cheyennes."

"No need to get skittish," said Steele. "There's only two of them, and they've barely got their growth."

This information made Winslow cock his head with sudden interest. "Young bucks, you say?"

"Yes, why?"

Winslow was silent for several moments, lost in reflection. "Young, you say. What do they look like?"

Something in the hardcase's tone alerted Steele. The rancher shrugged his beefy shoulders. "Look like? Hell, all Indians look alike to me."

"Then you ain't never stood a Pawnee next to a Flathead! Is one of the bucks tall for an Indian?"

Steele's eyes cut impatiently away. "The hell, you think I measure every renegade that rides through this valley?"

Winslow sniffed a rat here. He despised Hiram Steele and all other men, farmers or ranchers, who pounded their stake in one spot and worked it for life. But money talks and bullshit walks, was Winslow's motto, and Steele paid up every week in gold nuggets.

Still, this talk about young Cheyenne bucks cankered at him. He had seen what a handful of them did to Henri Lagace's mountain stronghold, from which Winslow had been lucky to escape with his topknot still attached.

"I'll tell you straight right now," he said. "When the men find out we're huggin' with Cheyennes, they'll want more money."

"Show me their dead bodies, and there'll be more money. Plenty more."

Steele walked to the front window and pushed the curtain aside. Beyond the main yard, several of his regular hands were erecting a big new pole corral.

"Whether it's bears or Indians," said Steele, "this next raid won't be stopped. I'll see to that. And when I set my mind to something, you can call it as good as done."

Only one sleep after they avoided the Bluecoat search party, the two Cheyennes spotted new signs of possible trouble.

A new pole corral was going up, yet there was no sign that Steele's wranglers were planning to ride out after wild mustangs. A corral this large could only mean that Steele planned to acquire a large number of horses soon.

"Steele's fed up with the penny-ante game," said John Hanchon that night when Touch the Sky and Little Horse visited the house and told him about the new corral. "He's going to raise the stakes sky high this next time, and drive us out. That corral is for my horses—there's not another good herd of wild mustangs between here and the Niobrara River, and Steele knows that."

Later, in the shelter of their brush lean-to, Touch the Sky lay on his back and watched the stars through the entrance hole. He thought again about the worry lines permanently etched into his parents' faces. And he thought about Hiram Steele, who drove him out of this territory for no other crime than being an Indian.

"Brother," he said to Little Horse in the cool darkness, "I am weary of always waiting for our enemy to act before we know their plans. This new corral, I must learn their plans for it."

"I have ears for this," said Little Horse. "But how? Will you turn into a bird and fly among them, listening?"

"Only Arrow Keeper's big medicine might turn me into a bird. But yes, I will go among them and listen."

He heard Little Horse sit up in his robe. His voice was low with seriousness when he said, "Brother, have you gone Wendigo? They will spit you and roast you over the embers."

"I will sneak up on the lodge where the men sleep," said Touch the Sky. "Whites always foolishly wag their tongues. Perhaps I will learn more about this corral, learn when and how they will attack my father's ranch. Black Elk was right, a warrior must always own the element of surprise."

Little Horse was silent for many heartbeats. Touch the Sky was right about surprise, of course. But this was a dangerous move, this plan to enter the vipers' nest.

"I agree," Little Horse finally said. "But I must go with you."

"I have no ears for this talk! But think, it is I who understand the paleface tongue. It will be easier for one to sneak in than two."

"It is no use, brother. You will reverse the wind

before you change Little Horse's mind. I go with you. Now let us talk about this thing."

Touch the Sky could tell, from his friend's tone, that he meant what he said. So the two friends counseled in earnest, glad at last for this clear course of action.

Little Horse reminded him: This mission would take place after the fall of darkness, that eternal foe of the Cheyennes. This was bad medicine. It meant they could not kill nor even attack an enemy without staining the tribe's sacred Medicine Arrows forever. Therefore, he argued, they must prepare an elaborate defense tomorrow, during the day. A defense designed to delay their enemies, should they be forced to flee, without requiring them to actually fight except as a last resort.

The next morning they selected a shallow, rocky basin as their emergency escape route. It lay directly behind the bunkhouse, separated from the pine log building by a meadow and a line of low hills. That afternoon a sudden thunder squall darkened the area and sent all the hands seeking shelter. The Cheyennes took advantage of the bad weather to prepare their escape. They worked well into the evening, chewing on jerked beef and dried plums to ease the gnawing in their bellies.

Touch the Sky had already studied the bunkhouse carefully, one evening when he and Little Horse had sneaked close to the main yard to estimate the number of men working for Steele. He knew that there was one window, just around the front corner from the doorway. It was covered with oiled paper, but one corner had torn out leaving an opening the size of a fist.

"I will be able to hear them," said Touch the

Sky as they prepared to approach the yard. "But I will be exposed in the moonlight on a side the sentry can see clearly. You must remain back behind near the corral as my lookout. If the sentry approaches, sound the owl hoot."

Little Horse agreed in a nod. Their danger was extreme because they had both decided to leave all weapons except their throwing axes back at camp as a gesture of assurance to Maiyun, the Good Supernatural, that they would not attack after dark as did the treacherous Pawnees. Their axes would be hidden at the edge of the rocky basin. If trapped or captured before they reached the basin, they had no defense.

Although the cream-colored moonlight exposed them, it also made for an easy journey on foot down from their campsite to the outlying pastures of the Steele spread. The two Cheyennes waited for occasional scuds of clouds to sweep in front of the moon. Then they would race closer to the bunkhouse, staying low to the ground and keeping their faces down as much as possible to cut reflection or glare from their eyes.

At the far corner of the last corral, Touch the Sky gripped his friend's arm and squeezed it. Little Horse nodded. For a long moment, crouched in the shadow of the corral poles, they felt united in their common goal of defeating their enemy. Every sense was alive, alert, and the copper taste of fear was mixed with the sweet, thrilling scent of victory for their people.

"Wait here, brother," whispered Little Horse. "I hear the sentry."

The smaller Cheyenne's keen ears proved right again. It was a full ten heartbeats before Touch the Sky heard the wrangler's mount approach-

Judd Cole

ing from the opposite side of the yard. The man made a pass around the bunkhouse and the main house, throwing a long, eerie shadow in the stark moonlight. Then he swung out toward the outlying sheds and pens.

"Slide easy like that paleface's shadow," said Little Horse, "and leave one ear listening for the owl, brother! And remember, you carry no weapons!"

Touch the Sky searched the yard one final time. Then he rose in a crouch and crossed the open expanse between the corral and the corner of the bunkhouse. He flattened himself against the building and inched closer to the opening in the oiled paper. A yellow beam of lantern light shot out like a stray shaft of sunlight.

He could hear the mournful twang of a Jew's harp. Snatches of conversation escaped through the hole like bugs.

"God strike me dead now if it ain't the truth! I did so meet the Queen of England!"

"Why prove up a homestead jist to see the gum 'ment boys give it all back to the Innuns?"

"You ask *this* white nigger, I won't poke no redheaded woman. They got a bush down there like a prickly pear."

Touch the Sky was about to find a more comfortable position, ready to settle in for a long wait. At that moment a hound trotted around the corner and spotted him.

A growl bubbled low in its throat.

The next moment it began a furious barking.

"The hell?" shouted somebody inside the bunkhouse. "Who goes out there?"

The door banged open and Touch the Sky sprang toward the corral.

"Fly like the wind, brother!" he said to Little Horse.

"Over there by the corral!" a man shouted. "Two of 'em, see?"

A couple of men had grabbed weapons as they ran outside. They opened fire. Slugs whanged past the Cheyennes' ears. Several men gave chase on foot while others raced for their stalled horses.

"Do not run in a straight line, brother!" said Little Horse. "It makes an easy target!"

They zigzagged across the open meadow and into the low hills, bullets nipping at their heels all the way. Now they could hear the ominous pounding of shod hooves as the first mounted wranglers gave chase.

Touch the Sky looked over his shoulder and recognized the sentry leading the group. He was closing fast, not bothering to draw his sidearm. Clearly he meant to move into killing range first before he wasted a cap.

They could hear their enemies' horses snorting now. They put on a final burst of speed and reached the edge of the rock-strewn basin.

Touch the Sky was first to reach the boulder behind which they'd stashed their axes. The sentry gave sharp spur to his mount, surging even closer as the two Cheyennes stopped to face him.

"No blood!" Little Horse shouted as Touch the Sky cocked his arm. The tall Cheyenne unleashed the double-bladed throwing axe. It spun end over end and sliced clean through one of the latigos of the sentry's saddle. The cinch immediately broke and the saddle slid quickly around, tossing the rider clear.

"Quickly!" said Touch the Sky. "Remember the route!"

They raced along the trail they had prepared earlier. Now bullets ricocheted from boulders as more riders closed in.

Suddenly, a horse crashed to the ground, its legs entwined in leather ropes the Cheyennes had strung there earlier.

Another rider bore down on them, close enough now to draw steel. He was drawing a bead on Touch the Sky's back when he raised one hand to swipe at an obstructing branch.

There was a noise like a whip cracking as his swipe released the powerfully bent branch the Cheyennes had rigged earlier. The force easily lifted him from the saddle and knocked him off his horse backwards. His spine snapped like old wood when he landed square on a jagged-edged boulder.

Enough men had gone down to slow the charge to a standstill. The two Cheyennes took refuge in a prearranged spot, a narrow cleft between one wall of the basin and a huge slab of slate.

"All right, men!" said Winslow's gravelly voice. "Steele was right after all! We got Cheyennes on the warpath agin us! That's enough for tonight. Round up the horses and tend to the wounded."

"What about Myers?" said one of the men. "His back is snapped clean. He's gone beaver."

The well-hidden Cheyenne warriors watched, in the stark light of the moon, as Winslow walked back to the spot where the wrangler named Myers had fallen. Without a word he drew his pistol and put a bullet in the man's brain.

"Bury him tomorrow," he said, "when you can see what the hell you're doing. And from now on, keep your weapons to hand. We got us some Cheyennes to kill!"

From the edge of the basin, well secreted in a dense thicket, Swift Canoe and River of Winds watched the drama between the whites and their fellow Cheyennes.

Several sleeps earlier, they had spied on Touch the Sky as he found the message from the Bluecoat in the cottonwood tree. Clearly he followed the pony soldier's orders. Immediately after finding the white man's talking paper, he and Little Horse had moved their camp closer to this second mustang spread.

Then, only one sleep earlier, Swift Canoe and River of Winds had followed the two friends as they again checked for messages in the tree. They had run away as soon as they spotted the Bluecoat patrol. Thus, they saw nothing that occurred between the white butchers and their fellow Cheyennes. But Swift Canoe had concluded that the soldiers were coming to meet with Touch the Sky and Little Horse.

River of Winds said nothing to his companion, who was already like a dog in the hot moon in his thirst for blood. But secretly he suspected that Swift Canoe was right.

"Brother," said Swift Canoe now, having watched wordlessly as the paleface coolly shot his wounded companion like a lame horse. "I have thought long over this thing. I have heard stories from warriors whom I trust, warriors who speak one way always. They say that the long knives often secretly attack their own people. This way they blame some enemy and profit from the spoils of war."

River of Winds was silent. But he too wondered the same thing Swift Canoe had come to accept as truth: Did this explain the apparent meeting yesterday between the Cheyennes and the Bluecoats? Had Touch the Sky and Little Horse agreed to make war against white settlers to create the appearance that Cheyennes were raiding away from their hunting grounds?

"Anything is possible," said River of Winds. "These stories you have heard from the warriors, they are true. But this does not prove that Touch the Sky and Little Horse are spies."

"I can tell from your voice, brother, that your own heart does not believe your words. These two are dogs for the white soldier who leaves talking papers in the tree! They not only sell the secrets of Yellow Bear's tribe to their enemy. They turn a powerful foe against the entire Cheyenne nation!"

"Anything is possible. We must report to the council soon. Until then, I think with my eyes and ears and nose and not with my head," said River of Winds.

"Brother, you have seen more battles and have more winters behind you than I. But sometimes you think too much with your heart too. You will have your proof, and soon. These two bucks learned the art of warfare from Black Elk. Look below and see how well they learned! But brother, even the blind buffalo can scent a wolf! How can your keen eyes not see it? These two Cheyennes are turncoats!"

Chapter Twelve

"The tribe is not content," Arrow Keeper said to the councillors and warriors. "Our chief has finally crossed over in peace, and this is a good thing. But the tribe is unhappy."

The old medicine man sat near the center pole of the council lodge, his red Hudson's Bay blanket drawn tight around his shoulders. Funeral rites for Yellow Bear were over. Now he rested high on a scaffold in a secret forest known only to the Cheyennes.

This council had been called to discuss the future of the tribe and the upcoming chief-renewal ceremony. The chief-renewal could not be held until all far-flung members of the tribe, now visiting with distant clans, could be summoned by word-bringers.

"The tribe is unhappy," said Arrow Keeper, "and I understand this thing. Good meat is scarce. Our annual Spring Dance has been delayed. We have not had our usual gathering to visit with distant clans after the long winter's isolation. We have not prayed to the Arrows and thanked the Great Spirit for these warm moons."

The old men nodded their agreement.

"Now our chief has crossed over, and we must accomplish these neglected things. The first step belongs to the Headmen. They must decide on an acting peace chief until the renewal ceremony."

Black Elk immediately rose. His long war bonnet held one eagle-tail feather for each time he'd counted coup. The crudely sewn-on flap of his dead ear gave him an especially ferocious expression.

"Fathers and brothers! I am your war chief. You have smoked the common pipe with me many times. May Black Elk die of the yellow vomit if he ever hides in his tipi while his tribe is on the warpath!

"Headmen, hear my words! Even now Arrow Keeper acts as our peace chief. He is a blooded warrior who has strewn the bones of his enemies on many battlefields! His wisdom is vast like the plains, his medicine strong as the grizzly! Be wise, Headmen, and call on Arrow Keeper to remain as our peace chief until the renewal ceremony!"

This was greeted with an instant shout of approval from both the warriors and the Headmen. The Headmen did not bother voting with their stones. A quick voice vote confirmed unanimous support for the old shaman.

"The tribe has spoken with one voice," said Arrow Keeper, "and I will obey. My first unpleasant duty is to remind all of you that the Lakotas soon leave on their hunt. I have received word from Arapaho runners that Pawnees are on the move north from their hunting grounds below the Weeping Woman River. We must take steps to fortify our camp and strengthen the outlying guard."

His last words were directed toward Black Elk. That warrior now said, "All braves must ready their battle rigs and keep them ready."

He turned toward Wolf Who Hunts Smiling.

"Cousin, you must train the junior warriors as quickly as possible! Soon we will have enough beaver pelts to take to the trading post at Red Shale. Then we will have ammunition."

Wolf Who Hunts Smiling nodded. His furtive dark eyes were ablaze now with the sense of his own importance. "My warriors will stand and hold when the battle cry sounds!" he said. "Can this be said for Touch the Sky and Little Horse? Now, when the tribe needs every warrior, where are they?"

Wolf Who Hunts Smiling had recently been speaking with several of the younger warriors, convincing them of the need to protect the tribe from outsiders in spite of the blindness of some of the elders. Now a few of them shouted their approval of his words.

"We are not here to discuss Touch the Sky," said Arrow Keeper coldly. "River of Winds and Swift Canoe will make their first report soon enough."

"It is never too soon, Father, to expose a turncoat! The sooner we kill these two-faced Cheyennes, the safer our tribe!"

This too was greeted with a chorus of shouts. Now, for the first time, anger glimmered in Arrow Keeper's tired old eyes. He surprised everyone by rising nimbly and suddenly unfolding a coyote fur pouch he had been hiding behind his blanket.

The lodge fell as silent as the forest where they placed their dead. Everyone knew what was in that pouch.

Arrow Keeper, his gnarled old hands never once trembling, unwrapped four stone-tipped arrows. Their shafts were dyed with bright blue and yellow stripes and fletched with scarlet feathers.

Arrow Keeper walked close to Wolf Who Hunts Smiling and thrust the arrows toward his face.

"Do you see these arrows, bloodthirsty Cheyenne buck? *These* are the sacred Medicine Arrows which you and all other warriors have sworn, with your life, to keep forever sweet and clean! And now, in the presence of the Arrows, will you speak boldly of shedding the blood of your own?"

Arrow Keeper's voice was brittle with anger and disappointment. Wolf Who Hunts Smiling was shamed. A hot flush crept up his neck and into his face as he saw all the warriors and Headmen staring at him, their grim faces sharing in Arrow Keeper's disapproval.

"But Father! Hear my words."

"Silence, cousin!" commanded Black Elk. "Your chief has spoken. Do not further sully our Arrows with your unmanly disrespect!"

Wolf Who Hunts Smiling obediently closed his mouth and sat down on the robe-covered floor of the lodge. But anger seethed inside of him. How he hated this tall Cheyenne stranger who always managed to make him look like a fool—even when he wasn't present!

"Wake up, niece! Must you always be dreaming?"

With a guilty start, Honey Eater forced her thoughts back to the present. The beadwork shawl she was supposed to be working on lay untouched in her lap. Her aunt, Sharp Nosed Woman, stared at her with an impatient frown.

"I am sorry, Aunt. Did you speak?"

Sharp Nosed Woman shook her head and muttered something under her breath. She was the sister of Honey Eater's dead mother, Singing Woman, who had been shot dead by Pawnees before Honey Eater's eyes.

Sharp Nosed Woman was a middle-aged widow who had lost her brave in the same attack which killed her sister. Honey Eater was required by tribal law, now that her father was gone, to live with her closest female relative until she married. Sharp Nosed Woman loved her niece. But she was a no-nonsense, practical woman who could not understand why girls would wear flowers in their hair or love a warrior who had nothing but his breechclout to his name.

"Yes, stone ears, I did speak! I asked if you are prepared to send an answer to Black Elk yet."

Honey Eater said nothing, though her pretty face mirrored her anguish and grief and confusion. She still wore the black shawl of mourning, and already Black Elk had sent the gift of horses!

"Niece, have you eaten strong mushrooms? Or did the Great Spirit grant you much beauty and the sense of a rabbit to go with it? You must marry! And none better than Black Elk. True, his dead ear is unpleasant to behold. But this is a small thing."

"I am not troubled by his ear," Honey Eater told her aunt impatiently. "Black Elk received that hurt defending his tribe. I would gladly marry a brave with ten times this many wounds, if in my heart I loved him."

"Loved him? Well, and have you looked at the goods piled outside of this tipi? *I* could love a buck capable of providing me with these things. Indeed, niece, I loved one who provided much less. And even *he* was a comfort on cold nights."

Sharp Nosed Woman smiled as she enjoyed some private memory. Then she made the cut-off sign, which one did when speaking of the dead.

"Your aunt did not marry so wisely as your mother. Do not play the fox with me, little one. Everyone in the tribe knows you love Touch the Sky. True, he is pleasing to look at. But do you see meat racks behind his tipi? How many blankets does he own?"

"How could he own anything?" said Honey Eater bitterly. "He has spent all of his time defending his life from enemies within his own tribe!"

"Is this a wise thing, loving a man with so many enemies?"

Before Honey Eater could reply, her name was shouted outside the tipi.

She recognized Black Elk's voice and realized the council must be over. She felt her throat constricting at the prospect of facing him. Honey Eater rose and crossed to the entrance flap, lifting it aside and stepping outside.

"Honey Eater," said Black Elk, one hand indicating the travois piled high with goods which lay near the tipi. By custom, no one could touch it until Black Elk had received his reply. "This is only a portion of the bride-price which I offer to your clan. The horses have already been selected, and I have made new bridles for all. Will you give me my answer now?"

Honey Eater had practiced for this moment. Now, eyes respectfully downcast, her voice pleasant but determined, she said, "Black Elk, I am a Cheyenne maiden. I know my duty to my tribe. I know also the respect due to so great a warrior as you. But I cannot give you this answer. Not yet."

"Why?" demanded Black Elk. "True, Yellow Bear's final journey has left you sad, and you need time to heal this grief. But Honey Eater, only think! I am not asking you to perform the ceremony right away, only to pledge your love to me. I want to hear the crier racing through our camp, telling all that we will marry! Tell me yes now."

She shook her head. "I cannot. Not until—not until River of Winds and Swift Canoe have reported."

"What?" Black Elk's eyes were fierce with jealous anger. "So you can learn about your tall young brave? Learn if he has been hurt or killed fighting for those who would kill all Indians like lice?"

"Black Elk, I do not have two hearts," Honey Eater said gently. "And my one heart is filled with him."

Again Black Elk indicated the pile of goods. The travois overflowed with new robes and furs, skins of soft kid leather, new tipi covers, highly prized white man's tobacco, bright wool blankets.

"What can *he* offer?" said Black Elk scornfully. "His brave love talk may move your heart. But it is buffalo robes which warm your cold bones! You are in love with a turncoat who fights white men's battles!"

"I cannot believe he is a turncoat," said Honey Eater. "He would not betray us! He would fight to the death for any Cheyenne in this tribe, including his enemies."

Black Elk fought hard to keep the rage from showing in his face. But his dark eyes snapped sparks at these words.

"You have sweet words for him! But you are still a child in these matters. Very well, we will wait until the report from River of Winds and Swift Canoe. Then we will wait no longer. You will announce your decision. Your war chief has spoken!"

Chapter Thirteen

Very early on the morning following the chase in the rocky basin, Touch the Sky and Little Horse briefly revisited the scene of their escape. Luck was with them: The whites had not found Touch the Sky's throwing axe. He spotted it in the trampled dirt and slipped it back into his legging sash. Then they rode the hidden game trails and long coulees which eventually connected with Hanchon property.

Touch the Sky wanted to talk to his father about last night's attempt to eavesdrop on Steele's men. The friends agreed that Little Horse would ride out near their former campsite to check the cottonwood for messages. Touch the Sky planned to ride close to his parents' house, then hobble the dun and sneak the rest of the way on foot. Even though the Hanchon wranglers had been told about him and the Bluecoats knew he was in the area, there was no sense alerting that Bluecoat sentry.

The Cheyennes agreed to meet again later that day back at their new camp on the hogback overlooking Steele's ranch. They split up at the rim of the Tongue River valley, Little Horse swinging up higher toward the rimrock, Touch the Sky descending into the fertile green quiltwork of the valley. Both riders stayed well into the trees and avoided skylining themselves or riding in the open.

Touch the Sky dismounted in the last belt of trees circling his parents' spread. From there he could see the mountains in the distance, aspen-gold in the lower elevations, still tipped white at their very summits with the snow that never melted. Between these majestic mountains and the verdant pastures, the foothills stretched out in ever-larger mounds that grew darker and seemed to shimmer in the distance. Dividing it all like a shiny strip of silver ribbon was the winding and looping river.

He hobbled the dun with rawhide and easily made his way to the house without being noticed by the yard sentry. It was still early enough to catch John Hanchon at the breakfast table.

"Well, maybe you didn't find out exactly when my horses are going in that corral," said Hanchon when Touch the Sky had finished telling his story. "But you gave Steele's gun-throwers one more proof that they aren't working for easy wages. Maybe they'll think twice before they steal them mustangs."

The optimism of his words was not reflected in his troubled eyes. Touch the Sky also noticed signs of increasing strain on his adopted mother's face. There were half circles of fatigue under her eyes, a new habit of glancing warily out of the kitchen window to see if any riders approached. He remembered a time when worry was a stranger to her face.

"Today," said Touch the Sky, "I'll move around Steele's place, keep an eye on his hands. If they're planning to move out tonight, there'll be signs of it. I don't think the strike, if one is planned, will be that soon, though. The corral isn't quite finished."

Later, as he rose from the table to leave, Sarah gripped both of his hands in hers.

"Son, listen to me. I want you and your friend to leave, leave soon. Oh, child, I'm so happy to see you again my heart could just fairly burst! But it's too dangerous for you here now. Soldiers are all around the area."

Touch the Sky glanced toward his father, expecting to see his mother's plea repeated in John Hanchon's face. Instead, Touch the Sky sensed the same feeling in his white father that he sensed in Little Horse: If a fight was unavoidable, they were keen for it. He had told his father what these men did to the Cheyenne people. *These men shed the blood of your own,* his father's eyes seemed to tell him now. *And if kin don't matter, what does? Law is slow and scarce out here, but justice must be swift and plenty.*

"We'll be all right," he assured his mother. He added proudly, "Don't worry about soldiers. I'm more likely to fall off my horse than get shot by one of *them.*"

Despite his proud boast, Touch the Sky was worried. At the moment Hiram Steele and his white dogs had surprise on their side—only *they* knew the what and where and when of that new corral. He had to try again to learn something. He spied his opportunity on the way back from his parents' spread.

He was approaching the campsite from behind a line of cedar and scrub pine due west of Steele's main corral. Two wranglers were lashing the last corner posts for the new pole corral. All that remained to be finished after that was the gate, and new logs had been stacked nearby for that purpose.

These were two of Steele's regular hands, not from the bunch that rode with Abe Winslow. Touch the Sky recognized them from the days when he used to make deliveries out here. He gauged the terrain between the tree line, where he was hidden, and the worksite. Mostly tall horseweeds, with here and there an open patch of knee-high grass.

It would be risky, he knew as he stared at the rifles propped up against the corral fence near the two men. One of them also wore a sidearm. Touch the Sky decided his Sharps would be too awkward in the weeds, so he left it lashed to his pony.

At first he made good time low-crawling, timing his most rapid bursts with the stronger gusts of wind to cover his movement. As he neared the two workers, he was forced to slow down. Sharp pieces of flint dug into his elbows and knees, pesky flies bit his face. Soon he could hear the occasional sound of their voices, but he couldn't make out their words yet.

His senses fully alert for signs he'd been spotted, he quickly scuttled across an exposed stretch of shorter grass. Then he was back on his face again, inching closer to the corral.

"Well, still, if the scuttlebutt I hear is true, then it's goin' too far."

"Did I say it wasn't? No, sir! What I'm saying is this. You open your mouth about it, it's the last complaining you'll ever do. Old Hiram is over his head this time. He'll rue the day he ever threw in with Winslow and his bunch."

"I'll say! What Winslow brags he's got planned for the Innuns, it ain't Christian. A Christian will by God fight and kill an Innun if he's bound to. But he don't take pleasure in the kill, nor in talking about how he plans to carve up the body."

"Christian! Tim, you're behind times! These ain't no Christians."

"That's clear from what they got planned for the Hanchons."

Touch the Sky turned his head and focused all of his awareness on hearing what the two men said next. But at this point he felt the ground vibrating. Lifting his head slightly, he spotted several more hands riding toward the new corral from the main yard. It angered him to leave before he learned the all-important missing fact: *when* the next strike was coming. But he decided not to push his luck against the present odds.

He retreated to his dun and swung wide north, sticking well behind the trees. The things he had heard left his insides a welter of anger and fear. Whatever Steele and Winslow had planned for them all, it would be as cruel and brutal as the men themselves. His father bravely talked the he-bear talk. But how could two Cheyennes and a handful of horse-wranglers stop men like this—men who had the weight of the U.S. Army behind them?

Amidst this wild tumble of thoughts, his mind

kept showing him images of Kristen Steele, her wing-shaped eyes the seamless blue of endless summer sky. Perhaps these thoughts explained why he unconsciously nudged the dun closer and closer to a small pond well beyond the wagon track which ran past Steele's house.

Abruptly, he touched the pony's neck to halt her. As he looked, where the track seemed to disappear behind a series of grassy hummocks, memories were unleashed like floodwaters. Memories of meeting Kristen here in their secret copse behind the pond. Memories of long embraces, warm kisses, plans for their future in this new land that was like fruit ripe for picking.

Those were plans for his life as a white man, he reminded himself now. And they were a mistake. He was a Cheyenne and must always live like one.

Nonetheless, he hobbled the dun in a stand of cedar and, avoiding open stretches, approached the copse.

The wind chose this time to suddenly gust stronger, rustling the leaves around him and wrinkling the surface of the pond. Thus he did not hear the soft crying noises from within the copse.

He stepped through the close wall of pines and nearly tripped on Kristen!

"Matthew, oh, my God! You frightened me so!"

His face flushed warm. "I didn't know you were here, honest."

"It's not that. It's just, I can't believe you're here. Don't you know Pa's men will kill you on sight? You're not safe here!"

Her hair tumbled over her shoulders in a golden confusion. A white linen skirt was neatly tucked around her legs as she sat against the trunk of a huge walnut tree. Touch the Sky dropped to one knee beside her. A quick glance told him that the letters scattered around her were from him. Blushing and dropping her glance from his, she quickly gathered up the letters.

Her eyes were red and swollen from crying. "What is it?" he said.

She shook her head. "You're up against so much right now. It's not right to bother you with my troubles. Matthew, listen to me! Pa and his men will kill you in a minute if they spot you anywhere around here."

"Sure they will. I'm a Cheyenne, ain't I? That's good enough reason to most people."

"And it's wrong! It's just wrong, and I won't stand for it! That kind of senseless, mean hatred is why I will never marry Seth Carlson or any man like him! I don't care *what* Pa threatens!"

It was out now, so she told him about the encounter with her father and Seth Carlson and her father's declaration: Either she agreed to marry Carlson, or her father would ship her back East to live with his sister.

"Carlson!" Touch the Sky spat the word out of his mouth as if it were a bad taste. "He isn't worthy to kiss your boot, let alone marry you!"

"He's a horrible man! He hates what he's ordered to hate. He frightens me. There's this mean glint in his eye, sometimes, when he looks at me. The same glint he gets when he talks about Indians. He knows how I feel about you, and it galls him."

She stopped there, but Touch the Sky finished for her.

"Galls him that you love a Cheyenne instead of him?"

She nodded, another tear zigzagging down her cheek.

"Oh, Matthew, I'm so scared for you! Pa is at that stage where he doesn't raise his voice anymore. He just keeps getting quieter and more dangerous. I've seen it before, and when he gets this way, he always gets what he wants."

"He's already taken enough from me. This time he *won't* get what he wants."

Matthew dropped down beside her, one arm encircling her. She turned toward him and leaned against his bare chest, her hair soft and still sun warmed.

Swallowing hard so she could speak, Kristen said, "Do you still think about me?"

He nodded, not trusting his voice.

"Corey doesn't answer me when I ask him if you've got a girl—you know, a Cheyenne girl. But not answering, I guess that's a kind of answer."

Red men don't kiss their women, Touch the Sky reminded himself then as he smelled the clean honeysuckle smell of her skin. But he wanted to kiss her, and bad, and he could tell she wanted it too.

A horse whickered, close by on the wagon road, and Touch the Sky was on his feet in a blink.

He peered out past the brake of pines and across the pond. Four riders sat their horses, rifles propped across their saddletrees.

One was Abe Winslow, and he was staring toward the copse.

"C'mon, Abe!" called one of them goodnaturedly. "You promised us two hours of hard drinking! Daylight's burning, Boss!"

"I'm tellin' you," said Winslowe, "I saw a redskin. Two of 'em, maybe more, I'm not certain there. It was sudden like, just in the corner of my eye. They was peekin' in at somethin' inside them trees."

"Well, they're gone now," said the other man. "We'll kill them later."

But Winslow urged his mount off the track and started around the pond. Silent but quick, Touch the Sky moved back beside Kristen.

"Pretend to be reading your letters," he whispered. "Just sit here and pretend to read."

Touch the Sky swung up into the sturdy lower branches of the walnut, trying not to shake them too much as he moved around to the back of the tree. He unsheathed his knife and held it ready in his teeth to free his grip.

Winslow reached the near end of the pond, halted, dismounted. Touch the Sky could watch him clearly through a tunnel in the leaves around him.

Winslow lifted his slouch hat long enough to give his head a good shake, throwing the filthy, wet-sand-colored hair back out of his eyes.

He drew a French-made grapeshot revolver from his sash. It was designed for close-range killing where aiming wasn't important and fired a 20-gauge shot load.

Touch the Sky transferred the knife from his teeth to his hand. Carefully, he maneuvered around until he was in position to spring out of the tree. But he could clearly see the other well-armed riders sitting on the far side of the pond, impatiently waiting.

"Christ Jesus, Abe!" one of them shouted. "I'm as dry as a year-old cow chip! We're working on Hiram Steele's time, what's your hurry?"

Even if he killed Winslow, there were three more

to fight—and Kristen sitting right there where lead would be flying!

"Easy," he whispered to Kristen. "Here he comes."

A few moments later Winslow stood inside the copse, staring at Kristen as if he'd just found a gold piece in the road.

"Yes?" she said archly. "Do you have a message from my father?"

Winslow grinned, baring green-rimmed teeth and gums the color of raw liver. "No need to play the quality miss with me, sugarplum. Some o' Hiram's wranglers already told me how you like them red bucks. No wonder they was peekin' in here—waitin' to see if it was their turn yet, I reckon."

It took a moment for his meaning to take. When it did, Kristen blushed to the roots of her hair and turned her face away.

"You are a filthy, disgusting pig," she said. "Leave me alone now or I'll tell my father."

Winslow laughed, brandishing the grapeshot revolver. "This here little gal will take care of your daddy quick, sweet corset. You remember that."

"Please leave me alone now!"

Winslow moved a step closer. Kristen seemed to shrink within herself, searching for more distance from him. Overhead, Touch the Sky silently began chanting a battle song, preparing himself to leap and kill in one smooth movement. He should be able to seize the grapeshot revolver before the other riders could react.

Winslow's voice had gone husky and intimate in a way that disgusted Kristen. "Tell me something, quality miss."

Now he stood towering over her. He leaned closer, his breath whistling in his nostrils. "Tell me this much. Is it true what I hear? I hear that a red man's jizzom is red too. Is that a fact? I mean, I figger you would know, bein' as how you meet with 'em out here."

Hatred welled up inside of Touch the Sky, raw and bitter and strong. But if he gave in to his urge to gut Winslow now, he endangered Kristen more than he already had. So he set his jaw hard, his mouth a straight, grim line, and held back. The moment to leap might yet come. And even as he thought these things, he wondered: Was Winslow just talking about her meetings with him, or just now had he actually spotted another Indian? Could it have been Little Horse? If so, why had Winslow mentioned there were two?

Kristen had turned her body protectively away from Winslow, refusing to meet his eyes. He laughed. He started to reach out to touch her hair.

Touch the Sky loosened his one-handed grip on the branch overhead, silently took in a long breath. *Between the fourth and fifth ribs*, he could hear Black Elk repeating. *That way it is straight to the heart. And you must twist as you thrust, tearing your enemy's guts.*

"Goddamnit, Abe!" shouted one of the men impatiently. "Are you draining your snake or what? We're ridin' on without you!"

He stared at the humiliated girl for another ten seconds or so. Then he turned and yelled to the men, "Hold your horses! I'm on my way!"

Then he looked down at Kristen again. "I'll be lookin' for you again out here. And you can tell that buck of yours his little trick in the basin was

143

a big mistake. His scalp is gonna hang off my coup stick!"

"Brother, did you not see?" said Swift Canoe. "The white dog peered in, then left without firing! He spoke to Touch the Sky and the yellow-haired white woman. Yet during the raid in the basin, they pretended to be enemies. This white has joined in the treacherous plan to make it appear that Cheyennes are on the warpath against the white nation!"

River of Winds said nothing, his eyes lost in serious reflection. The two spies were hidden in a thicket behind the copse. They had carelessly come near to being captured when, engrossed in observing Touch the Sky and the white woman, they had not heard the white dogs approaching.

"Only think on these things," said Swift Canoe. "We have seen Touch the Sky and Little Horse receiving messages from Bluecoat pony soldiers. We saw the soldiers again riding to meet them on the ridge. Now we have seen this paleface speak with him. Are you finally sure in your heart, as I am, that they have turned against our people? Do you not see that they have agreed to play the fox, to make the whites believe that Cheyennes are on the warpath?"

Though he maintained his silence, River of Winds did indeed agree now that this was true. He was finally convinced when he saw Touch the Sky making love talk with the woman whose hair had trapped the sun. After all, everyone back at camp believed his heart belonged to Honey Eater.

"Little brother," he said finally, "now I am one with you in your belief. But we have no orders from the councillors. I will leave before our shadows are long in the sun and ride quickly back to the tribe with this news. You will remain here, all eyes and ears. But you will *not* raise your weapons against Touch the Sky, do you hear my words?"

"I hear them, and I will obey."

But deep in his heart, Swift Canoe felt only a deep loathing for this turncoat who had killed his brother and now sold his people for gold. He knew well that, despite the tribe's sanction against shedding Cheyenne blood, they would respect any brave who killed this terrible enemy of the red man.

He would watch, while River of Winds raced north, for his opportunity.

Chapter Fourteen

Tom Riley adjusted his hat a bit as the midday sun crept straight overhead. The recruit platoon of horse soldiers stood at parade rest for the noon formation, their faces dusty and sweatstreaked from morning maneuvers.

Riley had spent most of his time lately on training exercises north of Fort Bates—a recent change of assignment which he knew Seth Carlson had arranged to get him out of the picture. But now he and his unit had returned for supplies and remounts.

One thing Riley detested about garrison duty was the endless list of Department of the Army orders and directives he was forced to read aloud each day to his men. He finished off a long list now, his voice raw and tired from shouting out commands all morning.

" 'Each year at this time,' " he read from a

sheaf of documents bearing the seal of the War Department, " 'the military is plagued with the same insidious problem at its frontier installations: those nefarious cowards sometimes known as snowbirds. These are unpatriotic men who join the Army during cold months for food and shelter, then desert with the arrival of spring.

" 'All legally enlisted men-in-arms are hereby advised: Snowbirds are also deserters, and if caught will be executed as enemies of their country.' "

"At least the Army kills you quick and clean," said one of the salty old NCO's who had fought in the Cherokee Wars back East. "Them goddamn Innuns'll cut off your peeder first!"

A few men laughed, but Riley let it go. They got enough harsh treatment from the likes of Seth Carlson.

He finished the latest batch of Army messages. Riley reminded the men of the regimental parade today at 1330 hours. Then he dismissed his men for their noon rations.

He was crossing the parade field, toward the bachelor officers' quarters behind the sutler's store, when Riley saw Hiram Steele ride through the main gate.

The big, broad-shouldered man sat straight in the saddle, looking neither to his left nor his right. His business often brought him to the fort. Riley knew it was not unusual for the rancher to visit the officer in charge of the stables, where he was apparently headed now. Nonetheless, Riley found himself swerving toward the complex of big, single-story buildings where the regiment's horses were stalled when not grazing.

He ducked behind the corner of a nearby barracks when Seth Carlson emerged from the Headquarters Building. The officer too headed toward the stables. He and Steele made a point of pretending not to notice each other.

Riley fell in behind a corporal marching a work detail and kept them between him and the stables until he'd crossed the parade field. Then, after confirming that Carlson and Steele were indeed meeting in one of the stable buildings, he hurried around behind it. A wooden loading arm protruded from the loft door, thick ropes dangling down. Riley gripped one of the ropes and climbed hand-over-hand up into the loft.

His boots silent in the thick-matted straw and hay, he crossed to the edge of the loft and glanced below. Normally a private or two would be cleaning out stalls or pounding caulks into horseshoes. But the soldiers had gone to the mess hall. Steele and Carlson stood near the stall where Carlson's new mount now chewed on a nose bag full of oats.

"How do you like him?" said Steele, nodding toward the strong, well-muscled chestnut he'd given the soldier to replace the black Carlson had been forced to shoot.

"I'm starting to think you *did* give me the best of your herd. He's fast and a strong jumper."

"That's an Indian-fighter's pony," said Steele proudly. "He's trained for steep slopes and mountain trails. That, and quick maneuvering. *This* animal would of sensed that prairie-dog hole and missed it."

"He'll get his first trial tonight."

"It's all set at your end then?" said Steele.

Carlson nodded. "It'll be me and three men from the dragoons, all of us in mufti. Now, I gave 'em my word: They're being paid to attack and burn the house and outbuildings, nothing else. We'll lay down cover fire on any wranglers in the yard, but it's up to your bunch to round up the horses and fight off Hanchon's men in the field. We have to hit quick and get the hell out."

Steele nodded. "If the redskin is around the house, he's yours. If he's out with the herds, Winslow can have him. I don't care who kills him, so long as he's put under. This strike will either break John Hanchon's will or kill him. I ain't out to kill him, mind you, just to drive him out of the mustang business. The choice is his."

"Speaking of choices," said Carlson, "has Kristen said anything more about—about what you talked about the other night? About us getting married?"

"She won't say boo to a goose since that night. She's stubborn and mule-headed just like her mother was. You want the straight, soldier? You or your men kill that Indian, hear? You kill that Indian, I'll by God make sure she marries you. Because, man to man, here's the way it is. Now *don't* mistake my meaning, we're in this thing together. But the plain truth is, I got a daughter that kisses redskins. And you are in love with a woman that's partial to a savage over you. We're both made fools of here. That Cheyenne is humiliating the pair of us."

Riley, peeking down over a bale of new hay, watched Carlson's smooth-shaven face set itself in hard, determined lines.

"I'll kill that red bastard, all right," he said, anger and jealousy clear in his tone.

One of the privates on work detail returned and the two men drifted out, still talking. Riley climbed back down from the loft and tried to order his confused thoughts. It was too late to place a message in the fork of the cottonwood for the Cheyennes. And Corey's place was an hour and a half's ride, the Hanchon spread at least an hour, two hours both ways.

The regimental parade was coming up in less than an hour. Harding was in love with the pomp and regulation and would never excuse him or any on-duty officer from leading his platoon through the drills. Any attempt to leave the fort now would draw suspicion, maybe even get him followed—thrown in the stockade, if Carlson got wind of it.

No. His best hope was to go through with the parade, turn his men over to the platoon sergeant immediately afterward, and then ride hard to the Hanchons with this new word, avoiding the sentry on Thompson's Bluff. He'd have to hope the raid was planned for some time late enough to permit establishing defenses.

Otherwise, the Hanchons were finished—if they survived with their lives. As for the Cheyennes, their fate was even clearer. They had no middle ground. They would either kill or be killed.

"So that's the long and the short of it, boys," said John Hanchon. "These aren't wranglers you'll be going up against, they're frontier hardcases used to cold-blooded killing. I can't rightly ask you to fight without telling you that. And I don't blame any man that walks out that door right now."

John Hanchon finished speaking and Touch the Sky felt a pall of awkward silence fall over the front parlor. The room was filled by an odd assemblage. The four remaining wranglers and

Wade McKenna, their boots crusted with dried mud from recent rains, stood nervously twisting their hats around in their hands. Tom Riley, still in uniform, stood slightly apart from them. On the far side of the room another little group was formed by Corey Robinson, Touch the Sky, and Little Horse. Sarah, over her loud protests, had been sent into Bighorn Falls to stay with Holly Miller, the seamstress.

Riley had ridden first to Corey's place, then dispatched the redhead to the Cheyennes' camp with the news. Little Horse had been reluctant to enter a lodge with so many whites. But he'd agreed when Touch the Sky said this paleface council was important. He listened carefully now while his friend interpreted the important bits of information. The wranglers occasionally aimed a curious glance toward them. The Cheyennes, however, carefully avoided any eye contact with them.

A hand named 'Braska Jones scratched his ear. Then he said, "I didn't sign on for no shootin' war. You're a good man, Mr. Hanchon, and that's God's own truth. I've put up with my share o' fightin'. But this tonight, this is gettin' down to the nut-cuttin'. I got family back in Omaha. I'll have to throw in my hand."

"Fair enough," said Hanchon. "You've been a good worker. I'll pay you off when we finish up here. Anybody else?"

"Ain't no mix of mine what 'Braska does," said Wade McKenna. "But young Riley here ain't from these parts neither, yet *he's* willing to put at 'em! The rest of us live in this valley. We've put down stakes and aim to stay. This ain't just your fight. Hell, I got plans for my own spread. We let Steele drive you under, none of us will be safe."

The other three hands nodded their approval of McKenna's words.

"All right then," said Hanchon. "It's settled. We don't know exactly when they're hitting us, just that it'll be well after dark. That means we go over the plan one time now and then just hunker down and wait. This is where I let a soldier take over."

Riley said, "There's nine of us total, counting me and Corey. Steele's regular hands will be busy rounding up and driving the horses. The shooting will be left to about a dozen mercenaries riding for Steele, and four soldiers who plan to attack the house and yard. I doubt if Steele himself will be riding.

"Me, John Hanchon, and you wranglers will ring the main herd behind cover. I'll direct fire. We'll be outnumbered, but they'll be riding in the open and expecting only a sleepy line rider or two to be out there. Shoot for their horses first so they'll be unable to cut out any mustangs."

Riley looked at Touch the Sky. They had already briefly discussed what the Cheyennes would do.

"These two are going to have the tough job," said Riley. "First of all, they'll be watching at Steele's spread when the riders head out. Then they'll get back to give us the word when and where the fight's coming to us. After that, they come back here and defend the house because the soldiers plan to attack right after the fight starts out in the pastures."

Riley turned to Corey. The youth had insisted on joining either the bunch in the pasture or the Cheyennes up at the house. But Riley had convinced him to perform a more important task.

"You, Corey, will ride back to the Steele spread. After Steele's men ride out, you're going to take that pole corral apart. If they do heist any mustangs, we'll make damn good and sure they got no place to put them. But watch out for any sentries while you're working."

Corey nodded.

"Everybody straight on the plan?" said John Hanchon.

McKenna and the hands nodded.

"Clean and check your weapons," said Riley. "There'll be a full moon, so stay covered down as much as possible. And remember, a rustler is useless on his feet. Shooting a horse is as good as shooting the man."

"I thank you all again," said Hanchon. "May God have mercy on all of us. It's going to be a hard fight."

"Brother," said Little Horse when the two Cheyennes were alone in the moonlit yard. "We are warriors and we cannot avoid this fight. But we have not dressed nor painted, we have made no sacrifice to the Arrows. And our sister has gone to her resting place in the west, leaving the sky to Uncle Moon."

Touch the Sky nodded, understanding. A Cheyenne was seldom considered a coward if he refused to fight after dark or without painting, so important were these things.

"We must try hard to avoid the kill," he said.

He glanced around the yard and the surrounding outbuildings, then considered the best possible approaches for attack. The most direct route from Fort Bates would be from the wagon track to the north. But the Bluecoat attackers would want to throw suspicion off the fort. Meaning the most probable direction of attack would be from the rim of the valley, down the long slope behind the house.

"Before we ride to spy on the white dogs," said Touch the Sky, "I will speak with my father. I think we should prepare more traps for our enemies."

But this talk of spying made him think again of something else. Something he had been worried about since hearing the tall, thin paleface named Winslow insist he'd seen two Indians peeking into that copse while he talked with Kristen.

He glanced carefully around, searching the blue-black twilight.

Little Horse saw him. "Still you fear the tribe has sent spies?"

Touch the Sky nodded. Little Horse too glanced carefully around. "I hope you are wrong, brother," he said. "Tonight we face a powerful enemy. We may die. If we have been declared enemies of our tribe, we cannot make the journey to the Land of Ghosts. We will be doomed to wander in the Forest of Tears alone forever."

"Then brother," said Touch the Sky, "let us make preparations, not words, for clearly we had better not die!"

Chapter Fifteen

Their preparations near the house complete, the two Cheyennes rode out together toward the Steele spread while the fat moon crept toward his zenith.

They stopped briefly at their hidden shelter on the hogback to prepare their weapons. Both Indians were silent now, absorbed in the silent task of preparing themselves for battle. They scooped clay out of the soil near the seep spring and darkened their exposed skin.

They were able to keep an eye on the house and main yard while they made these preparations. The first confirmation of the raid was the number of horses in the corral, many of which would normally have been stalled for the night by now. Steele's wranglers and Winslow's bunch, mostly keeping to themselves, stood in small groups smoking or checking their weapons.

The two Cheyennes crept downridge, moving even closer. Several times the door to the house swung open, and men would turn to look. Finally, when the two Cheyennes began to wonder if the strike was on after all, Hiram Steele stepped out into the buttery moonlight.

He nodded once, and Abe Winslow's rusted-hinge voice shouted out, "Grab leather, boys!"

The Cheyenne warriors quickly returned and untethered their ponies. Hugging the tree line, keeping a constant eye on the riders below, Touch the Sky and Little Horse tracked the marauders as they set out, riding two abreast strung out in pairs 50 feet apart—almost 20 men strong, a good-sized cavalry squad. But almost half of them were wranglers used to hard drinking and fistfights, not killing, Touch the Sky reminded himself.

Still, that left at least a dozen paid killers against Riley's force of six. Thus the Cheyennes wanted to learn more than just the exact time of attack—they needed to learn the approach route so the defenders could get in the best position. The initial moments of attack were the most important, Black Elk had reminded them constantly.

They held their ponies to a matching trot only until they were sure they knew the route—not down from the rim of the valley, but up from the coulees and defiles toward the main mustang herd in its summer pasture. The defenders would need to concentrate their fire at the open wall of the natural pen, through the coulee which approached it.

Once sure of this, the two red brothers nudged their ponies hard, pushing them recklessly but trusting them now after several sleeps of light duty. By now they had learned the swiftest routes through the valley. Soon they were well ahead of their enemy, long black locks streaming behind them as they urged their mounts even harder across open stretches of bottomland.

Touch the Sky quickly gave the word to his father and Tom Riley. Then, knowing time was stretching thin, the two Cheyennes raced toward the house. They hobbled their horses in protective thickets and moved into position, each kneeling behind sturdy young cedars behind the house. The trees grew near the bottom of the long slope leading down from the rimrock above.

This time they didn't have long to wait. The first rifle shots from the coulee told them the defenders had surprised Steele's riders. Soon a gun battle raged in earnest.

But the Cheyennes concentrated on the slope, where the silhouettes of four riders had just appeared at the crest.

Carlson was easy to recognize on the big chestnut Riley had told them about. All four riders wore civilian clothes. They fanned out slightly as they descended the slope, picking up speed until their mounts' hooves were hollow, rapid drumbeats.

When they were more than halfway down the slope, closing rapidly on the hidden Cheyennes, Touch the Sky snorted like a horse clearing its nose after a good drink. Little Horse snorted back, signaling that he was ready.

The riders bent low over their pommels, savagely spurring their mounts. The thundering grew louder. The Cheyennes could now make out divots of soil and grass flying as the strong cavalry horses tore up the ground.

At the last possible moment, when it seemed the riders were about to pass them, Touch the Sky jerked taut the rope stretched along the ground between his cedar and Little Horse's. With the rope lifted about three feet above the ground, he rapidly snubbed it around the cedar a few times to secure it.

One of the three dragoons rode a roan stallion. It hit the rope hard in mid-stride and tumbled forward fast, the rider's left arm snapping in two places when he landed on it. Moments later the panicked horse, struggling to regain its feet, planted a hoof square on the rider's chest and caved in his ribs as it righted itself and bolted back up the slope.

A ginger mustang carrying a second dragoon also went down, but less forcefully. Though the soldier was uninjured, his rifle was still in his saddle scabbard. The sight of his companion's crushed chest sent him fleeing in the direction of his mustang.

Carlson's fleet-footed chestnut and the remaining dragoon's powerful little Sioux-broken paint managed to leap at the last possible instant, clearing the rope. Intent on their mission, neither man slowed to check on their downed companions.

Carlson swerved toward the house, the mounted infantryman toward the bunkhouse. Both clutched rags soaked in kerosene and wrapped around sticks. The dragoon reached the bunkhouse first, halted his mount outside the door, slammed it open with a powerful thrust of his boot. The next moment he struck a sulphur match and the torch was ablaze. He flipped it inside the bunkhouse and headed toward the outlying stable, pulling another makeshift brand from his saddle pannier.

But Little Horse had raced into the yard behind the dragoon, staying out of sight. As the soldier, intent on lighting his second torch, slowed to burn the stable, Little Horse raced inside the bunkhouse and threw a mattress over the flaming brand.

He headed for the stable even as the dragoon raced about the yard with a third flaming torch, igniting hayricks. Hanchon had already told them not to worry about saving hay, just buildings.

It was Touch the Sky's job to deal with Seth Carlson. So far neither Carlson nor the dragoon was aware of the presence of the Cheyennes. With two hayricks flaming high, lighting up the house and yard like bright afternoon sun, they were slow to notice that the bunkhouse and stables were not engulfed in flames.

Carlson had reined in his horse before the house and lighted his torch. His arm was cocked back to throw it when two powerful hands gripped his left leg and jerked his foot from the stirrup. His right foot jerked free too, and a moment later he lay on his back in the dirt, the torch sputtering out.

The chestnut, spooked by the increasing flames in the yard and the sudden loss of its master, side-jumped hard and knocked Touch the Sky down before he could leap on Carlson. The officer was up on his knees, clawing his service pistol from its stiff leather holster, before Touch the Sky shook his head clear.

Carlson aimed, the Cheyenne leaped, the pistol spat fire as Touch the Sky slammed into him and bowled him over again.

They rolled once, twice, again in the dirt, grappling viciously. By the time Touch the Sky rolled on top of his opponent, there was a bright red crease of blood where the bullet had grazed the hollow just above his left hip.

The two archenemies fought like snarling wolves, ripping each other's skin, gouging eyes, even biting. The flames from the burning hayricks leaped and danced high into the sky all around them, casting eerie shadows as they fought.

So far Little Horse had managed to save all but the hayricks and one minor storage shack. Intent on defeating the dragoon without drawing blood, Little Horse was at first unaware that his companion was struggling for his life in the dirt.

Touch the Sky had strength and agility over the Bluecoat officer. But the pony soldier was heavier and had practiced the European style of wrestling while at West Point. Now he performed a deft little flip with his legs tensed, neatly tossing Touch the Sky aside.

Carlson's service Colt lay in the dirt several feet away, its primer cap spent. But now, as Touch the Sky scrambled after him again, the officer dipped a hand inside his tunic and came back out with a short-barreled .50-caliber hideout gun.

There was no time. Now he must either draw blood or die. But Touch the Sky was still resolved against killing at night, unpainted and unblessed by the Medicine Arrows.

Even as Carlson straightened his arm to fire, Touch the Sky snatched the knife from his sheath and flipped it at Carlson in one smooth, fluid movement. There was a sound like cloth ripping as the lethally honed blade sliced neatly into the wrist of the hand clutching the hideout gun.

The gun discharged its only slug, harmlessly sending it two feet over Touch the Sky's head. Carlson cried out in pain and clutched his wounded arm, too shocked to pull the knife back out. Touch the Sky picked up the service revolver and flung it far out into the yard.

"I am a better man than you, paleface!" said Touch the Sky. "Do you see that? You live now because I let you, white dog! The day is coming when we will meet on the true field of battle. And then your hair will dangle from my clout!"

Carlson yanked the knife free, almost fainting at the pain, and dropped it in the dirt. His wrist spuming blood, he turned quickly away and raced for his horse.

The yard was brilliantly lighted now as the hayricks crackled and sparked, shooting huge tongues of flame. But the house and main buildings were untouched, and this fact had drawn Abe Winslow's attention from the battle up at the pasture.

Things had fared badly for the attackers. They had been caught by surprise and several of his men were down, several more trapped. Steele's wranglers, spooked by all the flying lead, had taken to the hills or were crouched nearby in hiding. It was part of Steele's contingency plan that, should Winslow see that the house was not burning, he would ride down and do the deed Carlson had failed to do. Now, with lead flying thicker than trail dust, he was glad to get the hell out of there.

By now, between the noise of the flaming hayricks and the nickering horses in the main corral, Winslow was able to enter the yard unnoticed. Thus it was that, approaching Touch the Sky from behind, he saw the Indian defeat Carlson and send the officer packing.

Winslow slipped the grapeshot revolver from

his sash. He let his horse walk closer until he was at point-blank range. Then he aimed at the back of the Cheyenne's head.

"Brother, watch out!"

Winslow squeezed the trigger just as Little Horse's lance knocked his arm askew. The grapeshot revolver discharged its 20-gauge shot load with a deafening roar.

A moment later the dragoon, who had dismounted to pick up the carbine he had dropped, was sitting on the ground in shock and pain, gazing at the bloody stump of his left leg. The bone protruded like a shattered tree branch.

The soldier had never met Winslow. He had seen nothing. He knew only that this man now staring at him, smoking weapon in hand, had just blown his leg to hell and gone.

"You scum-sucking sonofabitch!" he snarled. And just before he passed out from pain and blood loss, he lifted his carbine, locked it into his hip socket, and sent a slug thwapping into Winslow's chest.

There was no time to rejoice in their victory at saving the house and driving off the attackers. Both Cheyennes made sure the flaming hay was in no danger of igniting buildings. Then they raced toward the high ground and the summer pasture, where the battle still raged. They were prepared to draw blood if necessary. But the shouts of encouragement from Hanchon's wranglers told them the fight went well.

"This is what I have seen, brothers and fathers. I did not ride south to condemn this tall stranger. But these are the things I have seen. I know this is a serious charge. But I believe in my heart that it is also a true charge. Touch the Sky and Little Horse are secretly aiding the Bluecoats! They are attacking paleface settlers under secret orders from a little soldier chief!"

River of Winds finished his long report and fell silent. His words left a shocked stillness in the council lodge. None was more troubled than old Arrow Keeper. Had this report come from Swift Canoe, he would have known it was delivered with more than one tongue. Swift Canoe's Wolverine Clan were known among the village as complainers who always shirked hard work and loved to stir up trouble.

But from River of Winds! Arrow Keeper trusted this brave's word and his keen sense of fair play. He would never speak in a wolf bark against another Cheyenne.

"I spoke straight-arrow all along!" said Wolf Who Hunts Smiling triumphantly. "He is not even a turncoat—he was a spy all along!"

The outburst of shouts from the younger warriors forced Arrow Keeper to fold his arms until it was silent.

"Brothers, hear your chief! I too am bothered by this word River of Winds brings. But still, much remains to be explained. If these two bucks are spies, then we must find out how this thing happened and how they have hurt us with our enemies. If they are innocent, we must give them opportunity to prove this thing."

River of Winds was instructed to join Swift Canoe again, then track the two Cheyennes, never letting them out of sight. River of Winds and Swift Canoe, Arrow Keeper insisted, must learn as much as possible about this dangerous alliance with pony soldiers.

Arrow Keeper was deeply troubled, and his concern was plain to the others. But deep in his heart he still resisted believing what was now obvious to all: that Touch the Sky and Little Horse had not only deserted their tribe for good, but were selling it out for gold. Arrow Keeper was well aware of the white man's ploy of creating "Indian attacks" to drum up war profits. Many Indians had already brought their tribes down for good with this treacherous service to the white profiteers.

The shaman was not surprised, after the council, to find Honey Eater anxiously waiting in front of his tipi.

"What was decided about Touch the Sky, Father?"

Honey Eater and everyone else in the tribe had already heard the charges against Touch the Sky and Little Horse—including the story about how he held a sun-haired paleface woman in his blanket and made love talk to her.

"Very little, daughter. The Headmen must learn more. These are very serious charges."

"Do *you* believe them?"

Arrow Keeper looked into the girl's agonized, hopeful eyes and felt a pang of remorse in his heart. "Honey Eater, I believe that River of Winds always speaks straight. I believe he saw what he tells us he saw. However, the meaning of what he has seen still eludes the tribe."

"But what else *can* it mean, when a Cheyenne holds a pretty young paleface woman in his arms? He prefers a blue-eyes over a Cheyenne!"

Arrow Keeper was forced to maintain silence. How could he dare build up the girl's expectations and risk ruining her chances for a good marriage? Time was running out for her. She would soon have to marry.

Reading all this in his troubled gaze, Honey Eater said, "Please tell me, Father, what do I do? Black Elk will wait no longer! Do I risk the anger of his clan again by sending the gift of horses back?"

Nothing in his medicine vision about Touch the Sky, Arrow Keeper reminded himself, predicted anything about a marriage to Honey Eater. All that was foretold was greatness for Touch the Sky as a war leader. Men who were marked for greatness were not always the best men to love.

Finally, his heart heavy, he said, "You must remember that you are a Cheyenne maiden. You must always do your duty, what is right for your tribe. Black Elk is a war leader who has been blooded for his tribe. He has many possessions, fine horses. True, he is perhaps too much tempered in the hard arts of warfare. But with the mellowing of age, he may also someday become a great peace chief. And he is respected by his people."

Honey Keeper nodded, though this was not what she wanted to hear. "Father," she repeated desperately, "should I become Black Elk's bride? Time has run out, he demands to know this day!"

But Arrow Keeper only shook his head, his face a mask of unreadable wrinkles.

"You must do your duty," he repeated.

"But is duty more important than my love?"

Again he shook his head. "Words are no good now, little one. Make your decision. Just remember: We live on through the will of the tribe. And the will of the tribe calls for you to marry Black Elk."

Chapter Sixteen

Today, thought Swift Canoe, *the turncoat named Touch the Sky will finally die.*

It had been four sleeps since the strange nighttime battle near the paleface lodge. While River of Winds made his report far to the north in Cheyenne country, Swift Canoe had watched the entire conflict unfold. The young Cheyenne had not, however, recognized the four Bluecoats without their soldier clothing. He assumed the clash was between white settlers only. And since Touch the Sky and Little Horse were still meeting with a young Bluecoat officer, clearly they were still the long knives' dogs even if they did cleverly defeat the raiders.

Swift Canoe lay behind a tree on the long ridge overlooking the Hanchon spread. For four sleeps now he had watched his fellow Cheyennes as they, in turn, continued to prowl about the territory between the two mustang ranches. But it appeared that they were finally ready to leave. Both were preparing to mount their ponies below, Touch the Sky speaking with the paleface man and woman who lived in the lodge.

Where, wondered Swift Canoe, would they ride to? Surely they were not treacherous enough to return to Yellow Bear's camp? Or was that part of the Bluecoat's orders to them?

River of Winds was due back shortly with their orders from the councillors. If he was going to finally do it, Swift Canoe told himself, it must be soon—this day. And against two such capable fighters as those two, he would get only one arrow off before he would be forced to flee for his life.

The Cheyenne who killed such an enemy of the tribe would earn the respect of many blood-ed warriors. It would not bloody the Medicine Arrows to kill a turncoat like Touch the Sky.

One arrow.

Swift Canoe checked the condition of his buffalo-sinew bowstring, selected the most perfectly fletched and balanced arrow from his quiver. He would wait until the turncoats' route was clear, then ride on ahead and find a good ambush point.

"I'm not sure *how* I feel about you leaving," Sarah Hanchon told her adopted Cheyenne son. "Part of me wants you right here like you used to be. The other part of me wants you away from here, where it's safer."

Touch the Sky nodded. He didn't want to admit that he too felt a similar confusion about where he belonged. Last night, in a dream, Honey Eater and Kristen had both turned into eagles who ripped him in half fighting over him.

"Actually," said John Hanchon, "it's safer around here thanks to the boys. At least for a while anyway. Best time to stay on, if they've a mind to."

The valley had been unnaturally quiet since the battle four days ago. The fight in the summer pasture had gone well for Riley and Hanchon. Most of Steele's wranglers had lit out, and many hadn't shown their faces in the valley since. With Winslow and several of his gun-throwers dead, the rest of the mercenaries had decided they had their bellyful of the Wyoming Territory.

But Touch the Sky had learned even better news through Tom Riley. Riley's letter, including copies of Carlson's falsified reports about Indian danger, had reached the territorial commander at Fort Laramie and drawn an instant response by special courier. Major Harding, red-faced at the reprimand he'd received from above, suddenly had a fire lit under him. He'd immediately complied with the order to form a special board of inquiry to look into the raids on the Hanchon spread.

Touch the Sky agreed with Riley—no charges were likely to be filed as a result of the inquiry. Steele had too much influence at the fort. But the simple knowledge that somebody was looking into it should give Steele pause to worry. More important, the irate territorial commander had insisted to Washington that a U.S. marshal and deputy be stationed at Bighorn Falls to handle civilian disputes. They were due to report for duty soon.

Seth Carlson, deemed grossly incompetent after

filing the inaccurate reports, had already been demoted to second lieutenant and reassigned to an even more desolate no-man's-land, the remote Army outpost called Fort Peck in the Montana Territory. Touch the Sky regretted not killing him. But at least he was nowhere near Kristen now.

To Little Horse, Touch the Sky translated Sarah's offer to stay. To his surprise, Little Horse smiled. He spoke in Cheyenne, asking Touch the Sky to translate. Touch the Sky was still surprised when he turned to his parents and told them:

"My friend says to tell you, 'My name is not War Eagle. It is Little Horse. Now I trust you to know it.'"

Sarah smiled at the smaller Cheyenne. Then, shyly, she pushed her son's black locks back off his forehead and said, "Matthew? You've never told your father and me your Cheyenne name. We want to know it."

For a moment he hesitated, self-conscious. He spoke the Cheyenne words and they repeated them several times.

"What does it mean?" asked Sarah.

"Touch the Sky," he replied.

The Hanchons both smiled at the same time. "I like it," said Sarah. "You certainly do measure up to it."

John Hanchon had given the two youths the weapons he'd lent them, along with plenty of ammunition in buckskin pouches. Their legging sashes were filled with dried meat and fruit for the journey north to the upcountry of the Powder. Sarah had thrown in a generous supply of the biscuits Little Horse loved. Corey had said good-bye earlier, stopping by with Tom Riley. If only, thought Touch the Sky, he could have had one more meeting with Kristen to say good-bye.

It felt like a nail was lodged in his throat when he finally told his parents it was time to ride. Sarah smiled brightly, but crystal teardrops beaded up on her lashes.

"The first time you left," she said, fighting to keep her voice under control, "you went out in the night and left us a note. I felt so empty and aching inside because I never got the chance to hug you good-bye. Now, I know you don't feel comfortable, a big strong Cheyenne being hugged by his mama! But you just step over here and give me that hug, Matthew or Touch the Sky or whoever my fine son is these days!"

He smiled and did as she requested, picking her right up off the ground and twirling her around. The gesture surprised Little Horse. Thinking it must be a white custom upon leave-taking, he too picked Sarah up and twirled her. He looked even more confused when the other three suddenly laughed at him.

John Hanchon folded one arm around Matthew, one around Little Horse. "We going to see you two again around here?"

Sarah looked at him, waiting hopefully for the right answer.

He didn't know what to say. He was a Cheyenne now, but making this journey might have cost him his place in the tribe. Arrow Keeper said a Cheyenne without a tribe was a dead man. But neither was it possible to make a life back here, where the white settlers refused to accept him.

"I don't know," he said honestly. "I don't know what's going to happen. If I can, you bet you'll see me again."

It wasn't the answer Sarah wanted, but it would have to do.

"Well, *we* plan on being here, son, thanks to you and Little Horse," said John Hanchon. "You two have a place here anytime you need it, the white homesteaders be damned! Keep your powder dry, boys!"

As Touch the Sky was about to swing onto his dun, Sarah ran close and hugged him again. Then, unable to control her sudden sobs, she raced off toward the house. When Touch the Sky turned to say his final farewell to his father, he was surprised to see that the older man's eyes were damp.

"We both love you, son," he said gruffly. "Now get on out of here before I make a damn fool of myself," he added. With a final wave of his thickly callused hand, he headed up toward the house to comfort his wife.

The two Cheyennes rode in silence for several minutes, pointing their mounts toward the northern rim of the valley. The elation of their recent victory had given way to the reality—they were riding back to an uncertain future.

Thinking these things, Touch the Sky glanced up toward the rimrock above them, scanned the thickly wooded slopes. Little Horse saw him and did the same. Both had been thinking the same thing since Abe Winslow claimed to have seen two Cheyennes who could not have been them: Whoever the council had sent to spy on them, they were good at their work. Were they perhaps two more of Black Elk's well-trained warriors?

These two, thought Swift Canoe incredulously, were as brazen as magpies! It appeared that they were actually heading back toward the Cheyenne camp.

Sure of the route they would follow for a while now, he untethered his pony and raced ahead until he reached a good vantage point where the trail curved around a huge shoulder of rock strata. He hobbled his pony well back behind the protruding formation so he'd be ready to flee. Then, climbing the rock shelves like stairs, he made his way to the top of the shoulder.

Perfect. He could see the land for miles and miles from here, and the two riders winding their way slowly closer.

He lay on his belly on the warm rock. He slipped the selected arrow from his quiver, lined the notch up with his bowstring. Then he held it down at the ready, waiting patiently, his face as blank and impassive as the rock he lay on.

The two Cheyennes were about to draw abreast of a huge stratified rock shoulder when Little Horse suddenly said, "Brother! Someone approaches!"

They nudged their ponies off the trail and into the thickets, then dismounted. Touch the Sky unlashed the Sharps and made sure a primer cap and bullet were loaded.

Again, Touch the Sky heard nothing at first, another proof of Little Horse's keen hearing. Then, faintly, he detected the lazy clip-clop of shod hooves. He slipped his finger inside the trigger guard and took up the slack, waiting.

A moment later Kristen rode around the bend on her swayback piebald.

"Wait here," he told Little Horse, his heart swelling into his throat and making words difficult.

Kristen's surprise, when he stepped out and caught the bridle of her horse, quickly turned to joy at seeing him.

"I was hoping to meet you! Corey told me you were leaving. Oh, Matthew, I just had to say good-bye!"

He helped her dismount, his eyes unable to feast enough on her spun-gold masses of hair and flawless white skin.

"I knew you couldn't come to my place, and I didn't want to risk riling Pa by getting caught coming to your parents' spread again. So I asked Corey which route you'd be likely to take."

"How is your pa treating you?" said Matthew.

"Things are better. He's been a little more humble since a bunch of his own hands quit on him after that raid. The idea of this U.S. marshal coming has got him worried. And Matthew? He *knows* I know. I confronted him with everything about what he tried to do to your mother and father. It's shamed him enough that he wants to make peace with me."

"But will he stay this way?"

Her pretty face was creased by a frown. Touch the Sky realized that her answer was the same one he had just given his mother.

"I don't know. I just don't know what's going to happen."

Tentatively, she reached one finger out and touched the mass of burn scar on his bare, flat, tautly muscled stomach.

"Matthew? Do you love the woman you're riding back to more than you love me?"

The question took him by surprise and left him without words. For a moment he recalled that dream again, Honey Eater and Kristen fighting

173

over him, literally tearing him in two, a piece for each world. He opened his mouth to answer when she suddenly raised one hand to his lips.

"Shush! Never mind, I don't want to know. Just remember this. I love you! I know it's impossible and all wrong, but I love you! Matthew, I can't predict Pa's moods. Do you understand me? I don't know how long I'm even going to be living here. If he throws me out, I'll probably never see you again. I can't stand that thought!"

She could no longer speak. Tears streaming down her face, she reached up on tiptoe and kissed his lips. Then, doing it so quickly he didn't even have time to assist her, she mounted and rode back in the direction she'd come, pushing the piebald to a surprisingly lively pace.

Touch the Sky watched her disappear, her kiss still lingering like a gentle touch on his lips. He was about to turn toward the thickets when, again, he had the sudden feeling he was being watched.

He glanced all around, unable to see much because of the huge rock formation beside him which loomed over him like a wide tower, blocking the sun. But the feeling was still there like a hand on the back of his neck. If the tribe had indeed sent spies, what did this mean?

He stepped across the trail. Little Horse stepped out to meet him, leading their ponies. Touch the Sky's eye caught something bright glittering in the dirt. He stopped, glanced down.

A blue silk ribbon. Kristen must have dropped it.

A heartbeat after he crouched down to pick it up, an arrow missed his head by inches and embedded itself firmly in the trunk of the aspen beside him. It struck so hard that the shaft was buried almost two inches into the trunk.

Despite the shock of it, neither Cheyenne moved for several long moments. Then they briefly examined the arrow and locked glances.

Neither brave was surprised to recognize Cheyenne markings.

Even when they heard a pony escaping behind the rock shoulder, they didn't bother to give chase. This close to the soldiertown of Fort Bates was no place for Cheyennes to be warring against each other. And neither warrior was interested in revenge at that moment. Revenge was a small thing in the face of the possible banishment or even execution which might await them at the Powder River camp.

"Brother," said Little Horse, his voice reverent with wonder, "that arrow should have put you under. But I have seen another arrow, the one buried in your hair. You were not meant to die just then because the hand of the supernatural is in this thing."

His mouth set in its grim, determined slit, Touch the Sky snapped the arrow in half and threw it into the thickets. He and Little Horse had fought honorably, following the Cheyenne way. They had at least given his white parents a fighting chance to survive in the valley. It was right to come here and fight.

But returning to his old life, seeing Kristen again, had once again left him feeling like a man with a foot planted in two worlds, unsure which one was his. And as they rode, gazing uneasily around, that broken arrow became an omen of the unknown fate which awaited them upon their return.

VISION QUEST

Prologue

Ambushed by Bluecoat pony soldiers near the North Platte River, Running Antelope and his band of 30 Cheyenne braves fought with reckless courage. But they were not painted and dressed for battle—nor were their arrows and lances any match for the soldiers' carbines and artillery.

The lone survivor of the massacre was Running Antelope's infant son. The child was taken back to the river-bend settlement of Bighorn Falls in the Wyoming Territory. His Cheyenne name had been lost forever. He was renamed Matthew and raised by John and Sarah Hanchon, owners of the town's mercantile store.

In 1856, when Matthew turned 16, tragedy struck: He fell in love with Kristen, daughter of Hiram Steele, the wealthiest man in Bighorn Falls. Caught in their secret meeting-place, Matthew was viciously beaten by one of Steele's wranglers. And Kristen's suitor from nearby Fort Bates, a jealous young cavalry officer named Seth Carlson, threatened to ruin John Hanchon's all-important contract with the fort unless Matthew cleared out for good.

Thus driven from the only world he knew, the youth rode north to the up-country of the Powder River, Cheyenne country, seeking the people whose blood he shared. Captured by Cheyenne braves from Chief Yellow Bear's camp, he was accused of being a spy for the whites.

Only the intervention of old Arrow Keeper, the tribal medicine man, saved him from death by torture. The elder had recognized the birthmark, buried past the youth's hairline, from a medicine vision: a mulberry-colored arrowhead, the mark of the warrior. This tall youth was destined to lead his people in a final, great victory against their enemies.

Renamed Touch the Sky by Arrow Keeper, the unwelcome arrival was hated by Black Elk and his bitter young cousin Wolf Who Hunts Smiling. Black Elk was furious with jealousy when Chief Yellow Bear's daughter, Honey Eater, made love talk with Touch the Sky instead of him. And Wolf Who Hunts Smiling symbolically announced his intention to kill the suspected spy, walking between Touch the Sky and the campfire.

Even after Touch the Sky and his white friend Corey Robinson saved the Cheyenne village from annihilation by Pawnees he was not fully accepted as a warrior. Then whiskey traders invaded Indian country, led by the ruthless Henri Lagace.

Not only did the whiskey peddlers threaten to destroy the Indian way of life with their strong water. Lagace and his men had taken to slaughtering white trappers in their sleep, making the murders look like Cheyenne handiwork. Thus they profited when the panicked Territorial Commission declared a bounty on the scalp of any Cheyenne.

Lagace kidnapped Yellow Bear's daughter and threatened to kill her if the Cheyenne went on the warpath against him. But Yellow Bear could not sacrifice his tribe to save Honey Eater. The only hope was to send a small Cheyenne war party, led by Black Elk, into the heavily fortified white stronghold.

Touch the Sky was told, in a medicine vision, that he must defy Black Elk or Honey Eater would die. He deserted the war party and infiltrated the white camp on his own. He was taken prisoner and brutally tortured. But his courage rallied the other Cheyenne to mount an heroic surprise assault.

They scattered the white devils and freed Honey Eater. Touch the Sky then pursued his enemy Lagace until he killed him, ending the scalps-for-bounty menace. But much of his valor went unwitnessed, and many in the tribe were still unconvinced of his loyalty.

Their suspicions only deepened when Touch the Sky's friend Corey Robinson arrived at Yellow Bear's camp with bad news for the young Cheyenne: Hiram Steele had conspired, with Lieutenant Seth Carlson, to take over John and Sarah Hanchon's mercantile store. Now the two had launched a campaign to drive the Hanchons from their mustang spread.

Touch the Sky, badly needed by the tribe and Honey Eater because Chief Yellow Bear lay dying, was torn in his loyalties. Tribal law would not permit Honey Eater to live alone if her father died—meaning she would have to accept Black Elk's brideprice. But in the end he realized his white parents' battle was his battle. He returned to Bighorn Falls accompanied by his friend, the battle-hardened young warrior Little Horse.

They defeated their white enemies, but a new battle raged for Touch the Sky, a battle in his heart: Returning to Bighorn Falls crossed his trail with Kristen's. Seeing her again rekindled his passion and left him hopelessly trapped between two worlds, at home in neither.

Nor did he and Little Horse realize, as they started back to Yellow Bear's camp on the Powder River, the trouble which awaited them. Spies had watched them during their battle, mistaking Touch the Sky's meetings with the sympathetic cavalry officer Tom Riley as proof the Cheyenne was a traitor to his people.

Chapter One

"Brother," said Little Horse, breaking the long silence of their ride, "I am glad to return to Cheyenne hunting grounds. But during our absence I fear our people may have turned their hearts to stone against us."

Touch the Sky, easily the taller of the two young Cheyenne, nodded his agreement. Both youths had halted their ponies side by side on the rim of a long, grassy slope which formed the east wall of the Powder River valley. Below, a huge fork marked where the Little Powder joined the Powder.

Touch the Sky lifted one sun-bronzed arm to point at the tipis far below them. They were arranged in clan circles beside the fork, casting long shadows now that their sister, the sun, was nearing her resting place. Down near the water, a group of naked children were throwing stones at birds. Squaws knelt beside the tripods out-

9

side their tipi entrances, cooking elk and buffalo meat.

"At least," replied Touch the Sky, "all appears well below."

Both Cheyenne youths understood his unstated meaning: *At least the tribe was not slaughtered while we deserted them to fight white men's battles.*

"Once the Councillors learn who we defeated," said Little Horse, "perhaps the tribe will think differently."

"Perhaps," said Touch the Sky, though doubt was clear in his tone. "But will they believe us when we tell them that the paleface devils who tried to destroy my white parents were among those who rode with the scar-faced whiskey trader, Lagace?"

Little Horse was silent at this, knowing they had nothing but their word to prove their claim. In the eyes of the tribe, they had deserted their people when Chief Yellow Bear was sick—a vulnerable time for attack by enemies.

They nudged their ponies' flanks with their knees, descending closer to Yellow Bear's village. With each step nearer, Touch the Sky felt invisible flies stirring in his belly. His eyes swept the camp constantly as he tried to spot Honey Eater.

Was her father better now, or had Arrow Keeper's strong medicine failed to cure him? Had their chief crossed over to the Land of Ghosts? Did Honey Eater too believe he had deserted his people? All these questions cankered at him as the two youths descended the long slope.

Touch the Sky was lean and straight, tall even

for a Cheyenne. He had a strong, hawk nose and jet-black locks cut close over his eyes to keep his vision clear. The warm moons were upon them now, with the new grass well up—both youths were bare to the waist and wore beaded buckskin leggings, elkskin moccasins, and soft doeskin breechclouts. Leather bands around their left wrists protected them from the hard slap of their buffalo-sinew bowstrings.

"Brother!" said Little Horse when they had covered perhaps half the distance to the camp. "Look!"

He pointed to the lone hummock, between the river and the rest of the clan circles, which was reserved for the chief's tipi. An old Cheyenne sat outside the entrance flap, smoking a clay pipe and watching the children play. The elder had long gray hair streaked with white and his face was a seamed mass of deep wrinkles, though still hatchet-sharp in profile.

But it wasn't the face of Chief Yellow Bear. It was Arrow Keeper, the tribal medicine man.

"Our chief has crossed over while we were gone," said Little Horse with conviction. "This can mean nothing else. Yellow Bear's tipi has been taken down and placed on his scaffold with him. Arrow Keeper is our new chief!"

Suddenly, one of the sentries hidden in the trees circling camp raised the wolf howl of alarm.

The two Cheyenne bucks stared at each other, realizing they had just been spotted—and that the wolf howl was always reserved for announcing the arrival of enemies!

Even before they could nudge their ponies into motion again, a group of warriors rode hard from camp to meet them. Now the crier was racing up and down through camp on his pony, announcing their arrival.

The fierce young war chief named Black Elk led the warriors. He was accompanied by his younger cousin Wolf Who Hunts Smiling. When they reached the two arrivals, they formed a circle around them with lances raised.

"The white men's spies have come back like dogs returning to their vomit," said Wolf Who Hunts Smiling. "They are the eyes and ears of the Bluecoats!"

Touch the Sky locked stares with his sworn enemy. Wolf Who Hunts Smiling was small but hard-knit, with a guarded, wily face and furtive dark eyes that missed nothing. Ever since his capture, Wolf Who Hunts Smiling had accused him of being a spy. And one night he had deliberately stepped between Touch the Sky and the campfire—the Cheyenne way of announcing one's intention of killing another.

"I have no ears for your lies," said Touch the Sky. "Words are cheap, the coins spent freely by gossiping old squaws. Where is the proof that I or Little Horse have played the white men's dogs?"

"*There* is the proof!" said Wolf Who Hunts Smiling, pointing toward the braves named River of Winds and Swift Canoe. "They were sent to spy on you. They saw you making big medicine with the Bluecoat war chief! They saw you make war against paleface settlers so that Cheyennes would be blamed for the attacks!"

"You speak in a wolf bark!" said Touch the Sky. But he and Little Horse exchanged shocked glances as they realized the horrible mistake the tribe was making.

"The Bluecoat we made medicine with is a friend to the red man," said Little Horse. "He was—"

"Silence!" commanded Black Elk, speaking for the first time since the party had circled them.

Black Elk had seen only 20 winters, but already his war bonnet was filled with the eagle feathers of bravery. He was big and, unlike many red men, heavily muscled. His fierce black eyes were made even more fierce by the partially torn-off ear which he had sewn back onto his own skull with buckskin thread. His hair, like that of the others, had been cropped off short in mourning for Chief Yellow Bear.

"You say my cousin speaks in a wolf bark," he said to Touch the Sky. "But *I* speak only the straight word. The Headmen have not yet voted against you, so I will not take you prisoner. Though the tribe is angry at Little Horse, this is his home. But *you* are not welcome here! Before you ride closer, surrender your rifle!"

Hot blood stippled his cheeks, but Touch the Sky obeyed. He slid the percussion-action Sharps, a present from his white father in Bighorn Falls, out of the buckskin scabbard he had sewn to his blanket. He handed it to Black Elk.

"If this is my home," said Little Horse, "it is also Touch the Sky's home. If he is not welcome, I am not welcome."

"Speak carefully, your place here is not assured," said Black Elk. "If you desire it, perhaps you can join your brother when he is banned from Cheyenne lands forever!"

Touch the Sky and Little Horse were both silent
as they were escorted the rest of the way down to
the camp. Black Elk's ominous words had evoked
the memory of something old Arrow Keeper had
once told them: *A Cheyenne without a tribe is a
dead man.*

The hostile stares and accusing faces of the
others, as they rode in, stirred unpleasant memories for Touch the Sky: memories of that day
when, beaten and lashed to a travois, he had
first been brought to camp as a prisoner and
suspected spy.

His present misery still wasn't complete, however, until he caught his first glimpse of Honey
Eater.

Again, just as he had when he was still called
Matthew Hanchon and saw her for the first time,
he was struck by her frail beauty—the high, finely sculpted cheekbones, the long, black hair braided with white petals of mountain columbine.

But it wasn't the mere sight of Honey Eater
that made Touch the Sky's heart constrict in
agony. It was the fact that, as she met his eyes,
she was staring past the flap of Black Elk's tipi—
and she was wearing the beaded bride-shawl of
a newlywed!

Two sleeps passed, though in his misery Touch
the Sky hardly noticed whether moon or sun owned
the sky.

Out of respect for Yellow Bear, he and Little
Horse had cropped their hair short like the other warriors. But Touch the Sky made no further
attempt to join tribal life, nor was he welcome to.

He kept to his tipi by night, spent most of his days in the huge rope corrals working his ponies—the same ponies he had hoped to offer as the bride-price for Honey Eater. Only Little Horse was friendly to him. Arrow Keeper seemed to be avoiding him.

He knew that the Councillors would soon meet to decide his fate. But curiously, in his sorrow he was indifferent to his future. Let the Headmen vote with their stones to kill him, banish him, it was all one to him.

The others ignored him, looking right through him as if he were *odjib*—a thing of smoke. The report by River of Winds carried much weight. His word was well respected, and he had a reputation for fairness.

Tragically, the meetings he had witnessed between the Bluecoat pony soldier Tom Riley and Touch the Sky were not what they appeared to be. The officer had secretly joined forces with the Cheyenne to help them fool the paleface army. But Touch the Sky knew he could never prove this.

True, returning to Bighorn Falls and seeing Kristen Steele again had rekindled the dormant feelings in his heart for her. Seeing her had once again plunged him into a crisis—was he a white man, a red man, or an eternal outsider? Then, that first sight of Honey Eater, upon his return, had convinced him he loved the Cheyenne maiden too.

She had once crossed her wrists over her heart for him—Indian sign talk for love. Now she was Black Elk's wife!

On the third night after his return, Touch the Sky was walking back to his tipi after bathing in the river. A familiar voice called to him out of the grainy twilight.

"Woman Face!"

Touch the Sky drew up short. He was near the center of camp, nearly deserted now as most of the tribe prepared their late meal. The hide-covered frame of the council lodge loomed out of the darkness like a still, shaggy buffalo.

Only Wolf Who Hunts Smiling still called him Woman Face—a mocking reference to his old white man's habit of letting his emotions show in his face.

"So? Have you finally decided to make good on your threat to put me under?" said Touch the Sky. "Best to look before you wade in further—your cousin has my rifle, but he did not take my knife."

"Why should I risk dirtying the Sacred Arrows by shedding your blood now?" said Wolf Who Hunts Smiling. "The Headmen meet tomorrow to discuss you. Thanks to River of Winds' report, you will either be killed or banished. Either way, I am satisfied."

So his fate would be settled tomorrow? He was ready.

"Yes, you are satisfied," said Touch the Sky. "Just as a filthy pig is satisfied to eat its own droppings."

"Brave talk, Woman Face. But perhaps if you were more of a man your sweet Honey Eater would not be lying naked right now with my cousin!"

Hot rage surged into his face. Touch the Sky reached for the obsidian knife in his sheath.

"Sing the Death Song, Cheyenne," said Touch

the Sky softly as he drew his blade, "then draw your knife. If I am to be banished or killed, let me earn my punishment now!"

In a moment Wolf Who Hunts Smiling's bone-handle knife was in his hand. "As you will, white man's dog! Tonight one of us crosses over!"

Wolf Who Hunts Smiling lunged. Touch the Sky pivoted hard to his right and felt his enemy's blade nick the leather band around his left wrist as it passed harmlessly by. Touch the Sky leaped on top of the small but powerful Cheyenne and wrestled him to the ground.

Wolf Who Hunts Smiling wriggled free, rose to his feet, raised his knife, and prepared to leap again.

"Stop!"

Both youths glanced toward the speaker, barely discernible in the faltering light.

Arrow Keeper!

"Listen to your chief, young Cheyenne bucks! I speak words I want you to carry away with you. I forbid this fighting. Have we not enough enemies outside the tribe trying to kill us? I am still the keeper of the sacred Medicine Arrows. Any Cheyenne blood shed by another Cheyenne stains the Arrows. I will not let you dirty the entire tribe!"

"But, Father," Wolf Who Hunts Smiling said, "he—"

"Silence! Return to your clan circle."

After Wolf Who Hunts Smiling had departed, his face a mask of hatred for his enemy, Touch the Sky sheathed his knife and likewise started to leave. But Arrow Keeper called his name. He turned around.

"Yes, Father?"

"Return with me to my tipi, I would speak with you about urgent matters. I have had a medicine dream. The vision tells me you will die soon!"

Chapter Two

"You will die soon," repeated Arrow Keeper, "unless you leave before the Councillors decide your fate."

They sat in the gathering darkness just outside the entrance of Arrow Keeper's tipi. The acting chief struck fire from a piece of flint with his knife, igniting a small pile of bark-and-twig kindling. Flames leaped up, highlighting the seams and ridges of Arrow Keeper's face and the youthful sculpting of Touch the Sky's.

"The chief-renewal finally draws near," said Arrow Keeper. "The scattered bands of Cheyenne have nearly all returned to our valley for the ceremony. Soon there will be a time of dancing, feasting, and gift-giving. The tribe will name a successor now that our chief has been summoned."

Arrow Keeper automatically made the cut-off sign, as one did when speaking of the dead. Nor did he pronounce Yellow Bear's name aloud—the dead might hear their name and speak back.

"Soon I will no longer be chief. Then your only friend besides me will be Little Horse. And some in the tribe have already turned their hearts to stone against him for befriending you.

"So what will you do, little brother? My power to protect you will be limited. True it is, I am the Keeper of the Arrows. For this important responsibility I am respected. But the younger warriors, those who gather about Wolf Who Hunts Smiling and Swift Canoe and some of the others, are speaking more openly against me. And against you."

Arrow Keeper nudged the end of a log into the growing fire. Then he said, "A medicine dream, two sleeps ago, told me that you must die if the Council is allowed to meet and vote with their stones. Many in the tribe have spoken. They will not feel safe if a Bluecoat spy is alive among us."

Touch the Sky's mouth was a grim, determined slit in the flickering light. "Do *you* believe I am a Bluecoat spy, Father?"

"How would you ask me this thing? Did I not watch you save our chief's life by killing the Pawnee dog, War Thunder, with your battle ax? Did you not descend into the belly of the beast to save Honey Eater from the white devils who sold strong water? I have always talked only one way to you, and I say this. You are a true Cheyenne warrior, one worthy to wear the medicine hat in battle!"

"Perhaps," said Touch the Sky, his voice bitter with betrayal. "But my bravery did not prevent Honey Eater from accepting Black Elk's brideprice."

"Little brother, she did not make this decision lightly. She came to me in agony, but what would you have me tell this good young woman who is now alone in the world? That she should forsake everything and wait for you, a suspected spy, and infuriate Black Elk and the rest of the tribe?

"It may not always be fair, but our law does not permit our young women such choices. She is Cheyenne and must follow the Cheyenne way. Even a stone goes on being a stone."

Touch the Sky knew these words rang true. But still he could not crush the bitter sense of betrayal, the knife-edged doubts about his own ability to ever be a Cheyenne.

Arrow Keeper, studying his face closely in the flickering light, read these thoughts.

"It is not just the vote of the Headmen which I fear," he told the younger Cheyenne. "It is your own misery and doubt about being a red man which must also be defeated. True death, for any Indian, is to be alone forever. This is why a red man would rather fall on his own knife than be hated by his tribe. In your heart you are alone, even when surrounded by others. You cannot go on this way, living in two worlds yet belonging to neither."

Touch the Sky nodded, knowing these words flew straight-arrow.

"But what can I do, Father? As you say, I am alone. Honey Eater is Black Elk's squaw. I have already asked too much of Little Horse."

"You are alone, yes. And for this very reason, I am sending you on an important mission in the name of the entire tribe."

Sudden curiosity muted the misery in Touch the Sky's face.

"A mission?"

"Yes. A vision quest. There will be no fatal council because you will be on a sojourn to sacred Medicine Lake, seeking a medicine dream of great consequence to the Cheyenne people. As acting chief, I have the power to order this thing."

"A vision quest," repeated Touch the Sky.

The old shaman nodded. "Yes. A journey to the center of the red man's world. You remember when I spoke words about the mark hidden in your hair?"

Touch the Sky nodded. In the hair over his left temple, buried past the hairline, was a mulberry-colored birthmark shaped like an arrowhead—the mark of the warrior.

"I have already spoken to you about the powerful vision I experienced at Medicine Lake. But now I understand that *you* too must seek the same vision. If the hand of Maiyun, the Supernatural, is truly in this thing, then He will send the vision to you too."

Touch the Sky was silent, listening to the wood hiss and spit as the flames devoured it. He recalled well the vision Arrow Keeper had once described to him.

The elder had spent three grueling days in the Black Hills, standing in cold lake water up to his neck while he stared into the sun. On the third day the vision came.

It was a powerful dream, much of its meaning revealed in symbols, yet much of it also painfully clear. The vision had shown, in awful detail, the suffering that was in store for the Cheyenne people at the hands of paleface intruders. Soon, during cold moons yet to come, the Cheyenne would be forced to flee north to the Land of the Grandmother, which the whites called Canada.

The wind would howl like mating wolves, the temperature would fall so low the trees would split open with sounds like gunshots. There would be no wood for fires. The only way to save some of the infants would be to slaughter ponies and remove some of the warm guts, stuffing the little ones inside to keep them from freezing. The elders would freeze with the Death Song still on their lips.

But the vision also prophesized the rise of the long-lost son of the great chief Running Antelope—a son who had been reported killed along with his father and mother many winters ago. This young warrior would gather his people from all their far-flung hiding places and lead them in one last, great victory for the Cheyennes.

"I believe this vision was a true vision," said Arrow Keeper. "Not strong medicine placed over my eyes by my enemies. I believe *you* are Running Antelope's son—the arrowhead mark proves this.

"But it is not enough that *I* have seen this vision. Just as one man cannot eat or drink or hold a girl in his blanket for another, he cannot inspire another with his private visions. *You* must experience the vision in all of its force at Medicine Lake. Only then can you resolve this terrible battle in your heart. Only then will you accept who you are and what must be done."

Touch the Sky thought about all of this for a long while. Arrow Keeper was right about the terrible battle in his heart. But though he trusted and respected the old warrior greatly, Touch the Sky could not believe that *he* was the young war leader of Arrow Keeper's vision. Surely it was Black Elk.

Touch the Sky finally nodded. "When must I leave?"

"Immediately. Before the sun begins her next journey across the sky. You must purify yourself in the sweat lodge before you leave and again when you arrive. I will announce at the Council that I have sent you on this mission to seek spiritual guidance for the tribe. Many will not be happy, but I have ordered the sentries to let you ride out."

"But Father, what if I fail in seeking this medicine dream?"

Arrow Keeper stared long into the fire. When he finally answered, his voice was surprisingly sad and gentle.

"Before you entered the whiskey traders' camp, did you not experience a powerful vision? What man has done, man can do. But I will not coat the truth with honey. You will either experience this medicine vision, young Cheyenne warrior, or I fear you will be killed in the attempt."

Darkness settled like a heavy quilt over the Powder River village. The night sentries were posted, ready to raise the wolf howl if danger approached. Fires blazed throughout camp, and the young braves began gathering to gamble and bet on the pony races.

Touch the Sky heard the noise recede behind him as he descended the long grassy slope to the bank of the river. He veered toward the dark mass of an isolated hut built right next to the flowing water. It was made of buffalo hides stretched tight over a willow-branch frame.

Touch the Sky stooped, ducked inside, and started a fire to heat a circle of rocks. When they glowed hot, he stepped back outside and quickly stripped. Then he filled a wooden bowl with cold river water and poured it on the rocks.

The hot steam was difficult to breathe, at first. But soon, as rivulets of sweat began to pour from him, he felt his muscles relaxing. The confused stampede of his thoughts settled down to focus on one goal: the vision quest Arrow Keeper was sending him on. The old shaman insisted this vision would convince him of his place and purpose. Therefore, Touch the Sky desired it more than anything else.

Still, Arrow Keeper's words lingered in his memory like an echo: *You will either experience the medicine vision or be killed in the attempt.*

He finally emerged, rested and glistening with sweat in the moonlight, and rubbed his body down thoroughly with clumps of sage. Now it was time to make his preparations for the journey to Medicine Lake.

First he walked down river to the huge corral marked off by buffalo-hair ropes. He spotted his spirited dun grazing in the moonlight. But Touch the Sky knew she needed to rest and graze, to heal her scarred hocks and recover from the hard service she had given him lately.

Instead, he slipped his hackamore onto a spotted gray with a beautiful white mane. She was his trophy after counting first coup on a Crow warrior during a practice raid when Black Elk was training him. The pony was well trained, yet like all Cheyenne-trained horses had not been spirit-broken nor water-starved and beaten, as whites did to their horses. He led the gray back to his tipi and tethered her with a long strip of rawhide.

He slipped inside and gathered his few possessions. Black Elk had taken his rifle, leaving him with his knife, his stone-headed throwing-ax, his bow, and a foxskin quiver full of fire-hardened arrows.

He gathered extra moccasins, and stuffed his legging sash with pemmican and dried plums and jerked buffalo meat.

He skirted the activity in the middle of camp, sticking close to the river as he rode out. Not once did he look back. But his heart felt like a cold fist of stone in his chest, and he had never felt more alone in his life.

Thus distracted, his mind set fully on his purpose, he rounded a dense river thicket.

A lone figure glided out of the thick growth and into the pale-as-ice moonlight, startling him and making the gray shy in fright.

In a moment his knife was in his hand. He was about to slide from his pony and meet the attacker when he realized his "enemy" was Honey Eater!

Ever since Touch the Sky's return from the fight in Bighorn Falls, Honey Eater had been distraught with worry and remorse. In her heart she had never stopped loving him, and she had secretly been watching him since his return.

She knew he did not understand—in order to marry Black Elk, she had convinced herself that Touch the Sky had deserted her and the tribe. River of Winds' report had confirmed this, including the information that Touch the Sky was making love talk to a paleface girl with hair like spun-gold sunlight.

Only then had she finally married the importunate Black Elk. And now Touch the Sky was back, and Honey Eater knew she could love only him. Seeing him make preparations to leave, and at great risk of discovery, she had slipped off to meet him as he left.

Touch the Sky, however, could know none of this. His first thought, when he spotted Honey Eater, was that she had taken her nightly walk to gather fresh white columbine for her hair. He assumed the meeting was accidental, and his foremost desire was to get away—get away quickly before his own love and sense of betrayal forced him to break down in front of her.

"Touch the Sky!" she cried out behind him as he dug his knees into his pony and sprinted off into the blue-black darkness. But a moment later he was gone, disappearing like a wraith.

Honey Eater did not realize, as she stood weeping beside the bubbling river, that her brief meeting had been witnessed.

Wolf Who Hunts Smiling and Swift Canoe too had been watching Touch the Sky, aware that he was departing camp with Arrow Keeper's permission. But they rounded the thicket only in time to see their enemy bolt away, as if suddenly discovered. They were not soon enough to see that his meeting with Black Elk's bride was accidental.

"Brother," whispered Swift Canoe, who was crouched behind a hawthorn bush, "do you credit what your eyes behold? Your cousin's wife meeting secretly with Woman Face!"

Wolf Who Hunts Smiling's face, in the silvery moonlight, was furtive and calculating. "I have eyes to see, brother. And look now how she calls after him! She has sworn the squaw-taking vows with Black Elk, but now turns her stallion into a gelding!"

"Black Elk will beat her and cut off her nose when he learns of this," said Swift Canoe. "He may sing the Throw-away Song or even take her out on the plains."

Wolf Who Hunts Smiling nodded, though this last was rare and very extreme. The Throw-away Song was a public divorce. But taking a woman out on the plains was the worst punishment possible for an unfaithful Cheyenne woman: It meant that any warrior in the tribe who wanted to was free to lie with her. Afterward, polluted, she would be left to die alone and in shame.

"Come," said Wolf Who Hunts Smiling. "We must report this thing to my cousin. Black Elk's pride will do more than punish Honey Eater—he will *never* allow Touch the Sky to live after this!"

Chapter Three

Wolf Who Hunts Smiling and Swift Canoe were unable to report their news to Black Elk immediately.

On the previous day the hunters had run into exceptional luck near Sweet Medicine Creek, bringing down three full-grown elks and a fat mule deer. So much meat to butcher and pack in required help from camp. And friendly Sioux scouts had recently reported that Pawnee patrols had invaded Cheyenne country—meaning an armed war party would have to accompany the hunters back with their valuable haul.

Black Elk had led the war party. They had not returned until their uncle, the moon, had journeyed well across the sky. Wolf Who Hunts Smiling and Swift Canoe lingered about impatiently the next morning, until Honey Eater finally emerged from Black Elk's tipi and started the cooking fire.

Soon after, Black Elk emerged and ate his morning meal. Afterward, he moved to the shade behind his tipi and sat to file arrowpoints, which he had fastened onto a cottonwood stick to hold them. The two young warriors finally approached him.

"Cousin!" said Wolf Who Hunts Smiling.

Black Elk looked up. He was still tired, and his face still puffy and lopsided from sleep. Even so, the ear sewn back onto his skull with buckskin thread gave him a particularly fierce aspect.

"I would speak with you," said Wolf Who Hunts Smiling.

"You have a tongue," said Black Elk impatiently. "Use it."

Knowing a storm was about to break, Wolf Who Hunts Smiling glanced toward the tipi and lowered his voice. Then he announced bluntly, "Honey Eater has been meeting with Touch the Sky. He holds her in his blanket. We saw them last night."

Black Elk had expected nothing like this. For a moment his face was blank, the words too impossible to believe. Then, abruptly, hot blood rushed to his face.

"You speak in a wolf bark! Everyone knows you hate Touch the Sky. I care nothing for the trouble between you and your enemy, nor what lies you speak of each other. But now you claim that my bride has sullied the Medicine Arrows!

"Cousin! A moment before, I told you that you have a tongue. Now, I swear by Maiyun, I will cut it from your head!"

"I speak the straight word! Swift Canoe saw them too."

Swift Canoe bravely met Black Elk's fierce dark eyes and nodded.

"Both of you hate him!" said Black Elk. But desperation had crept into his tone. Adultery was a serious charge, as serious—and almost as rare among the Cheyenne—as the murder of a fellow Cheyenne. No one would make such a charge lightly.

Abruptly, Black Elk threw down the arrowpoints and stood up, hurrying into his tipi. The two youths expected a storm from within as Black Elk confronted his squaw. But instead he emerged a moment later, holding a curled piece of red willow bark.

"Swear this thing you have told me," he challenged them, thrusting forward the piece of bark. "Swear it on the Sacred Arrows!"

They glanced down and saw a red-clay drawing of the four Medicine Arrows, two pointing vertically, the other pair crossing them horizontally. No Cheyenne would lie while swearing on the Arrows, even on a symbolic drawing of them. Without hesitating, both bucks placed their hands on the bark and swore their oath.

Finally Black Elk believed them.

The hot, jealous rage which consumed him almost caused him to rush inside and kill Honey Eater on the spot. But following hard upon his rage came another emotion: shame. How could he, a proud warrior whose bonnet was full of coup feathers, admit to the tribe that his squaw was secretly meeting the outcast spy?

He could divorce his wife on the drum, of course. And this was a great disgrace for any squaw, let alone a chief's daughter. The men in the man's clan would sing the Throw-away Song while the husband danced by himself, holding a stick in his hand. Dancing up to the drum, the man hit it with his stick.

Boom! "I throw away my wife." With those words a warrior could drum his wife away, making a public quit-claim to all responsibility toward the squaw.

But the entire tribe would soon learn why. And never would he be respected—a war chief who could not keep his wife from rutting with a white man's dog! Besides—despite her treachery, Black Elk still loved Honey Eater. Better to pretend nothing had happened. Better to eliminate the other half of the problem.

Better, decided Black Elk, to kill Touch the Sky.

True, the mysterious stranger had the fighting spirit of a cougar and had developed into the best warrior Black Elk had ever trained. But he did not respect the Cheyenne way. He was a threat to the entire tribe, as this blackest of crimes proved.

Once again Black Elk held out the red willow bark.

"You have long thirsted for Touch the Sky's blood," Black Elk said to his cousin. "If you and Swift Canoe will make a vow of silence about this thing you have told me, I will give you my permission to kill him. And I will help you do it secretly, so the tribe will not know it was you."

The two friends readily agreed and swore their vow.

Arrow Keeper had already announced to the Councillors that Touch the Sky had been sent in the direction of the sun's birthplace on a vision quest at Medicine Lake.

"Pawnee are said to be in the area," said Black Elk. "I will announce to the others that, as War Chief, I have sent you two out on an important

32

scouting mission. Ride hard toward the Black Hills and be waiting when this squaw-stealing dog arrives. Wash his white man's stink from our tribe forever. For the sake of our people, kill him, Cheyenne warriors!"

The Pawnee warrior named Red Plume halted the line of braves behind him by raising his streamered lance high over his head.

One by one, all six braves nudged their ponies up beside their leader's. From behind a huge pile of scree high up in the rimrock, they watched a lone rider below make his way slowly across the open tableland near the Powder River.

"Cheyenne," said a keen-eyed brave named Gun Powder, recognizing the distinctive red handprint on the pony's left forequarter.

Normally, at a distance, the distinctive cut of the hair was the quickest way to guess an Indian's tribe. But this youth had cropped short his hair in mourning, a practice common among several Plains tribes.

"We have been patient long enough," said Red Plume. "Yellow Bear has crossed over. The best time for a surprise attack will be during their chief-renewal, when all have assembled with their gifts for the poor. We need only wait until darkness, as we did when our people stole their Sacred Arrows. These white-livered Shaiyena fear the darkness."

Red Plume was referring to the great battle, many winters ago, when the Pawnee had captured the Cheyenne's Sacred Arrows. Though their enemy had eventually regained them, a hatred inspired by bloodlust had grown between the two tribes ever since.

The Pawnee, who called themselves Chahiksi-chakihs, "men of men," were naked save for clouts and elkskin moccasins. Bright red plumage adorned their greased topknots, which rose stiff and straight from otherwise shaved skulls. Their powerful bows, made from the wood of the Osage orange, were feared throughout Plains country.

"Our shadows grow long in the sun," said Gun Powder. "We have only to trail him until he makes his camp for the night."

In contrast to the Cheyenne and most other Plains Indians, the Pawnee liked to travel and attack after dark. Their priests taught that all energy derived from the stars and constellations. Therefore, the tribe possessed an extensive knowledge of the heavens and commonly employed star charts to move about freely at night. Other Plains Indians named the stars, but—fearing darkness—had not learned to navigate by them.

"No," said Red Plume. "We seize him now, in the open, before he possibly meets with others. And then we learn from him exactly when and where the chief-renewal will be. Until we know this thing, we cannot know the best time to bring in the main body for the attack."

Red Plume slid a stone-tipped arrow from his quiver and lined the notch up with the buffalo-sinew bowstring. The others followed suit.

Riding out of the blazing sun behind them to disguise their movement, the Pawnee descended from the high country with blood in their eyes.

His mind numb with sadness, Touch the Sky had ridden due east all day long, letting his pony set her own pace.

Vision Quest

It would still be several more sleeps' ride before he would spot the rolling, dark-forested humps of the Black Hills on the horizon. Medicine Lake was nestled high among the hills. He had visited the sacred center of the Cheyenne world once before, when Arrow Keeper taught him the rudiments of Cheyenne customs and religion.

All that seemed as distant to him now as a long-forgotten dream. So much had happened since then: He had become a warrior, slain enemies, earned his first coup feather, withstood vicious torture—and sworn his eternal love to Honey Eater, who had returned his vow.

But everything he had done, like Honey Eater's love, was nothing but smoke behind him. He was hated as much by the tribe now as on the first day of his capture. For them, the white man's stink could never be washed from his skin, though it was red skin like theirs.

The spotted gray shied when a rabbit darted across their path, bringing Touch the Sky back to the present.

With a start of guilt, he glanced all around the sprawling vastness surrounding him. For a long time he had been riding with no attention to where he was going. The plains stretched out endlessly before him, the green and ochre colors bleeding together now as the sun neared her resting place. The river snaked its winding way on his left. Mountain peaks cut jagged spires against the sky behind him, the shimmering sun backlighting them and forcing him to squint.

The gray acted nervous and skittish, even after the rabbit was long gone. Again Touch the Sky glanced behind him, blinded in the fierce light.

35

Scattered clumps of cottonwood trees could easily hide pursuers.

A premonition of danger moved up his spine like the ticklish touch of a feather.

He placed a hand on the gray's thick white mane and spoke gently to her. It was almost time to make camp for the night. He veered closer to the river, planning to find a good patch of graze in which to tether his pony.

Suddenly, a sharp tug just below his ribs was followed immediately by a white-hot pain in his left side that made him cry out.

Touch the Sky looked down and recognized a Pawnee arrowhead protruding from his body, the honed tip shiny with his blood!

Then his hackles rose when, with a thundering of hooves, his unseen enemies raised a triumphant war cry and charged him.

Chapter Four

Touch the Sky knew the Pawnee were excellent horsemen. He was as good as dead if he attempted to outrun them across the wide-open prairie and sage flats.

Instead, he veered hard to the north, toward the Bighorn Mountains and the Yellowstone with its protective thickets.

His side felt like it was on fire. But hearing the bloodthirsty whoops and yips behind him made him forget the pain. The gray surged forward, laying her ears back flat as Touch the Sky prodded her flanks with his heels.

She was well rested from the slow pace earlier. Now, as the stolen Crow pony opened up the distance between Touch the Sky and his pursuers, he realized what a magnificent animal she was.

By the time the sun dropped below the horizon, the Pawnee were no longer in sight behind him.

Touch the Sky slowed his mount from a gallop to a run to a canter. Despite the fall of darkness and the fiery pain lancing through his wounded side, he knew he was dead if he stopped. The Pawnee were in their element after dark. He knew they could read the star-shot heavens as easily as a Cheyenne read sign along a game trail.

He ate some dried plums from his legging sash. But increasingly, he became aware of an overpowering thirst. Distracted with worry when he had ridden out of camp, he had foolishly neglected to fill a bladder-bag with water. Nor, after this hard run, could the gray go much longer without drinking.

He knew this new course was unlikely to cross any water before he reached the Yellowstone. But he couldn't afford to waste time searching for it.

He slowed the gray to a long trot and held that pace. Constantly, he turned one ear to listen behind him. At one point, when the gray faltered slightly topping a rise, he halted her for a brief rest.

Wincing at the pain which flared up in his side, he slid to the ground and dropped down on all fours. Placing one ear to the ground, he listened long and carefully. He heard or felt nothing, and relaxed slightly until the next burst of pain jolted him back to the reality of his danger.

He knew he would have to deal with the arrow before the wound swelled closed around it. But he also knew that removing the arrow would increase the bleeding. And on the open plains, there was plenty of time to bleed to death.

He could tell, by the location of the Grandmother Star to the north, that the night was well advanced. Mounting again was even more painful than dismounting. Speaking gently to the gray, he stroked her neck. Then he nudged her flanks.

Reluctantly, expecting a long, cool drink of water as reward for her hard work, the tough little pony snorted in protest before she obeyed.

"He is bleeding, but not heavily. The blood has not yet stiffened. He cannot be far from here."

Gun Powder knelt atop a long rise where the Cheyenne had obviously stopped, judging from the prints, both hoof and moccasin. The blood was clearly visible in the unclouded light of a full moon.

Red Plume stared at a brave named Iron Knife, anger tightening his face.

"You squirrel-brained fool! How could you have missed the pony and hit the Cheyenne? For this you will forfeit a coup feather. He is no good to us if he bleeds to death!"

Iron Knife said nothing. He stared straight ahead and showed nothing in his face. He was ashamed of his failure with his bow. But he had no respect for Red Plume or his clan, not one of whom dared face his knife. There was much talk of taking his coup feathers away. Yet no one in the tribe had ever gotten close enough to pluck them out of his bonnet.

"It is a fast pony," said Gun Powder. "A strong pony. But without water it will weaken. We can catch him this night if we ride hard."

Red Plume nodded. Idly, as he considered the best course of action, he picked a louse from the grease in his top-knot and cracked it between strong white teeth.

"Then we ride hard!" he said. "Before the morning star is born, he will lie under our lances!"

Twice during the long night Touch the Sky heard the distant sounds of his enemy behind him. Reluctantly, his wounded side throbbing at the increased jolting, he pushed the thirsty and tired gray to a long gallop.

Thus he opened the distance between himself and his pursuers. But by now his thirst was so powerful it overshadowed the pain of his wound. He sucked on pebbles to keep moisture in his mouth.

Finally, as his sister the sun began to color the eastern horizon pink, he was unable to bear his thirst any longer.

There was nothing he could do yet for his pony. But Touch the Sky veered right from his course when he spotted a rocky spine rising out of the plains. It had rained recently. He recalled a trick that old Knobby, a former mountain man who was now the hostler back in Bighorn Falls, had told him about.

Slowed considerably by his stiffening wound, he dismounted, hobbled his pony, and picked his way up toward the boulders at the very top of the spine. As he had hoped, the hollows of the larger rocks still held precious drops of rainwater. Gratefully, he moved from boulder to boulder, lowering his lips to the night-cooled water and lapping it up like an animal.

It was only a few swallows, all tolled. But the water blunted the harshest edge of his thirst. Before he climbed back down to his pony, he scanned the plains to the south.

His mouth tightened into a grim slit when he saw riders profiled against the new day's horizon. They were the size of insects at this distance. But a slight lead on a thirsty and nearly exhausted pony meant nothing on the plains.

His wound throbbed with insistent pain as he climbed back down to his mount. Now that the sun was rising, he decided to veer northeast—riding into the new sun would make him a more difficult target next time the Pawnee attacked.

Speaking softly to his pony, explaining that there was no other choice, he mounted and reluctantly pushed northward.

"The Cheyenne buck stopped here to drink."

Gun Powder's voice was raised so it would carry down to the others. They sat their ponies at the base of the rocky spine, watching the keen-eyed warrior read the boulders for sign.

"He has ridden into the sun," said the Pawnee brave called Iron Knife. He squatted on the ground, examining the prints leading away from the spine.

"Our enemy has tough battle bark on him. He has decided we must *earn* the right to dangle his scalp from our coup stick," said their leader, Red Plume.

The warrior's tone showed approval of their quarry's survival spirit. The Cheyenne had raised their battle axes forever against the Pawnee. This one knew full well what fate awaited him if—*when*—Red Plume's Pawnee braves seized him.

There was no question that he would soon watch crows and vultures pick at his guts, pulled out of his body coil by coil before his own eyes. Pawnee scouting ability was respected even by the Bluecoats themselves. The red "men of men" were considered the U.S. Army's most capable mercenaries—they formed the backbone of special Indian-hunting units which had razed more than one Cheyenne, Sioux, Arapahoe, and Shoshone village.

Those who called this "treachery" had forgotten the ancient wrongs against the Pawnee. The Sioux and the Cheyenne had joined forces to drive them south from the Powder River country, hoarding the vast buffalo herds for themselves. Pawnee children died of starvation while, to the north, buffalo meat lay rotting.

Soon, thought Red Plume, the just anger of the supernatural father, Tirawa, would demand another bloody retribution from the Cheyenne. Not just this lone warrior or the annual ritual of sacrificing a captured maiden—often a Cheyenne—to the Morning Star. This time the entire Cheyenne nation must atone with blood.

"He is a warrior," said Red Plume. "A sly one. However, *nothing* lies between us and the river but empty plains. A frog is slippery—in the water. But it is easily crushed on dry land."

He glanced up at the spine again and gestured impatiently to Gun Powder. "Hurry! Now we ride hard and crush our frog!"

The sun was well up and casting short shadows. Dull pain throbbed like a tight tourniquet in Touch the Sky's wounded side. By now thirst had caked his mouth like parched alkali soil, a raw, dry grittiness that filled his throat and left his belly cramping.

The gray too was weak with water starvation. Even at a slow trot she faltered often. Now he had to fight her more and more to keep her pointed northeast—some instinct made her want to try another direction.

42

Finally, tired of fighting her, Touch the Sky gave her her head and let the gray set her own pace and direction. She veered sharply to the west, breaking from a trot into a lope which soon became a run.

Abruptly, she drew up short in a slight, wide, dry depression that formed a winding path across the vast prairie.

Puzzled, even through the increasing fog of his exhaustion, pain, and delirium, Touch the Sky stroked the pure white mane.

"This is a dry streambed," he told his pony. "The water is long gone. You smell a memory, just a memory."

But the gray nickered impatiently, turned her head, pawed the ground hard.

His jaw set firmly against the pain, Touch the Sky dismounted and sank to his knees, staring hard at the depressions where the gray had dug up the dirt.

It looked darker than dry earth should—and felt slightly damp to his touch.

He gouged his fingers into the deepest print and probed even deeper.

When his fingers came back out, there was mud under the nails!

Unsheathing his knife, ignoring the pain in his side now, Touch the Sky dug frantically. A few minutes of digging exposed a thin layer of seepage.

He dug deeper, and soon a little pool had formed.

Giving thanks to Maiyun and the four directions, Touch the Sky dropped his face into the pool. Forcing himself to take measured swallows, he drank his fill. Then he widened the hole and rose to let the gray follow suit.

His legs were still weak with hunger. Touch the

Sky ate some pemmican and dried fruit from his legging sash while the gray drank and rested. Now, he told himself, they must ride hard toward the valley of the Yellowstone. His wound had swollen dangerously tight around the arrow. It had to be removed, and he had to sleep.

The pony had grazed lush grass all spring. Now, refreshed by the water, she resumed her hard pace.

Touch the Sky rode until his shadow was lengthening in the westering sun. Finally, topping a long rise, he spotted the first coarse-barked cottonwood trees with their leathery leaves. He had finally reached the winding valley of the Yellowstone.

His enemies were still trailing him—the last time he had listened to the ground, he had felt them approaching at a rapid pace. Now he led the gray into the river and followed the current downstream until he was sure he had made it difficult for the Pawnee to pick up his trail again.

He rode up out of the water and into a protective line of thickets. This was Crow country. So first he checked the ground all around him. He read the old and fresh tracks of weasel, mink, wolf, and cougar and knew it was safe—animals would not be so abundant in an area where humans were.

Touch the Sky found a nearby clearing amidst the thicket. He hobbled his pony in the patch of browse. Then he set to work building a crude brush lean-to in which to hide. He covered it over with branches and brambles, until it looked like a natural deadfall.

He threw his buffalo robe inside. By now the sun was sending her last feeble rays up against the encroaching night sky. Touch the Sky was now prepared for that which he had been dreading.

First he found a stand of spruce trees and dug some balsam sap from one. From a red willow he peeled strips of soft bark. Then he returned to his brush lean-to and crawled inside.

Wincing, he snapped the fletching off of the Pawnee arrow. Then, setting his jaw, he jerked the arrow out forward in one sharp tug.

White hot fire licked at his side, and a field of black dots danced in front of his eyes. Hurrying to get it done before he passed out, he packed the ragged, angry edges of his wound with balsam. Then he bound it with strips of the bark.

His ministrations left him exhausted. He collapsed back into his robe. Within moments he was sleeping like a dead man, even as the nearby Pawnee searched desperately for his trail.

Chapter Five

He woke to clear morning light and the scolding of jays, angry at this human intrusion into their nesting grounds.

But the warbling song of the nearby purple finch told Touch the Sky no one else was lurking in the area. Cautiously, he rose to a sitting position in the lean-to. Pain jolted through his wounded side. He eased outside for a better look.

A cold apprehension iced his stomach when he saw the ragged, discolored edges of his wound. The balsam had eased the burning pain. But he had waited too long to remove the arrow—now the wound was contaminated deep inside. A greenish-yellow discharge oozed from the torn flesh.

He checked on his pony and led her down to the river to drink. Then he moved her to a new patch of browse, still hidden within the thickets.

Vision Quest

By midday he was light-headed. He realized he needed fresh meat for strength and to fight the infection. This close to the river, small game was plentiful. He killed a rabbit, gutted and skinned it, then used the same arrow he'd shot it with as a spit, running it lengthwise through the rabbit.

He built a small fire while the sun was highest, which made the smoke and flames hard to see. As soon as the meat was charred enough to eat, he put the fire out. He also followed the precaution, after he'd devoured the rabbit, of moving further upriver in case the smoke had been spotted.

Well past midday, a new brush lean-to constructed, Touch the Sky began to relax. By now it appeared that he had successfully thrown the Pawnee off his scent. They must, he decided, be well out of this area. But when he ventured closer to the water's edge, he discovered he was wrong.

He first spotted the tracks in a patch of lush marsh marigold. Many tracks, leading up and down the river bank several times. They were made by unshod Indian ponies, and judging from the sharp bend of the crushed marigolds, the latest set were made quite recently.

Meaning the Pawnee probably remained in the area, searching for him.

Knowing the lice-eaters' skill at tracking, Touch the Sky realized it was only a matter of time before they closed in on him.

He considered his plight. The infection in his wound would soon severely limit his ability to travel very far across wide-open plains. The Pawnee would simply trail him like wolves stalking a wounded buffalo, merely waiting for him to drop. Nor could he stay here in the river valley—even if he could stay hidden, his pony would eventually be discovered.

No, thought Touch the Sky—neither plains nor river valley would do. He glanced south, toward the snowcapped peaks of the Bighorn Mountains.

His best chance for survival now was to take to the high country.

The Ute tribe lived high up in those peaks. They had been driven there by Sioux and Cheyenne after it was learned they were cooperating with Bluecoat pony soldiers. However, the turncoat Pawnee were also currently at war with the Ute.

Touch the Sky knew it would be easier for him to flee alone unnoticed into the mountains than it would be for the Pawnee band. They were not likely to ride far up into the hostile high country merely to capture one enemy.

The country between the river valley and the mountains was mostly flat, sparsely forested tableland and plains. Despite the Pawnee skill with star charts, he knew his only chance lay in leaving after darkness fell.

Again he checked on the gray, leading her to water before he tethered her in a sheltered patch of graze. Then he tended to his wound. He cleaned it as best he could and repacked it with balsam. Afterward, he rested inside the lean-to, preparing for his journey.

Nightfall brought clouds and light rain, which quickly gave way to a starlit sky and a full moon. Touch the Sky went down to the river to drink and cleanse his wound one more time. By now his side had swollen even more, the jagged mouth of the wound oozing pus. He was light-headed, feverish, and his weak legs felt hamstrung.

The fat moon and all the stars worried him. Before he retrieved his pony he rubbed his body down with mud to cut reflection. Then he squatted and concentrated on the most important survival skill his warrior training had taught him: freeing his mind of useless thoughts and paying attention instead to the language of nature.

All seemed well. The sparrow hawks which thickened the treetops near the water remained undisturbed. Frogs sent out their eerie, croaking rhythm, the hum of cicadas and crickets was unbroken. Prowling owls hooted to each other across the shadowy expanse of the murmuring river.

Now the time was right. If Pawnee were lurking nearby, they had cleverly fooled even nature herself.

But as he rose and started back toward the lean-to, his wounded side protested with a painful throbbing. Once he was forced to stop and sink to his knees until strength returned to his legs.

Again he glanced toward the peaks of the Bighorns, dark shapes against the blue-black night sky. Would he even be able to make the ride in this condition? But he had no choice. It was either ride for his life, or surrender it here.

He dropped one hand to his medicine pouch and offered a brief prayer to Maiyun. Then he went to retrieve his weapons and his pony.

* * *

"He knew it was foolish to stay hidden here. His wound bothers him greatly, but he has wisely run to the mountains. The tracks are fresh, but so is his pony. It has drunk and grazed and rested."

Gun Powder rose from the set of prints leading away from the river thickets toward the outlying plains and the distant Bighorn Mountains.

"He avoided us well," said Red Plume, still sitting his horse. "We passed this spot many times, searching. Our Cheyenne buck knows how to play the fox."

"His pony," said Gun Powder, "was captured from the Crow."

He pointed to the prints. In the bright wash of a full moon, looking closely, he could see the slight cleft made by the back of the hoof—the distinctive print of the stocky mountain breed preferred by the Crow tribe, allies in battle of the Pawnee.

"If he counted coup on a Crow brave," said Red Plume, "he is a warrior of the first rank."

"Then, why not let him go?" asked one of the other four braves riding with Red Plume and Gun Powder. "We can capture another Cheyenne. Why ride into the teeth of our enemies, the Ute?"

"I too am not eager to face Ute in their stronghold," said Red Plume. "But only think on this thing. This buck we track knows by now that we are Pawnee. We cannot be sure that Yellow Bear's tribe knows yet that we are in the Powder River country. If we let him go, and he returns to his clan circle, the entire Cheyenne nation will soon know that we have slipped into their hunting grounds.

"No, brothers! Iron Knife failed his tribe when

50

he aimed wrong. Now there is nothing else for it but to finish the work Iron Knife's arrow has begun. And with luck, we will also learn the secret of exactly when and where the Cheyenne will be holding their chief-renewal ceremony."

Red Plume looked at Gun Powder again. "You say his pony is fresh. But as you also say, his wound troubles him greatly. Quickly, mount up! With this moon turning night into day, we can ride hard and catch him before he even reaches the mountains."

He rode hard across the open country, his mind playing cat and mouse with consciousness. At one moment the infection in his wound made him feel feverish; a moment later chills would sweep through him, turning the clammy sweat cold all over him.

Only the occasional stand of scrub pine and cedar broke the monotonous, vast emptiness around him. In the moonlight he felt vulnerable, constantly observed. He slowed to rest the gray. Almost immediately, a bitch wolf began slinking along behind him, tenacious but keeping her distance.

Then Touch the Sky realized: He was giving off the stink of death! Wolves never attacked humans—they merely trailed them when they sensed death was near at hand, patiently waiting for nature to provide a meal.

At one point, when he was perhaps halfway to the foothills, he stopped his pony at the top of a long rise. By now his side was hot and throbbing, sending fiery tentacles of pain throughout his body when he dismounted. Lining himself up with the huge yellow moon, he stared out across the wavering plains for a long time until he was sure he detected the movement of riders following him. They were outlined against the huge saffron moon behind them—vague, shimmering shapes that drew gradually closer.

The lice-eaters had picked up his trail! Touch the Sky spoke to his pony; then, face crumpling at the pain, he mounted and dug his heels hard into her flanks.

"Hi-ya!" He shouted the battle cry to rally both of them.

Later, he would have no memory of that grueling race across the flats with death literally at his heels. He drove the gray mercilessly until she faltered, then slowed to a long trot to rest her. He continued this pattern, never once stopping. At one point, he started awake and realized he had been unconscious—how long, he didn't know. But if he fell from the saddle now, in his condition, his scalp was as good as dangling from a Pawnee coup stick.

While he was still lucid enough to do so, he freed one of the buffalo-hair ropes he used as a long tether for the pony. Wrapping it around his waist, carefully avoiding the aching wound, he then ran it through the pony's hackamore and under her belly like a surcingle, a strap used as a handhold when riding a mean horse. He then tied it around his waist again, securing himself.

He rode as if through a thick but patchy fog. For moments his eyes would snap open and he could see the distant peaks of the mountains, looming closer each time. Then the undertow of delirium would suck him under again, and for long spells he was unconscious while the gray set her own pace.

Once, toward sunrise, he turned again to search the flats behind him. He didn't need the aid of the moon now.

The Pawnee had steadily closed the distance. He spotted them, skylined on top of a ridge against the lightening sky. He could count the shapes now—six of them.

Fear keeping him awake, he finally gained the foothills as the sun burst forth over the horizon. Soon he was following a winding trail which snaked its way steadily higher through meadows of beautiful columbine and bright mountain laurel.

Every time he glanced back, pain stabbing through his side, he could see the Pawnee even nearer. The morning sun glistened on their shaved skulls and greased topknots, highlighted the brilliant streamers flying from their lances. They had been riding six abreast, but now rode single file along the narrow mountain trail.

Somewhere above, thought Touch the Sky, lurked Ute eager to raise the hair of Cheyenne or Pawnee. How far would the lice-eaters pursue him?

Despite the lost ground, he decided to stop briefly so he and the gray could drink from a streamlet. He dipped his head under the surface of the ice-cold water, the shock momentarily sharpening his senses again. He unwrapped his side and tried not to give in to fear when he saw how red and savage and swollen the wound had become. A putrid stink like carrion assaulted his nostrils.

He immersed in the cold water, the pain momentarily abating. But already he could hear the distant shouts of his Pawnee pursuers, pumping blood into their eyes by singing their battle songs.

The rest did the sturdy mountain pony good. Soon she had gained back some of the lost ground as her superior breeding began to pay off in the higher altitudes. She was able to scamper effortlessly where Touch the Sky thought only sure-footed mules could go.

As they were about to break out above the tree line, the gray suddenly shied and nervously side-jumped. Fearing ambush by Ute, Touch the Sky instead spotted a black bear well back from the trail. It ignored him, rolling a log over to look for insects. He calmed his pony and quickly urged her higher—all horses instinctively hated and feared bears, and some had been known to panic, killing their riders in headlong rushes over cliffs.

He began to fade in and out of awareness again as they pushed even higher, past wind-wrung trees stubbornly growing from cracks in rocks. The faint trail gave way to rock-strewn, dangerous slopes which sometimes rose precipitously. Twice the powerful gray slipped and lost her footing. Jolted hard, Touch the Sky was forced to cry out at the explosion of fiery hurt in his side.

Despite his determination, he passed out for

some time. He woke only when the gray suddenly halted, refusing to climb further.

Then he saw why: a huge rock slide had wiped out much of the slope above, the mass of the boulders and rocks forming a huge choke-point in front of him when they reached a narrow defile. Though the narrow opening had stopped most of them, they had jumbled into and over it with overwhelming weight. Now the slide was balanced on the feather edge, ready to hurtle on downward at the slightest nudge.

A nudge as slight as the weight of one pony.

Touch the Sky carefully skirted the dangerous area, riding well to the left of the loose scree. But now he was so weak that only the rope rigging held him on horseback. There was no other choice: He would have to risk a hiding place long enough to rest.

Above the rock slide, a lone boulder had been stopped by a granite outcropping. Touch the Sky made for its apron of shade. He scarcely mustered enough energy to dismount and hobble his pony in the shade of the outcropping before exhaustion turned his limbs to water. He crawled behind the boulder.

He dropped into a fitful, troubling sleep, his breath rasping in his throat. Reality fused with dreams. He heard the Pawnee war cry, heard the harsh, sharp, precise twang of their osage bows. He heard women and children crying, dying horses nickering, smelled the sheared-metal tang of blood—rivers of blood.

Most disturbing of all was the unsettling image which plagued Touch the Sky during his delirium sleep: the image of a huge snake, a snake larger than any he had ever seen, its perfectly hinged jaws open wide as it swallowed a full-grown horse!

But then one of the dream noises became more real than the others, somehow seemed closer.

When his eyes snapped open, the sun blazed straight into them. At the same moment, no more than a good stone's throw down the slope, the triumphant Pawnee raised their voices in shrill war cries as they spotted his pony.

Chapter Six

Pushing their ponies hard, avoiding paleface wagon tracks, Wolf Who Hunts Smiling and Swift Canoe rode due east toward the Black Hills and sacred Medicine Lake.

They already knew this was Touch the Sky's destination. Arrow Keeper had made the announcement about Touch the Sky's supposedly important mission for the tribe. But Black Elk, their war leader, had given *them* an important mission too.

Only theirs was a mission of death.

Had they taken time to read the signs, they would quickly have learned that their quarry was being pursued in a different direction. But they couldn't waste valuable time—he had one sleep's lead on them. Their plan was to ride fast like hawks swept along in a fierce wind and arrive at Medicine Lake before him. Black Elk, however, had announced to the tribe that they were only riding south to the Platte River to scout for Pawnee.

Shortly after they were out of sight of the curious eyes of the sentries, Wolf Who Hunts Smiling said, "I know a shorter way."

He veered away from the familiar game trail and pointed his pure black pony northeast. The country here was more wooded and far less dangerous to ride because there were few prairie dog holes to trip a horse. However, it was occasionally patrolled by Bluecoat logging details from the soldiertown just south of the Little Missouri River.

"Brother," said Swift Canoe when they stopped to water their ponies at a buffalo wallow. "A thing troubles me."

"Then speak of it," said Wolf Who Hunts Smiling. His furtive, swift eyes constantly scanned the surrounding ridges and cut to their backtrail.

Swift Canoe could not quite admit that he had attempted to kill Touch the Sky but failed. It happened when Swift Canoe and River of Winds had been sent to Bighorn Falls to spy on Touch the Sky and Little Horse. Now he only said:

"Like yours, my heart is nothing but stone toward Woman Face. He killed my brother! I agree with Black Elk. He must be killed for the good of the tribe. But this one thing troubles me, this drawing of Cheyenne blood so near our sacred lake. Can we not kill him sooner and avoid defiling the Arrows?"

Wolf Who Hunts Smiling had thought of this too. As usual he said nothing when Swift Canoe accused Touch the Sky of killing his brother, True Son. Wolf Who Hunts Smiling, of all members of the tribe, knew full well that Touch the Sky had not caused True Son's death. But he also remembered seeing his own father turned into stew meat by Bluecoat canister shot. He hated all whites, and this "Cheyenne" intruder was one of their dogs!

Still—the act of murdering another Cheyenne, even a stinking turncoat, was so heinous that the same Cheyenne word for "putrid" was applied to murderers. This was because murder began a man's internal corruption. About the murderer there clung the rotten smell. Murder brought the tribe bad luck. There could be no success in war; there could be no bounty in the hunt because game shunned the territory. Murderers were not allowed to eat or smoke from Cheyenne utensils for fear of polluting them.

Wolf Who Hunts Smiling did not believe all the nonsense repeated by the tribal elders. But this belief about murderers was strong.

"Have you never thought," he said, "that the hand of Maiyun is in this thing? Have you never thought that it is *He* who has selected the place where this enemy is to go under?"

Swift Canoe remained silent, considering this. Wolf Who Hunts Smiling was a fiery, convincing speaker.

"Have you never thought," he added, "that the Supernatural is angry at this 'Cheyenne' who speaks more than one way? This 'Cheyenne' who does not believe yet has been sent to have a vision—mocking our God and our faith?"

Swift Canoe nodded. His nostrils flared as his

breathing increased to match his anger.

"You speak the straight word, brother!"

"Only think on this thing," said Wolf Who Hunts Smiling. "Has this stranger not placed strong medicine over the eyes of our elders? He rides into our camp, stinking of the white man's ways. But do the elders protect their tribe from this danger?"

Swift Canoe shook his head, dark eyes snapping sparks of bitter resentment. "They do not, brother! Led by Arrow Keeper's example they blind their eyes to his faults and show him special consideration."

"I have ears for this! Have *we*, who never once hid in our clan lodge while the war cry sounded, ever been honored by a tribal council as he has?"

"Never," said Swift Canoe. "They are too busy fawning over their pet to notice our bravery."

"Nor do we turn our war leader into a gelding by holding his squaw in our blanket. This white man's dog would rut on our Cheyenne women! Hear this, buck! This is not the killing of a fellow Cheyenne. We are killing a dangerous enemy for the good of the tribe.

"Now mount, warrior! The only 'vision' this dog will see is the sight of my lance spilling his guts."

Touch the Sky's bow and foxskin quiver lay beside him. He slipped the notch of a fire-hardened arrow onto his bowstring and drew it taut. Then he peered cautiously around the shelter of the precariously balanced boulder.

The Pawnee were taking up positions down the slope from him, below the narrow, rock-clogged defile. Clearly, they were not sure yet exactly where he was hiding.

Touch the Sky realized the gray was in a vulnerable spot. He laid his bow down. Without revealing his position, he reached out beyond the boulder and undid her rawhide hobble. Then he picked up a light, round stone and tossed it at her, bouncing it off her flank. Unhurt but startled, the pony fled back over the shoulder of the mountain, out of range.

Soon the Pawnee sent a scout up on the right flank, skirting the rock slide to get a good side view of the defile. They suspected, thought Touch the Sky, that he had taken cover somewhere in the defile.

It was important to keep them thinking that way.

Wincing at the powerful pain, he rose to his elbows and then his knees, bow in his hands. Again he drew the string taut as he sighted on the crawling brave.

The Pawnee rose for a moment, craning to peer around a scraggly bush. The next instant Touch the Sky's arrow pierced his left cheek, skewered his tongue, broke several teeth, and punched out through his right cheek.

Though the arrow effectively trapped his mouth shut, the Pawnee raised a hideous shriek of pain. He scuttled back down toward his waiting companions. Blood streamed from both sides of his face.

Touch the Sky was in too much pain himself to feel any elation. His shot had bought him some time—but what good was time if he passed out again?

This time, still thinking he was holed up in the defile, the Pawnee tried sending a point man up the scree-covered left flank.

This was an awkward angle for Touch the Sky, since he had to either face exposure or use his left arm to pull the bowstring.

His arrow missed the sentry by a hand's-breadth. But it sent the lice-eater scuttling back down the slope on all fours like a panicked bug.

Now the Pawnee hunkered down out of sight. For a long time Touch the Sky fought to keep his eyes open, tossed from one wave to another on a turbulent sea of pain.

The sun climbed even higher overhead, its rays finally starting to warm up the night-cooled boulder.

Still, the Pawnee waited.

His eyes trembled, then closed. His head slacked forward until his chin bumped his chest.

He started awake, fear like a metallic dust coating his tongue. But still no movement from below the defile.

The sun beat down on him mercilessly. Absently, he popped a few pebbles in his mouth and sucked on them to slake his thirst.

The sun inched toward her resting place, and still the Pawnee did not move. Again and again Touch the Sky caught himself fading out.

Finally, as the shadow of the boulder was lengthening in the late sun, Touch the Sky began to suspect the lice-eaters had tricked him. Perhaps they had left long ago.

Or perhaps they were even now preparing to rush over the shoulder of the mountain behind him.

Vision Quest

A sudden prickle of apprehension made him turn to look up the slope behind him. The Pawnee chose that moment to charge, shrieking madly, from their hidden positions below him.

There were five of them now. This time they avoided the flanks, scrambling straight up over the tumble of scree. Despite the danger of provoking another slide, they leaped nimbly from boulder to boulder. And now, as arrows whipped past his ears with a humming sound like bumblebees, he realized they had figured out his position.

He notched an arrow, launched it, notched another, and sent it flying. But he had little time to aim past shields, and his enemies danced like the mating Hako birds of their elaborate spring ceremony, throwing his aim off.

The first Pawnee, blood lust gleaming in his eyes, scrambled into the rock-strewn defile. Touch the Sky considered running in the direction he had sent his horse. But he knew he would never outrun them in his weakened condition.

"Yip-yip-yiii!" screamed the lead Pawnee. He raised a double-bladed throwing ax over his head to rally his comrades.

Another arrow glanced off the boulder. Reflexively, Touch the Sky drew back. As he did so, he lost his balance and fell against the delicately positioned boulder.

It moved slightly. Only one edge of the granite outcropping kept it from hurtling downward.

Downward!

"Yip-yip-yiii!" Closer. The Pawnee was halfway across the huge jumble of fallen boulders, his companions close on the heels of his quilled moccasins.

Willing strength into his exhausted body, Touch the Sky leaned one shoulder into the boulder and heaved.

Nothing. He shoved again, hard, until his wounded side flared in a protest of pain. This time the boulder moved a little, a rivulet of dirt sliding down the slope.

"Yip-yip-yiii!"

The lead Pawnee was so close that Touch the Sky could make out the beadwork on his medicine bundle.

Again he leaned hard into the boulder, the pain in his wound so great now that he almost blacked out.

Suddenly the outcropping crumpled, and a moment later the boulder was tumbling down the slope.

The lead Pawnee barely leaped aside in time as the huge boulder, a hurtling juggernaut now, slammed into the loose, huge pile of scree. For a moment all was silent, time suspended as the huge slide seemed to shudder like a beast waking up.

The next moment, the earth seemed to cave in on herself. There was a huge, grinding roar; a cloud of dust puffed up and blocked the sun; the mountainside became a living, heaving thing.

A startled shouting rose from the frightened Pawnee. Behind them, their panicked horses rolled their eyes until they were all milky whites, straining to break their tethers.

The last thing Touch the Sky saw was a Pawnee disappearing in a cloud of sliding dirt and rock. The Cheyenne gave quick thanks to the four directions of the wind. But he didn't remain behind to see the results of his man-made disaster.

His face melting into a mask of pain with each step, he ran up the slope behind him. Now his life depended on how far the gray had wandered.

Chapter Seven

"Scalp Cane was sent under," said the Pawnee brave named Iron Knife. "Roan Bear's legs have been broken. We will need to lash together a travois for both of them. I have removed the arrow from Short Buffalo's face. But he will be unable to ride for several sleeps."

Red Plume nodded. His face was drawn tight in profile as he turned to stare in the direction the Cheyenne had fled. Red Plume had led the charge and barely leaped aside in time to avoid being crushed in the slide. A huge, grape-colored bruise covered the side of his face where he had landed hard when he jumped.

"He has cut our number in half. And killed my best pony," he said bitterly. "The best battle pony I have ever trained. Now it is maggot fodder under those boulders. I must ride Scalp Cane's pony."

Both warriors knew well what he meant: Riding

the pony of a dead warrior was considered bad luck. Red Plume no longer took joy in this hunt. He had even lost interest in the prospect of wringing information from their most hated enemy, the Cheyenne. He only wanted to capture this red dog— to have the pleasure of staking him out spread-eagle in the blazing sun after slicing his eyelids off.

"Find his trail," he told Gun Powder. "I swear this on my medicine bundle. For the Pawnee blood he has spilled, we will smear his blood on our faces!"

Even as Red Plume swore his oath, Touch the Sky was backtracking past the Pawnee at dangerously close range.

At first, after he started the slide, luck had been with the wounded, feverish Cheyenne: The well-trained gray had waited patiently just past the shoulder of the mountain.

But soon his luck ran out. The mountainside down which the sure-footed pony climbed had abruptly sheared off in a steep cliff. Unbroken rock wall plunged straight down to a jumbled mass of talus, rock fragments, far below.

He rode desperately to either side, but the cliff wrapped around this entire half of the mountain. There was no choice but to double back, dangerously close to the rock slide and the Pawnee.

He knew some had survived. Touch the Sky had heard them shouting to each other after the first thunderous din had abated.

Before he rode back over the shoulder, he dug four small but thick pieces of elk hide out of the chamois pannier tied to his horse. Rallying himself against the pain, he slid off the gray. It was a slow, painful process, but he tied all four pieces to the gray's hooves with rawhide thongs.

Touch the Sky had first learned the trick from Arrow Keeper. Even though most Indians did not shoe their ponies, in the high country there was plenty of stone and flint. It could ring loudly when struck by a horse's hoof.

He stole back down the mountain, leading his pony through an erosion gully that came within a stone's throw of the Pawnee survivors. Luckily, they were busy tending to the injured. No doubt they assumed he was long gone.

He realized now that he could not possibly stay in the high country. The Pawnee had braved a Ute attack to follow him. They would never give up their search now that he had their blood on his hands. His best hope lay in getting as much head start as possible before his wound forced him to hole up.

His journey back down out of the mountains in the gathering darkness was tense but uneventful. Once he passed a spot where the Ute had set up racks to smoke fish. Every moment he expected to hear either the deep-chested kill cry of the Ute or the shrill and unnerving Pawnee shriek. But he finally reached the foothills and then the moonlit plain without being challenged.

His infected side was approaching its crisis stage. Again he drifted back and forth between waking and sleeping. Again he was forced to lash himself to his pony to keep from dropping off her.

At first the gray had been pointed east toward the Black Hills. But as Touch the Sky drifted into his feverish fancies, the pony was spooked by a coyote. She began to follow her own course toward the vast, empty northern country.

Touch the Sky rode, unaware of his direction or surroundings, until the weary gray faltered and simply refused to go further. By now, the sun long gone, fever chills wracked the Cheyenne's exhausted body.

He slid off his pony and nearly fell, his legs were so weak. Touch the Sky was too exhausted to hobble his pony. He found a huge boulder that still retained the heat of the day. He sprawled against it, hugging the hard, warm surface.

Again that night, as he passed in and out of the fog of delirium, he experienced the strange medicine vision of earlier: a vision of a huge, winding snake swallowing a horse.

He awoke in the desolate time just after dawn, when all the colors of the plains still form a gray, unbroken mass. His wound was festering. It leaked a greenish-yellow discharge that stank sweetly of rot and death. But the deep, exhausted sleep had rested him.

Stiff and sore, he climbed down from the boulder. His pony grazed a patch of nearby grass. She nickered in greeting.

Touch the Sky stared back toward the mountains, watching close for movement on the horizon. But he saw no sign yet of the Pawnee.

He was badly disoriented and realized he had drifted far off course. This far north the country was unfamiliar. He could not recognize the landmarks which would lead him to Medicine Lake.

His hopes sinking even further, he took in the vast, strange landscape. When his name was still Matthew Hanchon, he had read Zebulon Pike's famous charge: The land west of the Mississippi River was "the Great American Desert," arid and empty and useless. The mountain men's explorations had proved Pike wrong—though vast, it was a land of riches. And the red man was in the way of those riches, according to the whites.

Still, Touch the Sky understood why the whites back East called this a desert—this was territory so desolate and huge that a rider without a remount was a dead man if his horse foundered.

But Touch the Sky had to cross it, to find his way to Medicine Lake. He had to elude the Pawnee in search, Arrow Keeper insisted, of a vision.

He knew that the vision Arrow Keeper meant was not the brief, horse-devouring-snake image of his dream. It would be a vast and epic vision, the old shaman insisted.

But even if he sought and obtained a vision, thought Touch the Sky, it could still be bad medicine. Arrow Keeper had explained this to him when Touch the Sky sought a vision before attacking the white whiskey traders. Now the old medicine man's words crept into his thoughts like a whispered warning:

A medicine vision can be either a revelation or a curse. An enemy's strong medicine may place a false vision over our eyes, and we may act upon it, aiding our enemies and destroying those whom we seek to help.

Even as he thought these things, his wound throbbed ominously. He whistled and the gray trotted obediently over to him.

Getting on his pony was a major effort which left tears of pain in his eyes. He wanted to rest for a few more hours.

But fear prodded him as he recalled the fate of those who had provoked Pawnee vengeance.

Vision Quest

*   *   *

Touch the Sky rode until his shadow was long and distorted in the dying sun. Though he headed east, he had no idea how far south he needed to go nor when he needed to turn.

His supply of pemmican and dried fruit was gone. At one point, skirting a long spine of hills, he spotted a whitetail deer. He shot but missed, losing another arrow because he could not risk the time searching for it. He was dangerously low now, his quiver almost empty.

But he had a more immediate problem than even hunger: his wound. Now he was constantly feverish as his body tried to fight off the infection. By sunset he felt like one huge, exposed wound.

Now, with the instincts of a sick animal, he only wanted to hole up until the crisis was over. At this point either prospect—survival or death—was the same to him.

He stopped at a runoff stream which cut through a copse of trees. Touch the Sky turned the gray loose to drink. He was unable now to bend down so he could tether her. That night the exhausted, delirious Cheyenne crawled into a dense stand of spruce. Then he passed out on a deep mat of needles.

He didn't wake up until the sun had almost completed her morning journey. He was clear-headed, famished, and realized he had survived his crisis.

The wound was still stiff and sore. But the discharge was almost gone, and the swelling was down. Touch the Sky carefully cleaned it and wrapped his side with soft bark to protect it.

Now he faced that other life-threatening crisis, the worm that gnawed slower but just as sure: starvation.

Game on the plains was scarce this far north. As for buffalo, the herds had been lessened, and driven further and further south each season, by mass slaughterings at the hands of white hiders. They would skin the carcass, pack the tasty tongue in brine, then simply leave the rest to rot by the thousands in the sun. Sometimes the carrion birds overhead were so thick they blocked out the sun.

For two sleeps Touch the Sky rode on. The land grew more bleak and less varied as he bore first east, then southeast, trying to spot a familiar mountain or other landmark.

He encountered enough water. But now the grass grew thinner and less nourishing, and he worried about graze for his hungry pony. For himself he managed to find and boil a few bitterroots. In the open vastness he robbed the caches of field mice for their stores of wild peas.

Never did he tarry long in one spot. He knew the Pawnee were tracking him like shadows stalk the sun. And unlike him, they had the advantage of their star charts for night travel.

By the third day after he'd survived his wound crisis, Touch the Sky was dizzy and weak with hunger. Occasional stands of forest yielded sweet acorns, a handful of green wild plums, a bit of honey. Once fortune was with him and a scrawny prairie chicken crossed his path. He killed it with his throwing ax and ate the tough, stringy meat with enjoyment, sorry it was only a few mouthfuls.

The fire to cook the bird was his first in several sleeps. Fear of the Pawnee restricted him to cold camps only. Always now, when he rested or slept, he kept his knife and bow at hand. Always he kept his back to a tree or rock, covering all approaches.

Vision Quest

Eventually, when there was no sign he was being followed, Touch the Sky began to relax on that count. Had the lice-eaters supped full of him and the trouble he caused? Had they finally given up, assuming he must be dead?

Perhaps. But as he slogged ever onward, driving his reluctant, hungry pony, he couldn't help wondering: What did it matter if he'd eluded his enemies? Wouldn't it have been better to die fighting than to crawl to a slow, agonizing death on the open plains?

Better to die as a warrior than to die as he had so far lived: alone and belonging nowhere.

Chapter Eight

By the time Touch the Sky spotted the pony soldiers, it was too late to flee.

The midday sun burned hot and glaring from a sky of such a deep, bottomless blue it made him squint. He was crossing barren flats, a short-grass prairie broken by the occasional stand of scrub oak. He had dismounted to cautiously examine a long-deserted white outpost.

It was a group of sod houses with long roots trailing down from the roofs. They had been built in a circle for defense from Indians. The walls were loopholed to accommodate rifle barrels. A stone watering trough in the yard held several inches of rain.

Touch the Sky guessed that this had once served as a way station for the white man's huge, mule-team freight wagons. These were more and more numerous on the plains as the "Indian menace" meant more and more supplies for the Bluecoat army.

Little remained behind now. Touch the Sky found only some empty wooden crates and a pile of buffalo bones, all heaped in one corner of the largest sod house.

Hunger gnawed at his belly. First he turned his pony loose to graze the sparse grass of the yard and drink from the trough. Then he hauled some of the bones outside into the sunlight.

Touch the Sky cracked them open on the edge of the water trough. Then he used the point of his knife to gouge out the soft, nutritious marrow. What couldn't be reached with his blade he dug out with the point of a narrow stick.

This put little in his empty belly. But even that little bit rallied him. Now he thought of a trick Black Elk had taught his band of young warriors.

He debated. It might be risky. But it seemed so empty out here, it ought to be safe. He had seen it work once before in country such as this.

And if the Pawnee were tracking him, it hardly mattered—by now they knew exactly where he was.

Moving gingerly to accommodate his still-sore wound, Touch the Sky stacked some of the crates near the corner of one of the sod buildings. Then he climbed up and jabbed the stone point of his battle lance into the roof. Now the long red streamers flapped in the breeze.

Black Elk had thus attracted and shot a curious elk on the open plains, first tying a cloth to a stick. Perhaps, thought Touch the Sky, it would attract game now.

But instead of game, it attracted a Bluecoat cavalry squad.

Hours had passed with no luck. He gave up and was on the verge of whistling for his pony. Suddenly, a flock of frightened sparrow hawks shot by overhead.

Touch the Sky scrambled back up to the roof, careful not to skyline himself, and spotted the patrol. They rode out of the east in a fanned-out wedge formation, about a dozen strong. They were closing rapidly on the sod houses.

Outrunning them on his tired pony was out of the question. Even if he fled now, he would still be clearly visible on the open plain to the west when they reached the yard.

It was unlikely they had yet noticed the gray—she was blocked from sight by one of the sod houses. Touch the Sky whistled for her. When she trotted over, he led her behind the largest building. He could only hope the Bluecoats would make a quick check and ride on.

Otherwise . . . he slid his throwing ax out of his pannier. Otherwise, he had the element of surprise—at least one long-knife would go under with him. He had no doubt the soldiers would kill him. A Cheyenne this far from the Powder River homeland was considered a renegade. The talking papers called "treaties" had done nothing to soften the white man's heart.

It was then that Touch the Sky spotted the skunk.

It emerged from under a rocky mound near the yard, moving at the slow, leisurely pace of an animal that knows it need not bother running if threatened. Touch the Sky knew the foul-smelling secretion of its anal pouches could be whiffed from an hour's ride away. Clothing sometimes retained the stink permanently.

He had little time to consider his idea. Instead, he hurried across the yard, "attacking" the skunk.

The animal glanced back at him, then raised its long, thickly haired tail in warning. Steeling himself, keeping the wind at his back, Touch the Sky moved in closer.

The skunk turned its back, erected its tail, and began the forceful muscular contractions that shot forth the pale yellow spray. As it emptied its pouches, Touch the Sky hurriedly backed away. But still, even with the wind at his back, the powerful stink tickled his gag reflex and made tears spring to his eyes.

For a moment the wind shifted, seeming to swirl directionless. Then it steadied to a swift breeze blowing out of the southwest. As Touch the Sky, still gagging, eyes streaming, staggered back to his hidden pony, the overwhelming stench was wafted out across the plains.

The soldiers bore down on the way station, their sabers gleaming in the sun.

Their horses' iron-shod hooves tore out clumps of dirt and grass and flung them into the sky. The officer riding at the head of the wedge formation raised his saber. Now the men closed ranks and formed a skirmish line.

For a moment the sun was blocked, and Touch the Sky got a good look at the officer's face. His blood ran cold when he recognized that sneer of cold command—Lieutenant Seth Carlson!

Of course it made sense that he would encounter his old enemy this far north. Touch the Sky's soldier friend, Tom Riley from Fort Bates, had explained it. After Touch the Sky helped his white parents defeat Hiram Steele and Carlson, the officer had been reassigned to a desolate outpost up north.

Now Touch the Sky recalled his vow from that time he had refused to kill Carlson because it was nighttime, when killing should be avoided: that they would meet again by day, and that Touch the Sky would dangle the soldier's scalp from his clout.

Perhaps he would never live to dangle it, thought Touch the Sky. But if he was quick he could at least scalp his enemy before the soldiers killed him in turn.

Carlson's patrol thundered closer.

Touch the Sky slid his knife out of its sheath and gripped it in his teeth, ready. He gripped his throwing ax and watched from behind the largest house, peering cautiously around the corner.

The soldiers raised a triumphant shout as they drew closer, their blood up for adventure.

Touch the Sky quietly sang the Cheyenne Death Song even as he prepared to fight for his life. Clearly, his ruse with the skunk had been a foolish, desperate plan.

Suddenly he felt invisible fingers lift his hair: The wind had increased.

Abruptly, the noxious stink slapped the soldiers and their mounts in the face with the force of a punch.

Carlson didn't need to signal a halt. As one, the Bluecoats reined in their mounts. Two horses shied violently, one soldier leaned sideways from his saddle and retched.

It was an unwritten law of the frontier: Neither man nor beast challenged the skunk. The Bluecoats were no exception. After a hasty conference, one of them uncased a pair of field glasses. He quickly took a final look at the streamered lance.

Vision Quest

Then Carlson barked out a command, and they rode on to the north.

Touch the Sky gave thanks to Maiyun. But even as he rode on, bearing southeast, stomach cramping from hunger, he couldn't help wondering: Had he once again eluded a quick death only to suffer a slow one?

He was no longer aware of the passing of time. By sheer force of habit, he rode when the sun was up, stopped when the last rays bled from the sky.

By now the gnawing hunger had become a part of him. He could not think of a time when he had not felt it. His cheekbones, always pronounced, now protruded like the cheeks of a skeleton. His ribs were as gaunt as barrel staves.

From time to time he encountered green plums and serviceberries. He knew that some Indians would eat any insects they could find. The Cricket Eaters, or Digger tribe, could survive indefinitely on dried ants and their larvae. But when he dug a handful out of an anthill and tried to swallow some, he only retched it all back up.

For long periods now his mind wandered as if through dream time. Again in memory he saw Honey Eater stepping out of Black Elk's tipi, wearing her beaded bride-shawl. He saw Kristen Steele, her hair like spun-gold sunshine, waiting for him in the secret copse where they used to meet.

Both gone, dead to him now. Two women from two different worlds—neither of which would let him be free.

Another moon, another sun, another hungry ride while cobwebs of delirium tangled his thoughts. At some point he had begun cutting off the buckskin strings of his fringed leggings, slowly chewing them for their meager nourishment.

Another sleep passed, and this time it was difficult to rise and get going.

He was thoroughly lost, thoroughly hungry, thoroughly dispirited. As he trudged up a long rise in the late-afternoon sun, his hand drifted to the obsidian blade of his knife.

He could fall on his knife now, and end it all quickly. The Cheyenne tribe did not consider suicide cowardly. In fact, a warrior who fell on his own knife to avoid suffering an unclean or undignified death was considered brave and was welcomed in the Land of Ghosts.

He topped the rise. Stopped. Stared long and hard, his jaw slacking open.

Suddenly, like sun bursting forth from rain-drenched heavens, Touch the Sky felt new hope surge within him. Below, reflecting silver in the glare, was a winding river swollen from rain and runoff. A choke point had formed at a sharp bend in the river, a spot where debris formed a powerful barrier.

But this was not, Touch the Sky realized, just a river. Now he knew he was somehow on the right path to Medicine Lake—and that a major vision awaited him there. For this twisting, winding river was also the horse-devouring "snake" of his recent dreams—among the objects snared by the choke point were several dead mustangs!

Chapter Nine

"Even if he is riding as slow as an old squaw," said Swift Canoe, "he should have arrived by now."

Wolf Who Hunts Smiling nodded. "Perhaps Arrow Keeper gave him special instructions which have delayed him."

"Or perhaps," said Swift Canoe, disappointment keen in his voice, "some enemy has done our work for us."

The two youths had made a camp high in the thickly wooded hills considered the center of the Cheyenne world. Below them, Medicine Lake reflected a deep blue in the morning sun. Only an occasional breeze wrinkled the mirror-smooth surface of the water. From here they could see down to the barren plains below.

While they spoke, Wolf Who Hunts Smiling had been examining the bark of a pine tree. High up in the tree, well beyond the Cheyenne's reach, the bark had been clawed deep. This was true for trees all around the lake, he'd noticed. Wolf Who Hunts Smiling recognized the marks: It was the way a grizzly bear marked its territory and warned competitors away.

All bears were wanderers, but the grizzly covered more territory than most. This bear might be nearby or clear across the hills. Wolf Who Hunts Smiling needed to know—the powerful grizzly was impossible to bring down with arrows or even most rifles. And its long, vicious claws made it the king of frontier predators. He had once seen a grizzly bring down a horse by hamstringing it with one swipe of its paws.

But the Cheyenne was not just worried about their own safety. He also had a plan hatching—assuming Touch the Sky ever arrived.

"Come," he said to Swift Canoe. "We will check our snares for rabbits. Then we will circle the lake in case our fox slipped in during the night."

Today luck was with them. They had made their way down to the lake, leapfrogging from tree to tree. As Wolf Who Hunts Smiling bent at the water's edge to drink, he spotted them off to his right: a set of long, narrow tracks made by an animal that had five toes and walked by setting its heel on the ground like a man.

Grizzly tracks. And they were fresh, judging from the dampness still trapped inside them.

"Brother," he said in a low voice to Swift Canoe, "move carefully and quietly. Do *not* let the wind slip behind you."

Like the buffalo, the grizzly had weak eyesight but a keen sense of smell. In fact it was this keen sense of smell which Wolf Who Hunts Smiling had counted on when forming his plan.

A child could have followed the signs. Besides the huge prints, they encountered several ravaged places where the bear had ripped up stumps to lick up the ants underneath. They soon began to hear the crashing of tree limbs and undergrowth, the occasional deep woofing grunts. They emerged cautiously from behind a deadfall and Wolf Who Hunts Smiling raised his head.

"Stay where you are, brother," he whispered, "or sing the Death Song!"

But Swift Canoe needed no warning. Below them, reigning alone and supreme in a small clearing, was the largest, most ferocious-looking grizzly they had ever seen. It was a male, half again as high as the tallest Cheyenne in the tribe. It must have easily matched the weight of two fat ponies.

Even as they watched, the huge, brownish-yellow monster raked its mark high on the bark of a tree. The grizzly was dish-faced, high in the shoulders. The white tips of its fur looked like frost and gave the bear its names, grizzly and silvertip.

"Brother," said Swift Canoe, awe in his voice, "we must be careful. Brother Bear is still hungry from his long winter's sleep. I fear for our ponies."

"I have ears for this. We will smoke them in a cedar fire to disguise their smell."

But Wolf Who Hunts Smiling's face eased into a grin as his furtive, quick-darting eyes took in the grizzly's every move.

"What do you think, brother?" he said. "If Woman Face ever arrives, do you think brother bear should come around for a visit?"

Swift Canoe stared at him, comprehension slowly dawning on his face.

"But only think," said Wolf Who Hunts Smiling. "Bears are easily lured by smell when the wind is right. They can be led just as one leads a dog."

"And this way, *we* do not spill Cheyenne blood."

Wolf Who Hunts Smiling grinned again. "Yes. And if Arrow Keeper sends braves to find the body of his favorite dog, they will find only a badly mauled corpse. We can fulfill Black Elk's orders without sullying the Sacred Arrows."

Below, the grizzly sent a huge log flying into the trees with one careless swipe of its paw.

Touch the Sky watched ominous rain clouds pile up on the horizon like huge black boulders.

One part of him realized a terrible storm was coming on, that he ought to find shelter. The wind had picked up steadily, until the cottonwoods showed the light undersides of their leathery leaves. But another part of him was too exhausted and hungry to care.

His hopes had surged when he discovered the river with the dead ponies—horrible though it was, the discovery had confirmed his medicine dream. He had been convinced, then, that he was on the right course to Medicine Lake. Now, with the river long behind him, he was again lost in wide-open, unfamiliar plains.

And by now his hopes had ebbed. Had he actually even *seen* those dead horses in the river, or was it a trick of his failing mind? Or, if he had seen them, that snake-devouring-horses image was surely a false vision, placed over his eyes by enemy magic to torment him. Perhaps a Pawnee shaman was behind it, exacting revenge for the blood he had shed.

Vision Quest

He slogged on, mechanically chewing on the last of his buckskin fringes. His pony limped now, and he knew he should check her hooves for lodged pebbles. But the thought kept fading before he could act on it.

Lightning suddenly spiderwebbed the sky, jagged, bone-white tines that speared down from the clouds to the earth.

A sudden wind gust almost stopped the gray's forward motion.

Thunder muttered, gathered rolling force, crack-boomed through the heavens in a thousand crashing echoes.

The first heavy raindrops hurtled downward, cold spikes that nailed the sky to the earth.

At first the wind and rain felt good, reviving some of Touch the Sky's energy. Then it began to pour down in earnest—great, gray, driving sheets of wind-lashed rain which stung his face.

Within minutes his horse was nearly mired in mud. Each hoof came up slowly, making wet sucking noises as they pulled clear of the mud.

She stumbled, slipped, nearly went down. Touch the Sky could see nothing around him now, just the gray curtain of rain. Desperately he tried to spot some sort of sheltered place.

Purely by chance the gray practically stumbled into a small coulee. The walls had been eroded back by wind and time, providing some shelter. Perhaps, had he been more clearheaded, Touch the Sky would have thought better of taking such low ground in this heavy rain. But all he wanted was to get somewhere where he could open his eyes again.

If anything, the force of the rain increased after

he and the gray had pressed in tight against one wall of the coulee. Only spray reached them here, driven on the wind gusts.

When he first heard a new sound of rumbling, Touch the Sky thought it was more thunder gathering.

Then, when it grew steadily louder, vibrating the ground, he thought of the rock slide which had buried the Pawnee. Only when it was too late did he realize he was about to be engulfed by a flash flood.

A huge, foaming-white gout of water swept around a turn just ahead of him in the coulee. It bore down on him with inexorable speed and power, allowing him no time to run.

It felt like a powerful fist pummeling his head when the water slammed into him. It lifted Touch the Sky and his pony like debris and swept them along the coulee. The Cheyenne saw the sky and the walls of the coulee all tumbling together, felt himself bobbing along like the floater stick of an underwater beaver trap.

The next moment, his head slammed into a boulder and Touch the Sky's world went black.

As he lay, balanced on a narrow pinnacle between life and death, he experienced another strange medicine vision.

He heard women's voices singing. At first the words were not clear. Then, slowly, he became aware that the women were singing a Cheyenne battle song.

Now the blackness gave way to flickering firelight, a huge fire like those used for clan gatherings. Now Touch the Sky saw a circle of women, Cheyenne women, young and old.

Only, he couldn't actually see them—not their faces. For while they sang, their voices raised in stirring harmony, they kept their faces hidden behind huge eagle-feather fans.

That was the last thing Touch the Sky remembered: huge fans so like the eagle's wings, flapping steadily, mysteriously, rhythmically.

Chapter Ten

His eyes eased open and then immediately closed to slits against the merciless sun.

Touch the Sky felt a fierce, throbbing pain in his right temple. He raised his hand and felt the puffy bruise that had swollen his right eye nearly shut.

He groaned as he sat up, pain coursing through him. He lay beside a huge boulder at the wide end of the coulee. The flood water had receded, leaving the rocky floor of the coulee polished and clean.

Suddenly he recalled everything that had happened. His heart leaping into his throat, he whistled for his pony.

Obediently, she trotted out from behind a rock spur to his left. Mud coated her legs and belly, and a small cut marred the coat above her left foreleg. Otherwise, she had apparently weathered the flash flood well.

Vision Quest

Touch the Sky sat where he was, too weak and dispirited to move just yet. He was light-headed with hunger, and the gnawing complaint in his belly had become a steady, sharp pain.

As he sat there, eyes focused dully ahead of him, he became aware of a huge shadow which steadily circled the place where he sat.

Touch the Sky glanced up and saw, backlit against the sun, a magnificent eagle with a huge wingspan.

Immediately his skin goose-pimpled as he recalled his medicine vision featuring Cheyenne maidens with their faces hidden behind eagle-feather fans. Surely this was just coincidence. But Touch the Sky rarely spotted eagles in the low country like this. They nested high up in the mountains, above the rimrock. Only when prey was scarce at the higher elevations would they scour the flats for food.

Why was it circling this spot? Surely there was no game in the coulee, this close to a human. And eagles never attacked people except to defend their nests.

It was odd. But the pain in his bruised head claimed his immediate attention. He rose, fighting a dizzy rush of nausea, and staggered to a nearby pool of rain water that hadn't yet drained off. He soaked his new wound in the cold water, feeling almost instant relief.

The arrow wound in his side was still stiff and sore, but the infection was gone now. Earlier Touch the Sky had pulled up some yarrow roots and pounded them into a paste, which he carried wrapped in cottonwood leaves. Now he rubbed the last of it on his wounded side.

He glanced overhead when he had finished: The eagle still circled in the same spot.

As if it were waiting for him to set out again? But that was foolish, he scolded himself.

Foolish or not—when he set out on his pony, still bearing southeast, the eagle followed them.

For most of that day, as Touch the Sky's shadow lengthened in the sun, the eagle remained circling overhead. Now even the hunger and pain could not mute Touch the Sky's growing excitement. This was not nature's usual way: The hand of the Supernatural was in this thing.

Even so, hunger threatened to soon do him in. He was so weak that it was an effort just to stay sitting on his horse. A stab of guilt lanced through him as he recalled older Cheyenne telling stories of the times, during the short white days of the cold moons, when the tribe had slaughtered their horses for meat. Even if he could bring himself to do so, what would he do afterward? How would he survive out here without a pony?

Thus ruminating, he was slow to realize that for the first time the eagle had stopped following him. It had veered off to the right behind a slight spine of hills.

Touch the Sky halted his pony, watching it.

Had he been wrong, then? Was this after all just an oddity and not part of his vision?

If so, why did the eagle now return and then once again fly back behind the spine—as if telling him to ride that way?

Touch the Sky swerved to the right and circled around to the opposite side of the spine. As soon as he rounded the last hill, he spotted it: a wickiup, a style of hut used by various Southwest Indian tribes. It was an oval-shaped frame of branches covered with brush. They were temporary shelters, used by hunters and scouts. This far north, it could well have been built by scouts who were looking for wild horses, which were more scarce in the deserts and semiarid flats to the south.

Clearly it was old and long deserted. Forced to summon strength to do so, Touch the Sky dismounted and walked closer to investigate. The wickiup was empty.

The eagle circled patiently overhead.

Puzzled, Touch the Sky looked up at the bird, then down again at the abandoned hut. If it had led him here, why?

The eagle deviated from its pattern to swoop low over the top of a lone cottonwood behind the hut. Touch the Sky walked over to the tree and glanced up into the branches.

He squinted. There appeared to be something hanging from a limb well past the fork in the trunk.

Summoning strength he was sure he no longer possessed, he shinnied up the tree to investigate. He discovered a tough elkskin pouch which had been tied to the limb. When he opened it, he realized why: It was a generous cache of dried venison!

Indians commonly cached food during good times, often for larger groups which planned to follow them or to ensure food for their return trip. Touch the Sky was far too grateful to spend much time wondering how the meat got there. First he gave thanks to Maiyun and the four directions. Then, even before he climbed down, he tore into one of the hunks of dried meat.

Later, as he continued his journey while the eagle still followed overhead, Touch the Sky thought long and hard about the mulberry-colored birthmark hidden in his hair and Arrow Keeper's epic vision.

He thought too about the time when he and Little Horse had been riding back to the tribe after their fight against Hiram Steele and Seth Carlson in Bighorn Falls. Just as Touch the Sky had bent to pick up a scrap of ribbon Kristen Steele had dropped, an arrow had missed him by inches.

Brother, Little Horse had said, his voice reverent with wonder, *that arrow should have put you under. But you were not meant to die just then because the hand of the Supernatural is in this thing.*

Could it be? thought Touch the Sky. Could Arrow Keeper and Little Horse be right? It still seemed impossible that he had been selected to fulfill tribal destiny.

But if he were not fate's deputy, thought the young Cheyenne as he again glanced overhead at the eagle, what was the meaning of all this?

"He was here, but not for long," said the Pawnee brave named Gun Powder. "No fire was made, and there are no droppings. Also, he is starving—see here where he cracked old buffalo bones open to eat the marrow."

Gun Powder rose from his crouch. He pointed out across the plains to the southeast, behind the sod-house complex.

"Once again, like a bird following the ancient migration route, he has gone in this direction. He is lost, but he knows where he wants to be."

"We will not let him escape us by starving," said Red Plume with conviction. "That is too easy."

"He makes no attempt to cover his signs," said

Gun Powder. "He believes we have given up the chase."

Now the brave named Short Buffalo spoke, though with difficulty. His words were slurred, the result of his still-swollen tongue and ravaged mouth—the work of the Cheyenne arrow which pierced his cheeks. As he stared toward the fugitive's escape route, his eyes were smoky with rage.

"Red Plume spoke true words. We will *not* let him starve! Place my words close to your hearts, warriors. May I die of the yellow vomit if this Cheyenne dog eludes us again! Short Buffalo will use his guts for tipi ropes!"

Only four from the original Pawnee band remained—Red Plume, Gun Powder, Iron Knife, and Short Buffalo. After the rock slide, they had used their mirrors and their lookouts to flash messages back to the main group, now waiting below the Niobrara River. Braves had been sent to collect the dead Scalp Cane and the wounded Roan Bear, whose crushed legs meant a travois had to be built. Short Buffalo, whose face and mouth had been nearly ruined by the arrow, insisted he was well enough after two sleeps' rest to accompany them again. Another five braves had joined their original group.

"If he is lost," said Red Plume, "and wounded and starving, he is as good as gone under. Ride quickly! Pawnee blood has been shed by our enemy. If he dies before we kill him, we are shamed!"

For the rest of that day the eagle flew slowly overhead, leading Touch the Sky across the vast, unfamiliar plains.

He had finally begun to recognize familiar landmarks. Those three mountain peaks which rose from the horizon like a trio of lone sentries: They were called the Three Sisters. He recognized them from the days when Black Elk led him there for warrior training.

When, near sunset, the eagle swung due east, Touch the Sky did not hesitate to follow. Exhausted, he made a simple cold camp beside an old buffalo wallow. He ate several strips of the nourishing dried venison. Then he rolled into his robe and slept a deep, dreamless sleep.

The eagle was still there in the morning, circling, patiently waiting.

Finally, when his shadow was long in front of him, Touch the Sky drew near to the eerie, darkly forested humps of the Black Hills. Night had already fallen, and the eagle was a mere shape against the blue-black sky when the young Cheyenne reached the shores of a remote, high-altitude lake.

A three-quarter moon and a fiery explosion of stars made luminous silver light reflect off the water like pale mist. He could hear the eerie cry of loons out on the lake. Touch the Sky had been here only once before in his life. But he was sure this was sacred Medicine Lake—site of Arrow Keeper's original vision, the same vision the younger Cheyenne had come to seek.

When he thought to look again, the eagle was gone.

Touch the Sky thanked Maiyun and the directions of the wind.

Then he tethered his pony in a lush patch of graze, using a long strip of rawhide to give her enough play to reach the water. Tomorrow, he reminded himself with guilt, he would inspect each foot—

hoof, pastern, and fetlock—carefully. The gray was limping steadily now. She needed rest, good forage. At least white men, he thought, could reward a good pony with a nose bag full of oats.

For a moment, as he unleashed his belongings from the gray, she shied nervously. She had seemed skittish since arriving; once, as they neared the lake, she had hunkered on her hocks and refused to move. He had been forced to dismount and gently persuade her until she moved again.

At first, bone weary himself, pain throbbing in his injured side and bruised head, he had assumed his pony was simply ill-tempered from exhaustion and her limp. Now, though, as the cry of loons echoed behind him, he too sensed some dangerous presence in this seemingly pristine and uninhabited area.

He scratched his pony's withers until she had calmed again. But as he did so, he looked cautiously all around him, watching for firelight or movement. However, all appeared well.

Now, as his uncle the moon crept toward his zenith, he searched for a safe campsite. Once again Fate seemed to treat him as a favorite child: After very little searching he found a small, dry, apparently long-deserted cave, judging from the unbroken brush crowding the entrance. It was located well back from the shoreline.

He used his knife and a piece of flint to start a small fire just inside the cave's entrance. This was not for cooking or warmth, but to explore the cave before he decided to stay there.

Good—the flickering yellow-orange light revealed no recent prints inside the cave, animal or human. The cave had a fairly wide, high entrance.

But it quickly narrowed at the back into a tiny, constricted space where he had to kneel.

Convinced it was deserted, he gathered plenty of wood and kindling and brought it inside. The well-lit night sky, and an ample supply of dry aspen and birch limbs, simplified his task.

He hauled his weapons and buffalo robe inside. Exhausted though he was, he was not yet ready to sleep. His quiver held an extra supply of arrow shafts he had cut from a dead pine. Now, in the wavering firelight, he carefully honed the shafts and hardened the points in the fire.

Soon, the grueling ordeal of invoking the medicine dream must begin. The Pawnee were only at the back of his mind now. He was sure they had given up on tracking him—how much could one Cheyenne buck be worth to them?

True, he reminded himself, he had shed Pawnee blood, and all Plains tribes placed a high value on vengeance. But if they had wanted him, surely they would have killed him long before this.

Still, even as his eyelids finally grew heavy with sleep, a quick lance of foreboding stabbed through him. He suddenly had the feeling that human eyes were watching him from behind the dark cloak of the night.

Once again he stepped outside, watching and listening to the night. But nothing seemed amiss.

Chiding himself for a white-livered coward, he got a firm purchase on his courage. Then he stepped back into the cave.

Chapter Eleven

"Wake up," said Wolf Who Hunts Smiling. "Today we kill our enemy!"

Swift Canoe rolled out of his buffalo robe, instantly wide awake despite the lopsided shape of his sleepy face. He remembered the night before, watching every move when Touch the Sky had arrived and made his camp.

Most Indians were late sleepers. In order to rise with the sun, Wolf Who Hunts Smiling had drunk much water the night before so his aching bladder would rouse him.

"He should sleep long yet," said Swift Canoe. "He was exhausted when he arrived. Did you see his ribs protrude?"

Wolf Who Hunts Smiling nodded.

"True, he is weak from hunger. But count little on this. Though I hate and despise him, I admit Woman Face is strong and capable. We must work quickly and be careful."

"I am more worried about Brother Bear than Woman Face," said Swift Canoe. "We might easily lure him to *us* instead. Should we not after all do this thing ourselves?"

"This is no time to show the brains of a rabbit," said Wolf Who Hunts Smiling impatiently. "Recall, if our plan works, *we* do not sully the Sacred Arrows by drawing Cheyenne blood. Too, Arrow Keeper will surely send someone to find Woman Face. This way they will find mauled remains, and we will not be suspected. Not all in the tribe believed Black Elk's story that we were sent out to scout Pawnee."

"I have ears for this. But if the plan does not work'?"

Wolf Who Hunts Smiling's dark, furtive eyes met his friend's. "If the plan does not work, we kill him ourselves."

They were camped high on a thickly wooded hillside behind Medicine Lake. The sun had not yet risen, and the early morning sky was still the color of flint. The sweet song of the larks greeted them as they set out toward a tall cedar located halfway between their camp and the shore of the lake.

They had already selected this tree because, from its top branches, one could see the entire area all the way down to the plains. From this tree they had discovered the grizzly's den and some of the creature's favorite hunting routes.

When they reached the tree, Wolf Who Hunts Smiling quickly climbed to the top. The sun was starting to rise from her birthplace, and far below on the flats he saw prairie falcons circling, hunting for squirrels.

Closer at hand, all was quiet at the entrance to Touch the Sky's cave. And further, past the far end of the lake, it was also quiet near the rocky entrance to the grizzly's den.

Wolf Who Hunts Smiling was patient. All bears were early risers when not in hibernation. He watched every spot where he had seen the grizzly prowling, looking for movement, not shape.

Finally he spotted it. The huge silvertip had torn open an anthill. He was letting the ants run up his paw before he licked them off. This way the bear avoided sand and stickers. Each time its tongue shot out, Wolf Who Hunts Smiling saw large, sharp canines.

At first the Cheyenne's heart sank. The wind was to the grizzly's back, blowing away from the entrance to Touch the Sky's cave.

But then the grizzly began ambling toward the opposite shore of the lake, into the face of the wind.

Wolf Who Hunts Smiling nimbly climbed back down to the ground.

"Quickly!" he told Swift Canoe. "Now we follow our plan!"

Two sleeps earlier they had located a deer run which led to the shore of the lake. Every morning whitetail deer came down to the water to drink. The two Cheyenne had already constructed a blind of dead brush and limbs.

They slipped quietly up to their hiding place and peeked around it toward the lake. A doe and her fawn were drinking.

Wolf Who Hunts Smiling had recently made a strong new bow from oak. Now he pulled an arrow from his quiver and slid the string into the notch.

The doe stepped a few paces into the clear water and her fawn followed. Wolf Who Hunts Smiling remembered Black Elk's lesson: Always try to shoot game when it's in the water. That way, if the first bullet or arrow doesn't kill it, its escape will be slowed so the second shot can bring it down.

But he needed no second shot. His first arrow pierced the fawn's soft flank and struck warm vitals, dropping it in the water. The startled doe was gone in several quick bounds.

Quickly the two Cheyenne hauled the fawn ashore. Swift Canoe unsheathed his bone-handle knife and opened the fawn up from throat to rump. Meantime, Wolf Who Hunts Smiling climbed the lookout tree again to make sure the grizzly was still downwind.

It was.

They dragged the bleeding fawn to a high ridge located between Touch the Sky's cave and the prowling grizzly. The wind, a stiff, steady breeze, was directly behind them now.

From this high ground they could see the huge, yellow-brown grizzly, though the nearly blind bear could not possibly spot them. They watched it rise, sniff the air, then stand rooted as the breeze wafted the smell of the bleeding fawn.

"Brother," said Swift Canoe triumphantly, "he has fixed on the smell. And have you ever seen a bear this huge?"

"Hurry!" said Wolf Who Hunts Smiling as the dish-faced monster began lumbering toward them.

Lugging the bloody carcass between them, they raced back toward the entrance of Touch the Sky's cave. Wolf Who Hunts Smiling drew another arrow, ready to kill him if they woke him up. But they managed to leave the fawn just inside the dark cave entrance without alarming the sleeping Cheyenne within.

Then they raced away like a pair of scalded dogs, heading for the safe vantage point of their camp.

"Brother," said Wolf Who Hunts Smiling, "it is like stealing eggs from a nest on the ground."

"True. The very sight of Brother Bear at his cave entrance will turn Woman Face Wendigo!"

Once again Touch the Sky slept a deep, dreamless sleep as his body regained some of its depleted strength.

But at first, when a deep, angry bellow woke him like a kick to the face, he was convinced he was indeed dreaming: A gigantic grizzly, its curved claws dripping gobbets of bloody meat, nearly filled the entrance to the cave!

Touch the Sky had placed his robe near the back of the cave. Now he reflexively pressed even tighter against the wall, his heart leaping into his throat.

He spotted the fawn, now tossed aside in the bear's rage as it encountered the overpowering smell of a human. Perhaps it had intended to cache it here. Had the Cheyenne, after all, mistakenly selected a bear's den?

But that was impossible, he thought—there had been no smells or other obvious signs of animal occupation. And though they were still early in the warm moons, it was too late for a grizzly to be emerging from its hibernation-like sleep.

Still—clearly this one was mean and ravenous as a bear waking from its winter sleep. Many grizzlies had experience with white hunters and had come to hate humans. Now, as this one pressed even closer to the frightened Cheyenne, Touch the Sky spotted a gnarled scar where a bullet had caught the bear high on the chest.

Touch the Sky's scalp was sweating, fear had turned his limbs to stone. A paw swiped past his face, only inches away. He knew those hard-as-steel claws could rip a horse open in one swipe.

Again the grizzly's angry bellow, another pass of the lethal claws. The wind from the near miss fanned Touch the Sky's face. He could smell the bear's stinking breath every time it bellowed.

Luckily, however, the cave was apparently too small as it tapered toward the rear. Touch the Sky felt a little strength returning to his limbs as this fact sank in. The grizzly could fit only its head, forelegs, and part of its high shoulders past the entrance.

But clearly he was trapped here so long as the bear chose to remain.

Desperately he eyed his weapons. As always, he had slept with them close to hand. But his bow would be useless in such tight quarters, he didn't even have room to draw the string back. His throwing ax and knife would be equally useless, like attacking Bluecoat artillery with rocks.

Besides—a grizzly was almost impossible to kill without a huge-bore rifle.

The bear grunted as it squeezed even tighter into the entrance. Its eyes were charged with blood lust.

The claws barely missed him this time. On the second swipe, they caught the edge of the buffalo robe and shredded it.

Touch the Sky pressed flat against the cool stone wall of the small cave. The smell of the grizzly was overpowering, its breath hot and moist on his bare skin.

He tried to fight down his panic so he could think. Now he recalled Arrow Keeper's stories about Cheyenne who had made medicine talk to animals, taming them and even becoming their friends in the wild.

"Brother Bear," he said, his voice calm and friendly, "I am a red man! It was white hunters who tried to put you under and left that hurt on your skin. The red man lives like his brother the bear, wild and hunted, safe nowhere!"

The grizzly quieted, as if the Cheyenne words were a strange but soothing music.

"Brother Bear! Why kill me? Look at my lean body—I am stringy and tough from hunger, like winter-starved game. The tender meat on that fawn will be better in your belly."

Suddenly, however, his voice seemed to further enrage the grizzly. This time one set of claws actually took a nick out of his right knee, sending a burning pain up his leg.

Touch the Sky fell silent, hoping to simply outwait the bear. But though it eventually backed out of the cave, it refused to leave the entrance. Periodically, it would suddenly become enraged and thrust its way back in, hoping to catch the Cheyenne in a careless moment.

This went on for some time. Outside, the sun rose higher and sent more light into the cave. Touch the Sky's back and legs were severely cramped from the long crouch against the back wall. He knew he could not maintain this position much longer without pushing his tired, weak muscles to collapse.

And the only way to fall was forward, into the bear's claws.

Better to take a lesson from Black Elk's warrior training: When attacked and all seems lost, become the aggressor, not the victim.

He had been eyeing the pile of kindling and wood for some time. Like his weapons, it lay close to hand. The plan he had in mind was dangerous—might in fact very well kill him. But it was the only hope he saw.

Each time the grizzly backed out of the cave, Touch the Sky would hurriedly draw wood and kindling close. And each time he did so, the bear in turn bellowed in fury and thrust back into the cave. So it took the Cheyenne quite some time to assemble enough material for a fire.

He struck a spark from his flint and ignited a pile of kindling. Then he piled on wood. During all this the bear continually tried to rip him with its slashing claws. Twice they tossed burning wood from the fire; each time the Cheyenne threw it back in.

There was enough air for a fire, but no ventilation for the heat and smoke. Tears sprang to Touch the Sky's eyes as smoke billowed into them. The heat singed his skin and he coughed hard, wracking coughs as acrid fingers of smoke and heat tickled his lungs.

The bear too coughed. Then, as more and more smoke accumulated, it backed out of the cave.

Now, thought Touch the Sky.

Pulling his shredded robe out from under him, he brought it down over the fire for a moment, lifted it until the flames leaped up again, then brought it down again. He was making a smudge fire like the kind used to chase off mosquitoes.

Huge black clouds of smoke billowed from the cave entrance now. Gagging, his eyes streaming, Touch the Sky heard the enraged beast bellow as it backed further away. If only he could hang on a little longer, he told himself, make a little more smoke . . .

Outside, the wind suddenly shifted. A moment later the thick pall of smoke was sucked back into the cave.

It caught Touch the Sky flush and pressed the last breath of air out of the cave. He could see nothing through the tears streaming from his eyes. All he knew was that he was suffocating. Now there was no question of hanging on a bit longer, now it no longer mattered where the bear was. Either he got out or he died of suffocation.

Deciding to take his chance with the bear, he screamed the Cheyenne war cry to nerve himself.

Then, the Death Song on his lips, he sprang forward through the entrance to the cave.

Chapter Twelve

"Look!"

The Pawnee brave named Gun Powder pointed south across the empty plain. The sun was still new on the eastern horizon to his left, a dull yellow ball without warmth. In the direction he pointed, the Black Hills were just now starting to take form against the skyline.

The newborn sun provided enough light to make the dark, puffy clouds visible as they rose above the hills like escaping bubbles.

"Smoke! We have no lookouts this far east," said Red Plume, their battle chief. "They cannot be made by our messengers."

"This is not talking smoke," said Gun Powder with conviction. "No tribe uses such signals. Our fox has carelessly built a fire and revealed his den."

"*I* am for Cheyenne blood!" said Short Buffalo,

thrusting his battle lance high.

Though his words were brave, they were badly muffled because of his wounded mouth. Several braves were forced to turn their heads to hide their wry smiles.

"Scalp Cane gave me ponies after the Apache stole my clan's herds," said Iron Knife. "Now he has crossed over unclean thanks to this Cheyenne buck. Roan Bear has only nineteen winters behind him. But he will never walk straight like a man again, his legs are so twisted. I will *drink* this Cheyenne's blood, not merely smear it on my face!"

"You do well to speak in a kill-cry," said Red Plume to Iron Knife, contempt clear in his tone. "You, the eagle-eyed brave who missed a pony's rump with his arrow!"

Several other warriors laughed. Rage smoked in Iron Knife's eyes, but he set his face one way and held it, ignoring the others and looking only at Red Plume.

"In the Medicine Bonnet clan, we are taught that a good Crow pony is worth more than a good Cheyenne buck. This one time I may have missed with my arrow. But my knife, once drawn, always strikes vitals."

The challenge was clear in his tone, and Red Plume knew Iron Knife had spoken straight. Red Plume was a good battle leader, quick on his feet and able to think clearly even when the enemy's unnerving war cry sounded. But Iron Knife was a killer to be reckoned with in a blade fight. Red Plume already regretted his harsh words just now. He also rued his promise to take back one of Iron Knife's coup feathers as punishment for his bad shot. This was no time to push the hot-tempered brave further.

"Your clan teaches wisely, then," said Red Plume. "We are Pawnee brothers of the Kitkehanki, men of men. And we are united against our enemy!"

He and Iron Knife crossed lances and the rest of the warriors raised their shrill war cry. They had ridden through much of the night, easily tracking their quarry. By now they knew he was headed for the Black Hills and the Cheyenne's sacred lake—no doubt expecting help from their God.

Short Buffalo's swollen and torn face was a constant reminder to the others of this elusive Cheyenne buck's dangerous skill. One of the new arrivals to the group, a warrior named Sun Road, had joined the Pawnee group known as the Skidi when they attacked Yellow Bear's camp one winter ago. Sun Road swore this tall buck they sought now was the same who had killed the Skidi battle leader, War Thunder.

The Pawnee warriors dug their heels and knees hard into their ponies, their minds set only on vengeance.

At first, when he burst forth from the smoke-filled maw of the cave, Touch the Sky could see nothing. His eyes ached and streamed tears, his throat and lungs cried for air. But each time he gasped, they purchased only raw, burning pain.

He dropped to the ground, helpless, choking, expecting death at any moment. But steel claws did not rip his muscles from his bones nor spill his guts in one swipe. Nor was he picked up, like a limp rag doll in a terrier's jaws, and dashed to pieces on the rocks.

Smoke was still rising in wisps behind him when Touch the Sky realized that, for now at least, the bear was gone. His eyes were still streaming and blurred. But he could see now that the grizzly was nowhere close by.

Still—he was far from safe, he reminded himself. The huge predator was no doubt still in the area around the lake. Bears were highly territorial and did not quit an area easily. Now it had even more reason than ever to hate humans.

Touch the Sky had no weapons that could bring down a grizzly. His only hope for survival lay in avoiding and outwitting the ill-tempered monster.

Finally, a cool breath bathed his aching lungs. Another.

Slowly, Touch the Sky sat up in the grass.

Across the lake, where his pony was tethered in lush graze, there was a sound like a sturdy tree limb snapping.

Across the lake . . .

. . . where his pony was tethered!

Touch the Sky leaped to his feet. He turned around slowly in a circle until he felt the breeze steady in his face. It was blowing from the north: meaning his pony was almost certainly downwind from the bear.

He hurried back into the cave and grabbed his bow and quiver of new arrows. Then he raced down toward the shore of the lake.

Trees grew close to the water, obscuring his view of the little sheltered cove where he'd left the gray. Touch the Sky leaped over fallen trees and gnarled roots, swerved to avoid bramble thickets and boulders.

Another tree limb snapped, leaves were violently shaken.

A sudden, frightened nicker was followed by an angry bellow.

Too late!

Desperation sent more strength surging into Touch the Sky's legs. His wounded side protested with a jolt of pain each time he leaped a log or root.

The gray's panicked whinnying was unrelenting now. More limbs snapped, leaves rattled, the grizzly's deep bellows seemed to pulsate the air and vibrate the ground.

Touch the Sky cleared the last trees and reached the cove. On the gently sloping grassy bank, rearing at the end of its tether, the gray held the grizzly at bay with her wildly flailing hooves.

The horse's frightened nickering sounded more terrifying than the anguished cries of mortally wounded Cheyenne on a battlefield. Touch the Sky was upwind, and the bear hadn't noticed him yet. It was too intent on killing the horse.

There was nothing else Touch the Sky could do. So he slid a fire-hardened arrow from his quiver and notched it to his bowstring. There was no hope, of course, of killing or even seriously hurting the grizzly. But it had to at least be distracted—or Touch the Sky had an impossible walk ahead of him across a no-man's-land.

He took cover in a swale behind a spruce thicket.

Vision Quest

The grizzly was not so blind that it would fail to make out his human shape at this close range.

The gray nickered, reared, kicked out with her forelegs.

The grizzly's right paw swiped. The claws raked furrows in the pony's muscle-corded chest. The bear reached back for a second, more deadly blow.

Touch the Sky let fly his arrow. It struck the grizzly's shaggy, yellow-brown fur just below the left shoulder.

The beast's surprised grunt was followed by a roar much louder than its usual woofing bellow. Enraged, but also frightened, the grizzly crashed into the trees and fled.

His pony was so terrified that Touch the Sky was forced to talk to her for a long time before he could approach her. He finally got her calmed down. Then he led her into the cool lake to bathe her new wounds. They still bled, but were not deep.

This was a bad omen, thought Touch the Sky. This sojourn to Medicine Lake had proven to be a disaster from its very beginning. He had hoped the arrival of the mysterious eagle signaled a change in his fortunes.

Now—in addition to angry Pawnee, neglected wounds, and a half-starved body—he had an enraged grizzly to contend with. Arrow Keeper had not made this mission sound so complicated and dangerous when he explained it back at camp.

Again, as Touch the Sky led his horse back out of the clean lake, he felt a cool tickle of premonition move up the bumps of his spine like a feather.

"I *told* you hunger would make him no less dangerous," Wolf Who Hunts Smiling said bitterly.

"Did you see how cleverly he eluded Brother Bear?" said Swift Canoe. His tone was begrudgingly respectful. "Not once did he show the white feather."

"He is a warrior," said Wolf Who Hunts Smiling. "But he is no Cheyenne! He has brought contamination to our tribe. We are bound by Black Elk's orders."

Both youths were crouched behind a hawthorn bush just down ridge from their hidden camp. The lake lay even further down below them.

"I tried to kill him once," said Swift Canoe, fitting an arrow to his string. "But he ducked just as I shot. This time I will sink my shaft into the quick of him!"

Wolf Who Hunts Smiling made no move to stop his friend. Despite his talk of Touch the Sky's being a spy, the main reason Wolf Who Hunts Smiling hated him was envy. Clearly Arrow Keeper was preparing the tall stranger for a leadership position within the tribe. But Wolf Who Hunts Smiling had his own ambitions for the tribe, and had already begun winning younger warriors over to his way of thinking. He hoped to soon form his own military society within the tribe and challenge the Headmen, who were not keen enough to take the fight to the encroaching white men.

Even so, just as Swift Canoe had eased his bowstring back, Wolf Who Hunts Smiling took his arm in a grip as strong as an eagle's talons.

"Hold, brother! Look, down on the plains!"

Swift Canoe glanced down the forested hillside, looking where his friend pointed. His jaw fell slack with surprise.

Both Cheyenne immediately recognized the distinctive topknots of the approaching riders: Pawnee! They counted nine riders, coming from exactly the same direction that Touch the Sky had chosen.

"They are tracking Woman Face," Wolf Who Hunts Smiling said with conviction.

"You must be right, brother! See how they fan out now? See how they dismount? They are hobbling their horses."

"They hope to surprise him."

"True," said Swift Canoe. "But lice-eaters will not content themselves with one kill if more Cheyenne are available."

The nervousness in Swift Canoe's tone was clear, as was his meaning. Wolf Who Hunts Smiling thought for a moment, then nodded at his companion's words.

"There are too many of them for us to fight," said Wolf Who Hunts Smiling.

"Woman Face is too far down to see them until it is too late for him. Now is the time for us to ride down the back of this hill and flee."

Wolf Who Hunts Smiling considered this. He hated to come this far, wait this long, come this close, only to flee now. But if a grizzly made an area dangerous, Pawnee made it doubly so. Staying here much longer meant that he and Swift Canoe risked capture themselves.

"I have ears for your words," said Wolf Who Hunts Smiling.

His quick-darting, furtive eyes raced back and forth between the approaching Pawnee and the unsuspecting Cheyenne below. "Let us ride. A little smoke will not save Woman Face this time. Let the bloodthirsty Pawnee finish what Brother Bear has begun."

Chapter Thirteen

The Pawnee, still unaware of the grizzly's presence, silently formed a ring around Medicine Lake. Despite their proud boasts and their eagerness to seize this deadly enemy, they were warriors of the Kitkehahki branch of the Pawnee—raised near the river the whites called the Republican. They were highly disciplined fighters who valued obedience to their battle chiefs. They would wait for the signal from Red Plume before they showed themselves.

And that signal would not come yet, for Red Plume was curious.

He had already discussed this loner Cheyenne with Gun Powder, his best scout and most battle-tested brave. Gun Powder, like Red Plume and all true warriors, respected a worthy enemy. Both Pawnee agreed: This Cheyenne was on a special mission to invoke strong medicine. Strong medicine which might be turned against the Pawnee nations when they combined for the massive raid during the upcoming Cheyenne chief-renewal ceremony.

Better to find out, thought Red Plume now as he lay behind a thick oak, watching. The Cheyenne buck was clearly visible now. He was younger than Red Plume had expected—perhaps 18 or 19 winters behind him. He was tipi-pole thin with starvation and moved as if tired. But he was also tall, even for a Cheyenne, and his wide shoulders hinted at a sturdy frame when well fed.

Red Plume absently dug a louse out of the stiff grease in his topknot and cracked it between his strong white teeth. Of all the tribes he knew, the Cheyenne perhaps more than any other feared being separated from the rest of their tribe. So terrible was solitude to them that rarely would they banish even a murderer.

So whatever this one had been sent to do, it was important, thought Red Plume.

The Pawnee war chief frowned when he saw Iron Knife stick his head out too far from behind a dogwood tree. Disciplined or not, the proud warrior had been humiliated by his miss with the arrow. Now he ached to make amends by gutting this Pawnee-killer. But he would have to hurry to wrest that pleasure from the injured Short Buffalo, who had first claim to his blood.

Hold off, said the look Red Plume gave both impatient braves. *Your time approaches. For now, just watch and learn.*

His sister the sun was not yet far above the eastern horizon when Touch the Sky began constructing the willow-branch frame.

Vision Quest

You must purify yourself in the sweat lodge before you leave and again when you arrive.

Arrow Keeper's words returned in memory and guided Touch the Sky's purpose. While he worked, one ear was cocked for warnings of the bear's return. The Cheyenne knew he was still too weak to attempt the grueling ordeal of invoking a vision. This day he would sweat himself clean. Then he would paint his face, meditate, rest, and eat, regaining strength.

He bent the flexible willow branches into shape, lashed them together with buffalo-hair ropes. He returned to the cave and carried his now-tattered buffalo robe back. He draped it over the frame.

You will be on a sojourn to sacred Medicine Lake seeking a medicine dream of great consequence to the Cheyenne people.

Touch the Sky built a hot fire of aspen and oak inside the crude frame hut. One by one, he heaped rocks in a circle about the fire and let them heat for a long time. Only when they finally began to glow red did he strip out of his breechclout and leggings and moccasins.

He filled his buckskin legging sash with cold lake water, then returned to the sweat lodge. Before he lifted the hide and went inside, he paused to glance all around the lake.

He felt eyes watching him—unseen but close.

He glanced toward his pony, tethered nearby. She had calmed since the confrontation with the silvertip bear. But now she too watched the trees all around them, wary. Her ears flicked forward, listening.

You must experience the vision in all of its force at Medicine Lake. Only then can you resolve this terrible battle in your heart. Only then will you accept who you are and what must be done.

Touch the Sky went inside and dumped the cold water on the glowing rocks. At first the hissing steam nearly scalded him. But soon it cooled enough to comfortably breathe. He sat cross-legged in the swirling wisps of steam, feeling his pores expand and ooze cleansing sweat.

He sat for a long time, until his mind was empty of thoughts. Finally, as the rivulets of sweat began to cool against his skin, he left the sweat lodge.

He wiped down with clumps of willow leaves, followed this with a cooling plunge in the lake. Then he dressed again.

Near the water he dug red-bank clay out and put some on a piece of bark to dry a bit in the sun. He crushed ripe blackberries and mixed the juice with yarrow paste to make black dye. He mashed brown wild turnip roots with blades of lush green grass, grinding them together between rocks to produce a yellow paint.

Touch the Sky painted his forehead yellow, his nose red, his chin black—the Cheyenne battle colors. Warriors painted this way when making their sacrifice to the Medicine Arrows before battle. Touch the Sky would remain painted until he experienced the vision—assuming he was destined to receive it.

But Father, what if I fail in seeking this medicine dream?

You will either experience this medicine vision, young Cheyenne warrior, or I fear you will be killed in the attempt.

Touch the Sky finished painting and headed back toward the cave. Now he would eat some more venison, then inspect his pony's hooves before he began the final rest and meditation for his vision quest.

Suddenly a hideous shrieking broke out all around him.

A moment later a circle of well-armed Pawnee braves was closing in on him, their eyes fierce with blood lust.

"Our young fox shook the hounds for many sleeps," said a Pawnee with a huge red plume in his topknot. He advanced closer, speaking in the mixture of Lakota Sioux and Northern Cheyenne dialects he had learned from prisoners. "But now he has led the hounds to his very den!"

He said something rapidly in Pawnee to the others and the rest stopped. Only the brave in the red plume advanced closer toward Touch the Sky.

"I know your tribe well enough to know you are painted for an important ceremony, I speak one way and tell you honestly, I grew alarmed as I watched you. If I tolerated this thing much longer, would you succeed in bringing strong medicine down on Cheyenne enemies? For I believe as Gun Powder preaches: All red men worship one God by different names. Only, the Cheyenne chose to starve our women and children by hoarding the buffalo! For this we war, buck! Now you have blooded my warriors, and your blood is the price of their souls."

"You drew first blood!" Touch the Sky retorted. "Have the Cheyenne sold themselves to the Bluecoats as scouts to hunt down red men? Have *I* starved a Pawnee woman or babe? Has *this* Cheyenne fired on your elders or ever raised his war lance against any Pawnee except in defense of his tribe?"

"He has indeed, Red Plume!" said one of the warriors who had joined Red Plume's band after the rock slide. "I fought in the raids one winter ago against Yellow Bear's camp. *This* tall buck is the one who sent War Thunder over!"

The speaker realized he had spoken the name of a dead man and now made the cut-off sign, asking forgiveness of Tirawa, the Pawnee Father.

"Do you deny this thing?" Red Plume demanded.

Touch the Sky held his mouth in a straight, determined line, showing nothing in his face. By now he had learned well the lesson of Old Knobby, the former mountain man who had befriended him in Bighorn Falls: If captured by Indians, *never* let them see your fear. Begging them for mercy only ensured a slow, agonizing death by torture.

"I deny nothing!" he said defiantly. "Once the war cry sounds, I am for greasing *any* enemy's bones with my battle paint!"

These brave words earned looks of respect from several of the warriors, including Red Plume and Gun Powder.

"I have no ears for this," said another brave. But Touch the Sky barely understood him—not only were the words unfamiliar, the Pawnee's mouth was cruelly mangled. Then the Cheyenne saw the ragged holes in both cheeks and realized this was a victim of his powerful new bow and fire-hardened arrows.

"Look!" added the wounded Pawnee. "Even now his eyes search for boulders to bring down upon us! But a woman's trickery will not save him this time."

Touch the Sky's mind worked furiously. Fighting them was out of the question, as was running. Nine of them circled him, one facing him no matter where he turned. For the present, it was necessary to gain more time to hatch a plan.

"Boulders!" he said loudly, mustering scorn. "For killing Pawnee? Give me a handful of pebbles!"

"Hold, Iron Knife, or forfeit your war bonnet!"

The leader with the brilliant red plume spoke just in time to prevent a warrior from sinking his knife to the hilt in Touch the Sky. It was a French dragoon's bayonet with a deep blood gutter carved in its iron blade to facilitate rapid bleeding.

"Pebbles! For a buck who has barely left the dug, you talk the he-bear talk," said Red Plume. "Are you like a cat who spits and makes a war face but does little else?"

Touch the Sky had to do something, and quickly. The others were impatient to gain vengeance for their fallen comrades. They were clearly tiring of his blustering talk.

Invisible fingers tickled the left side of his face, and Touch the Sky realized the wind was shifting. The wind . . .

Where was the silvertip? It had disappeared behind that long ridge north of the lake. So far, they had all been downwind, assuming it was still north of the water. But now the wind blew straight out of the south. It would carry the human smell along with the smell of their horses, hobbled below.

Despite their precise star charts and their scorn of red men who feared the dark, the Pawnee were vastly superstitious. Touch the Sky's friend Corey Robinson had once saved Yellow Bear's tribe merely by posing as a madman—Pawnee warriors considered insane whites to be the strongest bad medicine in their world.

This was his only chance, Touch the Sky decided. A slim chance was better than a sure death.

"I know nothing of spitting cats!" he said in a brazen, challenging tone. "My name is Bear Caller. I have been sent here by my tribe's shaman because my magic is strong medicine."

"Your magic! Do you carry the famous Cheyenne bloodstone which makes your prints invisible to an enemy?"

The scorn in Red Plume's tone made several other warriors laugh.

"Not this," said one of them. "This buck knows the secret words which turn horse droppings into pemmican!"

Even Short Buffalo and Iron Knife, impatient to gut this dog, laughed at this.

The wind still blew from the south. *Hurry*, Brother Bear, thought Touch the Sky.

"I told you, I am Bear Caller. My people call me this because I am of the Bear Clan and the bear is my brother. I can summon the ferocious grizzly to kill my enemies!"

"And *I* am called Bird Follower because I can fly across the sky!" said Iron Knife. "You are like the whites, speaking many bold words which mean little."

"Summon this ferocious grizzly," said Red Plume. "Show us this strong medicine."

The wind was a steady, stiff breeze now. But had the bear moved on? thought Touch the Sky desperately.

The Pawnee mocked him mercilessly when Touch the Sky loosed an imitation of the grizzly's hungry woofing sound. He repeated it several times, a barking cough from deep in his chest.

"Oooff!" said one of the warriors, imitating their prisoner. "Oooff, ooff-ooff!"

The rest laughed so hard that one or two of them fell upon the ground.

"See how the silvertip rushes to aid his brother," said Red Plume. "Your medicine is indeed powerful."

More laughter. But at that moment the enraged bear hiding in the woods whiffed the overwhelming smell of humans and horses violating his territory. The roaring bellow it unleashed reminded Touch the Sky of buffalo bulls locked in combat.

Tree limbs crashed, there were more bellows. As one, the nine Pawnee turned to stare toward the ridge.

The monster that suddenly appeared on top of the ridge stretched out to his full height on his hind legs. He bellowed his rage, then started lumbering clumsily but with impressive speed toward the group of intruders.

Had they acted in concert, the Pawnee could have brought the grizzly down with their arrows and lances. But the one thing which could quickly destroy their battlefield discipline was strong magic. And this Cheyenne had just summoned a silvertip to his aid, right before their eyes! His magic was indeed strong—the strongest they had ever seen.

The Pawnee panicked and fled downhill toward their horses. This headlong flight distracted the bear. Touch the Sky raced toward his own pony, now rearing against her tether as the grizzly drew nearer.

Touch the Sky untied the rawhide tether and leaped onto the gray, speaking soothing words to fight her panic. Then, as the angry bear routed his enemies, he rode into the dense cover of trees.

Chapter Fourteen

Honey Eater sat just outside the entrance flap of Black Elk's tipi, watching the unmarried girls crossing camp toward their sewing lodge.

How much like fresh flowers some of them looked! And though she was as young as many of them, how much older and wearier Honey Eater felt when she watched them skipping and laughing. The tribe prepared them, almost from birth, for the great rite of passage to womanhood: marriage. And yet, who spoke of this misery and heartache she felt now?

Some of them waved to her, and the young beauty waved back, putting on the gay face that was expected of a great chief's daughter. She missed her friends from the other clans. They would spend much of their morning learning the domestic arts of the tribe from the older squaws. Much gossip and teasing would take place as the girls learned such skills as the highly prized art of Cheyenne beadwork. It was considered the finest on the plains, and the Cheyenne women jealously guarded their secrets.

Honey Eater was finishing an elk hide on pumice stone, softening it for the awl and thread. Inside, Black Elk still slept. He had been up most of the night with the rowdiest warriors, gambling and betting on pony races. He had been cold and remote with her ever since Touch the Sky had been sent on his mission by Arrow Keeper.

Touch the Sky . . . where was he?

Again she let the elkskin fall around her lap as her thoughts wandered. She had tried to be a good Cheyenne wife, to keep her mind free of thoughts for any brave except Black Elk. But she was a simple creature with only one heart—and her one heart was filled with love for the tall youth who had sworn his love for her aloud even as white devils tortured him.

Was he even alive? *Why* did he have to return from Bighorn Falls after she had given up all hope? After River of Winds made his report about Touch the Sky and the golden-haired girl he held in his blanket, she had tried to turn her heart to stone toward him.

But always, at the back of every dream, she heard his voice from that night when he was sure he was about to die: "Do you know that I have placed a stone in front of my tipi?" he had called out to her. "When that stone melts, so too will my love for you!"

The stone was still there—still unmelted. She checked every day.

It was her father's death, thought Honey Eater,

unconsciously making the cut-off sign. His passing and tribal law had left her no choice. She had only accepted Black Elk's gift of horses after Arrow Keeper reminded her. Her duty was to the tribe, and the tribe expected a chief's daughter to marry Black Elk.

The hide flap over the tipi entrance was lifted aside and Black Elk stepped outside. He was naked save for his clout. He glanced down at the unfinished hide and frowned.

"Have you made this the work of your old age, woman? I need new moccasins. Do you expect a war chief to go about looking as if he has neither meat nor racks to store it?"

"I am sorry," she said guiltily.

She stretched the elkskin tight in her fingers and began scraping it over the rough stone. Secretly, though, she was weary of this constant boasting about war. All it ever brought was pain and loss and terrible suffering. Could men find nothing else to worship?

"You dream far too much," said Black Elk. "Your thoughts are seldom on your work and your duties as a wife."

These words hung in the air between them like harsh smoke, accusing her. He had not mentioned Touch the Sky by name, but they both knew what he hinted at.

"My duties?"

She tried to keep her voice submissive as she pointed to the tripod where his elk steak waited for him, dripping succulent kidney fat. "There waits your breakfast. I have made your tea just as you like it. I have also made you new clothing for the chief-renewal. Your war bonnet is the finest in the Cheyenne nation, your horse blanket embroidered like no other. I cook your meals, rub your aching muscles, sew your new moccasins. How, then, have I neglected my duties?"

Black Elk scowled, looking fierce. His severed, dead flap of ear looked like wrinkled leather. "Do not take this tone with me! I am your husband and your war chief! If you have done your duty, then tell me you have my son in your womb."

Honey Eater averted her eyes. "I cannot catch a baby as if it were a toy thrown to me."

"No. But a cow must rut before she can become heavy with calf. You have no desire to lie with your own husband. I have felt how you pull back from my embrace. Is this what you call doing your duty?"

Honey Eater was silent. His words held some truth, and she felt her guilt. It was a Cheyenne squaw's obligation to put her husband and her tribe before her own needs. But her body rebelled against her conscience: She could not even pretend pleasure with another man so long as it was Touch the Sky she burned for.

Black Elk read the confession in her silence. Rage filled him for a moment. He felt the helplessness of a powerful warrior confronted with a situation where physical skill was not enough. But he found some comfort in the thought that, by now, Touch the Sky should be gone under— sent to his death by Wolf Who Hunts Smiling and Swift Canoe.

Again, his rage deep and black at the memory, he recalled his cousin and Swift Canoe swearing on the Sacred Arrows that Honey Eater was meeting with Touch the Sky in secret, that he was holding her in his blanket. He found it hard to accept, yet—they had sworn on the Arrows! His jealous rage had overcome even the Cheyenne dread of drawing tribal blood.

Before Honey Eater could reply, Arrow Keeper crossed to their tipi. Black Elk rose respectfully to greet their peace leader.

"The last word-bringers have returned to camp," he said. "All of the far-flung clans below the Platte River have been notified of the chief-renewal. I have decided the ceremony will be held in the middle of the Moon When the Cherries Ripen. It will take place near our old winter camp in the Tongue River valley."

Black Elk nodded at this important news.

Arrow Keeper pulled his blanket tighter around his shoulders. The old shaman's silver hair was still thick, his eyes sharp despite the leathery mask of wrinkles surrounding them.

"Have your cousin and Swift Canoe returned yet with a report on the Pawnee?"

Black Elk's eyes fled from his chief's. Arrow Keeper noted this. He had not been fooled when Black Elk, shortly after Touch the Sky rode out toward the Black Hills, had sent Touch the Sky's worst enemies on a "scouting mission."

"Not yet, Father," said Black Elk.

True, thought Arrow Keeper, River of Winds' report was damning and seemed to prove Touch the Sky was either a turncoat or at least a dog for the white men, cooperating in their treachery. But Arrow Keeper refused to believe appearances. And secretly, he knew Black Elk respected Touch the Sky too much to kill him like this, sullying the Arrows, without further proof.

No, thought the old shaman as he glanced at Honey Eater—here was the reason for Black Elk's shameful order. The girl was innocent, of course. But the Cheyenne way did not always allow for innocence.

"Perhaps," Arrow Keeper finally said, "your two young warriors have lost their way. Or perhaps they have met an enemy who fights better than they."

Both men understood the elder's hidden meaning. Arrow Keeper turned to leave. Then he turned back around and once again held Black Elk's eyes with his.

"If they do not return soon," he said, "Touch the Sky may arrive before them."

Hot blood crept into Black Elk's face. But he said nothing, holding his face impassive. Honey Eater stared at both men in turn, trying to read the real meaning of this strange conversation. Arrow Keeper watched Black Elk a few moments longer, disappointment keen in his eyes.

"Thankfully, Maiyun has His own battle plan," said the old shaman. "I have seen a vision and I will hold by it. What must be will be, and no mortal warrior can change this."

The next moment, like smoke caught on the wind, he was gone.

Chapter Fifteen

Near the spot where the Weeping Woman River oxbowed, Wolf Who Hunts Smiling and Swift Canoe rode into serious trouble.

The two Cheyenne youths had chosen this place to water their ponies. They were unaware that, recently, paleface miners had built a camp here. This followed the discovery of a modest amount of gold trapped in sediment pockets at the river's bend. The color had long since been exhausted by eager miners. But rumors and gold fever still drew dozens of desperate whites.

Now, bitter and frustrated, they welcomed the opportunity to grant a taste of vigilante justice to these marauding renegades.

The Cheyenne had topped a long rise and spotted the buckboards, canvas pyramid tents, and Indian-style tipis. White men swarmed like ants, and some of them spotted the two riders before they could retreat out of sight.

"They will ride hard," said Wolf Who Hunts Smiling as a group of whites raced to mount up for the chase.

He had heard Black Elk and some of the Headmen speak of this thing. Soldiers of the Southern Dog Cheyenne had attacked and killed miners along the Platte. There were only a few of these Dog Soldiers, drunk on strong water and following the battle chief named War Horse. But white men needed only a few small acorns to conclude that a tall oak forest was in their way.

Wolf Who Hunts Smiling had been right—the white miners rode hard, dogging them like shadows. But their horses were fat from graining and lazy from prolonged grazing. Whites trained their horses for obedience, not endurance. They were good for short bursts of power and speed, not the sustained run.

Soon the iron bits of their mounts were flecked with foam. Meanwhile, the leaner, smaller, more spirited Indian ponies were opening the distance.

The miners abandoned the chase near sunset. The two Cheyenne found themselves in unfamiliar country, their ponies exhausted. The terrain was mostly hills covered with long Sudan grass, interspersed with jagged, red-dirt ravines.

They were skirting the steep bank of a dried-up creek when a startled fox bounded across their path.

Swift Canoe's paint, riding nearest to the creek, shied in fright and side-jumped. The left foreleg came down on clay and the bank crumbled, tumbling horse and rider down a steep decline to a dry, rock-strewn bed of hard-baked clay.

Vision Quest

Even out of sight up above, Wolf Who Hunts Smiling heard the sickening noise when the pony landed head first, its neck snapping fast and clean. By the time he dismounted, calmed and hobbled his own pony, and climbed down, the paint was heaving—great, wracking death gasps. Bloody froth bubbled from its nostrils.

Swift Canoe had been thrown clear. But he was just now regaining consciousness. And his broken right arm lay at a ridiculously impossible angle to his body. Wolf Who Hunts Smiling winced when he saw a jagged stump of white bone protruding through a tear in the skin. It was a serious break. On the plains, it was a potentially deadly wound.

"Brother!"

Swift Canoe's strained voice hinted at the incredible pain. He had glanced at his pony, then his wound, and lost the color in his face.

"Look here! My pony is dead! And my arm! Brother, help me, I fear I am gone under!"

Swift Canoe's fear of dying showed now in his eyes. Wolf Who Hunts Smiling felt his face twist in disapproval. This was a bad situation, truly. But he was of the Panther Clan, as was his cousin Black Elk. The men of that clan placed high honor on never showing fear in their voice or face.

"Any good warrior may find himself upon the ground helpless," said Wolf Who Hunts Smiling. "There is no shame in this. But you are a bull, not a cow! Do not whine like a woman. Are we not both Cheyenne? Do we not take care of our own? Cease this talk of fear and death!"

But his words were wasted—Swift Canoe no longer heard him. The pain had washed over him in ever-increasing waves until numb shock took over. He lay with his eyes wide-open but glazed, unseeing, while his teeth chattered like an elk-tooth necklace.

Wolf Who Hunts Smiling considered: Swift Canoe's Wolverine Clan were complainers and shirkers, true. Their women were notorious for hiding their meat rations, after a hunt distribution, and then lining up for a second allotment. But Swift Canoe, while certainly no battle leader, had counted coup and taken scalps like a man.

Besides—he was a loyal follower, and Wolf Who Hunts Smiling needed loyal followers. He was even more ambitious than his cousin Black Elk. He was not content, as Black Elk was, to serve as a war chief who ruled only in battle. He wanted to head his own band. He would lead the fight to drive the white dogs from the peaks and valleys and plains of the Shaiyena homeland.

For this, he would need loyal followers like Swift Canoe. Like Black Elk, Wolf Who Hunts Smiling was covered with hard bark. But he was also wily like his name—he must try to save Swift Canoe.

He thought about a travois. But what would he construct it from out here on the plains, no trees in sight? Besides, that would be too much weight for even his sturdy black, across such a distance.

Leaving him now and riding for help was also a bad plan. Wolf Who Hunts Smiling was not even sure where they were, nor how many sleeps it would require to find the tribe. The only sensible choice was to remain with him. He would tend to the wound and slaughter the dead pony so they would have meat—albeit raw meat, since they lacked wood for a fire. When Swift Canoe was able to survive on his own, Wolf Who Hunts

Smiling could then return to camp and send help back for him.

He was worried, though. True, they had shaken the white miners for good. But they had made no effort to cover their trail when they fled from Medicine Lake. What if the sharp-eyed Pawnee picked up on their sign?

Wolf Who Hunts Smiling thought of the Colt Model 1855 rifle in his buckskin scabbard above. He had plenty of bullets and percussion caps since the tribe had begun exchanging the season's beaver plews at the trading post in Red Shale. If lice-eaters attacked, he was at least in a good defensive position: open country in front of him, a deep creek bed behind him. He would sell his Cheyenne scalp dearly.

Thinking of the Pawnee made him also think of Woman Face. By now his enemy should be either dead or dying.

Swift Canoe groaned, begging for water.

Dead or dying, Wolf Who Hunts Smiling told himself again as he climbed the steep bank, struggling for hand- and footholds, back up to his pony and the bladder-bag of water. But by now he had begun to wonder if the rumors about Touch the Sky could possibly be true.

The rumors about strong medicine guiding his fate and protecting him.

Eluding the angry silvertip was only one of many times when the tall stranger had knocked Death from his pony before the Black Warrior could count first coup on his mortal soul. Wolf Who Hunts Smiling hated him. What right did he have, riding into a Cheyenne camp with the stink of murdering whites all over him? He drank strong water with whites, he laid secret plans with them, he left talking papers for their Bluecoat pony soldiers in the hollows of trees. He even held one of their yellow-haired squaws in his blanket and made love talk! Besides—clearly Arrow Keeper had great plans for this tall stranger. Plans that Wolf Who Hunts Smiling's ambition would not abide.

This two-faced, many-tongued interloper deserved whatever fate the Pawnee had chosen for him. But now, as he climbed over the bank and stared out across the rolling plains, Wolf Who Hunts Smiling felt it again: the nagging suspicion that, in spite of everything, he would face his enemy again.

His cousin, the lake, lay calm and still when Touch the Sky finally began the ordeal of invoking a medicine dream.

He had no fear of the Pawnee returning soon. Much time had to pass before any lice-eater would visit an area known for bad medicine. They would face bullet or blade bravely. But at the first hint of enemy magic, they showed the white feather.

He had rested through the night, preparing for this day. To supplement his supply of venison, he had killed a plump rabbit and enjoyed his first taste of fresh meat in many sleeps. Now the wound in his side was merely a dull ache, like a bad memory blunted by time.

Though he rested well that night, sleep eluded him for a long time. He found his mind carefully considering the question of red man's medicine, the Indian's way of dealing with the supernatural. Some of the stories the elders told were foolish, of course. No Cheyenne believed all of them. But had he not seen proof of Arrow Keeper's big medicine?

Vision Quest

There was the time when Pawnee attacked Yellow Bear's camp. Touch the Sky had watched a lice-eater fire point-blank at Honey Eater, twice. But Arrow Keeper had thrown his magic panther skin over her just before the warrior fired, and the bullets went wide. And once Arrow Keeper had blessed Touch the Sky's horse with power, speed, and endurance—had the dun not flown like a fierce wind across the plains, easily catching the whiskey trader Henri Lagace on his magnificent cavalry sorrel?

Before his sister the sun rose for the day, Touch the Sky built a huge fire beside the lake. With the eerie tongues of orange flame casting his shadow against the trees, he began the rhythmic dancing that helped an Indian focus his mind. He moved in a wide, loose circle about the fire. He rattled stones wrapped in soft bark and lifted his knees high to the steady cadence of "Hi-ya, hi-ya!" His mind began to grow quiet; intrusive thoughts drifted into a fog that blew away.

With the first rays of dawn, Touch the Sky stripped naked. He touched his medicine bundle one last time, drawing strength from the badger claws within. Then he took his place atop a lone hill at one end of the lake. While sandpipers and other small shore birds stared at him curiously, he stood silent and stone still.

The dancing had already prepared him for the trance state which must happen if he were to endure the upcoming ordeal. He felt it coming on, a gradual but steady shutting down of the body as it moved into a state almost like hibernation. His muscles grew heavy and slack as they lost all unnecessary tension. His mind was clear, totally

137

aware, not lost in the past or the future but existing now in the becoming that was the gateway to visions.

He stopped fighting the pain and discomfort, lost his fear, felt no hatred or jealousy or envy. Time and place became a river, flowing all around him, at first, then carrying him with the current.

He stared, unblinking, into the sun now, feeling no pain, doing no damage to his eyes. Gradually, as she tracked higher across the blue dome of the sky, his head tilted to follow her. His shadow was long behind him, grew short, now stretched out longer again in front of him as the sun finally eased toward her resting place. But the Cheyenne felt no sense of time passing, no reminder that he was rooted to the earth.

And then, at some point, he simply blinked once, and he was aware again in the usual way.

His body felt stiff, and the location of the Grandmother Star told him the night was well along. The air felt chilly, a harsh wind blew steadily from the north. But without debating it, Touch the Sky walked down to the lake and waded in.

The water was torturously cold against his sunbaked skin. But he kept moving out until the water reached his chin. Then, again, he untethered his mind from its usual awareness, freeing it from the little day and letting it seek the Vision Way.

Arrow Keeper had once told him how most people misunderstand visions. They assumed that visions came easily to the sick, sad, and dying because they were weak in their minds. They were not weak, Arrow Keeper insisted, they were *ready*.

And now, after his long ordeal on the plains, the dancing, his long day staring into the sun—

Touch the Sky too was ready.

First came the voices. But not dead voices from a dead past. Living voices guiding him now, here, on the upward path known as the medicine dream.

Old Knobby, the hostler at the feed stable in Bighorn Falls: *The Injun figgers he belongs to the land. The white man figgers the land belongs to him. They ain't meant to live together.*

John Hanchon, his white father: *I've worked until I'm mule-tired, but I still go to bed scared every night.*

He heard more voices, his mother and his friend Corey Robinson and Kristen Steele and the brevet officer Tom Riley and Little Horse and Honey Eater. And he felt no fear when the ghosts of the dead paraded past—Chief Yellow Bear, High Forehead, True Son, all trying to warn him, trying to tell him something. But he couldn't quite make out the words.

And then words gave way to sounds and mind pictures. He saw horses rearing, their eyes huge with fright, while red warriors sang their battle cry. Rivers of blood flowed everywhere, cannons roared, steel clashed against steel. From across the vast plains red warriors streamed, flowing like the blood they must soon shed. One brave led them, his war bonnet streaming coup feathers. But Touch the Sky could not see his face.

He saw glimpses of the ice-shrouded lands to the north. He saw the faces of his enemies, Hiram Steele and Seth Carlson. He saw a long ragged column of starving Cheyenne, again being led by the mysterious brave whose face he could not see.

Then, once again, he blinked, and he was aware of everything around him. Aware in the little day. But it was as if the night had been painted in brilliant hues, glazed in ceramic.

Overhead, the same eagle that had guided him here now circled gracefully, a ghostly silhouette in the moonlight. On shore, watching him with intent curiosity, was the huge grizzly. Only, now it showed no anger. It simply watched him with open curiosity. The moonlit lake shimmered like black ice, the eerie cries of the loons seemed to extend, distort, now grow distant and low, now shrill and close in his ears.

When the voice of Chief Yellow Bear came again, high, clear, right in his ears, Touch the Sky felt no fear.

"We who have crossed over," said this voice from the Land of Ghosts, "know everything that will pass. I have seen you bounce your son on your knee, just as I have seen you shed blood for that son and his mother.

"Touch the Sky, place these words close to your heart forever, for they will save the Shaiyena nation: *When all seems lost, become your enemy!*"

The voice faded, the mind pictures returned, and now Touch the Sky again saw the mysterious warrior leading his people. Only this time the war leader turned for a moment to look back, the war cry on his lips, and he recognized himself.

Touch the Sky wasn't sure how much longer he stood rooted in the frigid lake. But at some point he became aware that his teeth were chattering, his muscles cramped with cold. Stiff muscles protesting, he waded back to shore. As he stepped up out of the water, he spotted the eagle one last time:

140

It completed one full circle of the lake, then headed out across the plains.

He walked back to his clothing. Then, as he reached down for his clout, he froze.

Nestled atop his leggings was the object of his second vision during the journey here, the symbol of courage and fighting spirit in battle: an eagle-tail feather. He touched it—it was still warm from the eagle's body heat.

Only now, as the numbness in his body finally wore off, did the full significance of his medicine dream sink through to Touch the Sky.

There was no longer any question of it. Arrow Keeper was right. The hand of the Great Spirit was indeed involved in this thing. He could not be sure of the meaning of everything he saw. Image had piled upon image, sound blended with sound, and the events of many years seemed telescoped into the intensity of a moment.

But Arrow Keeper was right. His arrival at Yellow Bear's tribe was not some random happening. That birthmark hidden behind his hair—it was not some random marking. Touch the Sky could not be sure of his part, but Fate had already written a role for him. A great role, but one with many great responsibilities and hardships.

Touch the Sky understood and accepted all this. Just as, once and for all, he accepted his destiny as a Cheyenne. Holding the feather in one hand, he vowed to return and face his tribe again no matter what.

Chapter Sixteen

"It is as I feared," said Wolf Who Hunts Smiling. "The lice-eaters were not content with killing Woman Face. They followed our sign, and now the fight comes to us."

The sun glowed straight overhead out of a cloudless sky. But even squinting, Wolf Who Hunts Smiling could see the group of riders approaching straight toward them. They had stopped, one of them dismounting and kneeling to the ground—clearly he was reading sign.

The Cheyenne's horse was picketed below in the creek bed. Wolf Who Hunts Smiling had used their two buffalo robes and a few arrow shafts to rig a small shelter from the sun. Swift Canoe lay inside it now, sweltering in the breezeless heat.

"Brother, my arm is useless," Swift Canoe called up to him, "or I would join you. You can kill me now and ride hard and perhaps outrun them."

Vision Quest

In fact Wolf Who Hunts Smiling had already considered this plan. But it was too late now. The night before he had dug for a long time in the creek bed, finally discovering a thin layer of alkali-tasting water. If he rode out now, in this unfamiliar country, when would he next reach water?

Besides—these were Indian ponies, not the lazy plugs ridden by whites. He would never stand a chance of outrunning the Pawnee.

No, he was safest right here. Let his enemy come at him. They had no shelter for a hidden attack. He would pick them off like prairie chickens, well protected in his natural breastwork of the creek bed. His pony was safe below.

Again he carefully inspected his bullets and primer caps in the soft kid pouch at his elbow. A grain of sand could clog up the Colt's firing mechanism.

"I have no ears for this talk of killing each other," he said to Swift Canoe. "I plan to grease Pawnee bones with war paint! One bullet, one enemy."

"*This* is the he-bear talk!" said Swift Canoe. "We are the fighting Cheyenne!"

"If the fight goes bad and they send me under," said Wolf Who Hunts Smiling, "remember that you have your knife and one good arm—sing the Death Song and fall on your own blade. You do not want to be captured by lice-eaters."

But his warning was unnecessary. Swift Canoe, like all Cheyenne warriors, lived in dread of Pawnee torture. His knife was already in his hand.

By now the riders were almost in long-arm range. Wolf Who Hunts Smiling inserted a primer cap into the loading gate of the Colt. He had no intention of waiting until the Pawnee were close enough to discover them. His hope was to keep them back out of rifle range.

And to pray to Maiyun for a full moon and a starlit night. The Pawnee were in their element after dark.

He sighted on one of the riders, ignoring the smaller target presented by the brave and aiming instead for the middle of his pony's chest. He inserted his finger inside the trigger guard and slowly took up the slack.

Red Plume signaled a halt while Gun Powder dismounted and examined the ground for signs.

"The white men quit chasing them some time back," reported the Pawnee scout. "They slowed their mounts—the tracks are closer together and not so deep. Now they are riding easy."

Red Plume nodded. "Then we should catch them soon. This is not Indian territory and they will be lost. Be they Sioux or Cheyenne, *this* time we take prisoners. By now the Cheyenne tribe has decided on a time and place for their chief-renewal. A Sioux will know this thing as well as his cousin the Cheyenne."

"The riders are Cheyenne or Sioux," agreed Gun Powder. "Crow ponies have a cleft hoof. The Arapaho and Shoshone have both traveled toward the Land of the Grandmother to the north, following the buffalo herds. We are too far south for these to be the prints of Mandan or Hidatsa."

"And you are sure the trail started at Medicine Lake?"

Gun Powder nodded. "Near the same time as we arrived. The dirt is still not crusted in the tracks."

"This means they played the rabbit when they spotted us. I suspect these two are word-bringers. No doubt they had a message for the bear-calling shaman."

Red Plume had lost enough face when the Cheyenne youth with the powerful medicine had sent him scrambling with the rest of his braves, fleeing like children afraid of the Wendigo. Now they had exhausted one full sleep in an impromptu council, debating whether or not to follow this trail. This time it would be different. This time the men of men would demonstrate why they were the most feared warriors in all the Plains Indian country.

Before he could give the order to ride, however, Short Buffalo spoke up. Though his words were still muffled and indistinct because of the wounds to his mouth, this time no one laughed. His words were too serious.

"Brothers! Hear me! You know me. We have hunted and traveled the war path together, and visited as friends in our clan lodges. You know my clan, and you know my society!"

Absolute silence followed this. Every brave present knew that Short Buffalo was a member of the Death Arrow Society, a Pawnee military society which attracted only the most courageous—but also only the most reckless—of warriors. Each member of the Death Arrows carried a black-painted arrow always in his quiver. That arrow could never be drawn save on one condition: that it must draw blood. If the brave failed to kill his enemy with it, then he was required by the society's law to kill himself in expiation.

Every buck present, including Red Plume,

knew the significance of his action when Short Buffalo now slid the black arrow from his quiver. By that action he had pledged his life for the rare honor of overriding normal tribal law or even the commands of his war leader. Red Plume was bound by the manly heroism of such an act: Short Buffalo had sworn to kill, and he would be allowed to do so on his own terms. Failing this, he must die.

Every brave present was inspired by Short Buffalo's act.

"Mount!" Red Plume commanded Gun Powder. "Now we teach our ponies about hard riding!"

He sounded the shrill Pawnee war yip, and the rest of the braves repeated it. They dug heels and knees into their ponies, urging them to a hard run. Their greased topknots gleamed in the stark sunlight, and several had streaked their nearly naked bodies with vermillion dye.

Short Buffalo raced out ahead of them, his war lance held high. No one heard a shot nor detected a puff of muzzle smoke. But a moment later, a piebald pony next to Short Buffalo collapsed as if its bones had turned to water.

Touch the Sky had made good time during the first morning after he left Medicine Lake, bearing due west toward the Cheyenne camp at the fork where the Powder River joined the Little Powder. But a Bluecoat cavalry patrol ambushed him near Beaver Creek and flushed him far into the even more desolate terrain of the southern country.

The solders gave up past midday. His horse was well rested and fed, and Touch the Sky had filled his sash with fruits and nuts to supplement the rest of his venison. This delay in unfamiliar country seemed a trifling thing now after all he had endured.

Then, toward sundown, he heard the first shots.

They came at regular intervals, as if one person were firing and reloading, firing and reloading, using cool battlefield discipline. A long pause, the thunder of hooves, another interval of regularly spaced shots.

A series of red dirt ravines pockmarked the area. Touch the Sky was able to stick mostly to the cover of these as he slipped closer. Finally he emerged from one and cautiously peered out from behind a long, low, grass-covered hummock.

The sight sent blood throbbing into his face. It was the same group of Pawnee who had planned to kill him back at Medicine Lake!

From his present location, Touch the Sky could not see whoever it was they were engaging in a harassment attack. Two ponies lay dead on the ground, a third kicked in death agonies. One Pawnee lay still, apparently dead, another bled from a wound in his arm. They were grouped behind the war leader called Red Plume. Evidently they had retreated to a spot just out of the defender's effective range.

Even as Touch the Sky watched, a brave dug heels into his pony and rode out from the group. He raced in a zig-zagging pattern toward what Touch the Sky now recognized as a creek, the lip of its bank barely visible from where he watched.

The rifle spoke its piece, the Pawnee charged on, still swerving and doubling back across his own path on his surefooted pony.

Another shot, another miss. The pony raced closer.

A third shot, and the pony was down. Almost without missing a beat, the agile rider raced on foot back toward his companions. A final shot kicked up a yellow plume of dust at his retreating heels.

Touch the Sky wondered who was under siege. It sounded like a lone fighter, unless his companions had been killed or injured. No white settlers or Bluecoats would travel alone out here. It was almost surely a red man. With the exception of the Ute tribe, any enemy of the Pawnee was a friend of the Cheyenne. And Touch the Sky knew no mountain-dwelling Ute would be in this area.

He studied the lay of the land and tried to guess in what direction that creek might twist and wind. Then, sticking to the jagged ravines and hiding behind hummocks, he went in search of it.

He found it without much trouble while the sun still gave light. Touch the Sky hobbled his pony and proceeded along the dried, baked-clay bed cautiously. He heard several more shots, the sound drawing near as he advanced.

His heart raced faster as he approached a sharp bend, close now to the sounds of rifle shots. He rounded it slowly, hugging the steep bank and staying in its apron of shade.

For a moment his head denied his eyes when he recognized Wolf Who Hunts Smiling dug in at the top of the bank. He was sighting out toward the Pawnee with the Colt that had once belonged to Touch the Sky. Below, his anxious face protruding from a crude hide shelter-half, was Swift Canoe.

Vision Quest

Swift Canoe clutched his bone-handle knife in his hand.

"Brother!" Wolf Who Hunts Smiling called down to him. "I fear it will soon go badly for us. I think the lice-eaters are finally tired of being picked off like nits from a buffalo! They are massing for the charge! Let them come, I am for them! But only this, brother: If they should hit me and only wound me, do not fall on your knife until you have made sure I am gone over. Do not leave me for them to take alive."

"I swear this thing, Cheyenne warrior," Swift Canoe promised.

Touch the Sky did not stop to wonder why the two Cheyenne were marooned this far from the Powder River camp. Nor why their path had crossed that of the same Pawnee with whom he'd tangled. Their courage, in the face of such a dire threat, impressed him.

He hated both of them. And both had tried to kill him. But they were behaving like true warriors now, and were they not Cheyenne? His battle with them was a battle within the tribe—this was an enemy from without, one who attacked in darkness and killed women and children while they slept in their robes.

He could not just let them die. Nor would it save any of them if he joined the fight beside Wolf Who Hunts Smiling. There were still a half-dozen good braves thirsty for blood. This was not a time for fighting.

Touch the Sky climbed to the top of the bank and carefully peered out, getting his bearing. Then he dropped back down and followed his back-trail, heading toward a nearby ravine.

*   *   *

"It is settled," said Red Plume. "Short Buffalo has spoken and I have spoken. He will ride in alone. We follow. He draws first blood or dies. But we have waited long enough. I care not if Mother Night would protect us, I am for blood now! We attack now, as one!"

Short Buffalo was tired of words. His horse leaped out from the others and raced toward the creek. It was a roan mare, trained to turn buffalo herds and nimble on its feet. Short Buffalo borrowed a trick from the Cheyenne and rode low hugging his pony's neck to make a small target.

The agile pony leaped over one dead horse, another, swerved right, left, swept past the dead Pawnee. One shot missed. A second dropped the roan and its rider when they were less than a stone's throw away from the creek.

Unlike his comrades, Short Buffalo did not retreat out of range. He sounded the war yip and raced into the teeth of his enemy.

Desperate but moving with calm competence, Wolf Who Hunts Smiling loaded one of his last bullets and primer caps. He waited until the enraged Pawnee was blocking the sun, then squeezed the trigger.

There was a brief sizzling sound when the primer cap misfired.

"Sing the Death Song!" shouted Wolf Who Hunts Smiling to Swift Canoe even as he frantically clawed his own knife out of its sheath.

Short Buffalo leaped, thrusting his stone-tipped lance at Wolf Who Hunts Smiling. The small but quick and strong Cheyenne lunged to one side and avoided the lance. At the same moment, he brought his knife up to meet Short Buffalo.

The Pawnee impaled himself and tumbled into the creek, his war cry transformed into a death shriek. But the impact had knocked Wolf Who Hunts Smiling down too. And above, he and Swift Canoe could hear the rest of the attackers thundering closer.

Deciding it was better to die above fighting, instead of trapped down there like a cowering child, Wolf Who Hunts Smiling climbed back over the bank.

Just as he emerged, a furious bellow from his right drew everyone's attention.

Wolf Who Hunts Smiling's jaw dropped open in astonishment when Touch the Sky—not even armed—emerged from a ravine and ran straight at the Pawnee. The ridiculous fool was woofing and growling like a silvertip bear, as if that should somehow frighten blood-lusting Pawnee warriors! Had he gone Wendigo?

But his astonishment turned to pure shock moments later, when the Pawnee showed the white feather and tore off across the plains!

Red Plume knew the Pawnee nations were in trouble now. See how this mysterious, bear-summoning Cheyenne shaman arrived out of thin air to protect his own? Until they knew more about him and his powerful medicine, Red Plume knew he must recommend to the council that all plans for attacking the Cheyenne chief-renewal be canceled.

Chapter Seventeen

The Pawnee were soon mere dust devils on the horizon. Wolf Who Hunts Smiling stared at his tribal enemy as he crossed closer toward the creek.

A sudden thought weakened his knees: Where was Woman Face's horse, his weapons? How could he simply have appeared out of the earth like a thing of smoke?

How, wondered Wolf Who Hunts Smiling, unless this was not Touch the Sky but his ghost?

All in an instant, it made horrible but logical sense. The Pawnee *had* tortured and killed him! Why else would they have fled, the very first moment they spotted him, like dogs with their tails on fire?

It also made gruesome sense that Touch the Sky's ghost would now imitate the silvertip. Was this not the animal his Cheyenne enemies lured to kill him? To Wolf Who Hunts Smiling, as to most

Indians, ghosts who return to the body-world are revenants—spirits bent on revenge.

Thinking these things, Wolf Who Hunts Smiling forgot his recent stern lecture to Swift Canoe about courage under pressure. He also violated the manly code of his Panther Clan: Fear turned his face white, his eyes huge. His lips trembled as if he had suddenly been thrown naked into a snowbank. Clearly, he wore his terror in his face.

"Leave this place!" he said in his bewilderment.

He made the cut-off sign even though he knew such mild white magic was useless against a spirit manifestation.

Touch the Sky, now totally bewildered himself, stopped. He stood perhaps 20 paces back from the bank of the dried-up creek. Wolf Who Hunts Smiling had hollowed out a crude rifle pit. Only the upper part of his body was visible. Now and then a frustrated Swift Canoe called up to him, desperate to learn what was going on. Wolf Who Hunts Smiling ignored him, busy fending off complete panic.

"I fought with you, I drew your blood," said Wolf Who Hunts Smiling. "And true it is I walked between you and the fire. But I never crept up on you from behind like a cowardly Mandan or came for you in your sleep like the treacherous Comanche! When you were trapped in the whiskey traders' camp, I fought like ten warriors to free you. True, I wanted to kill you. But in a fair fight, warrior to warrior!"

This talk amazed Touch the Sky. He watched Wolf Who Hunts Smiling again make the cut-off sign. Clearly his enemy was convinced beyond all doubt he had returned from the Land of Ghosts.

But why did he think this thing? What could have convinced him he had been killed?

Then, a heartbeat later, he understood.

He understood everything.

Now it was clear to him what these two Cheyenne—his sworn enemies—were doing in this desolate no-man's-land so far from camp. *Now* he understood why that grizzly had so suddenly shown up at an uninhabited cave. He also knew how that freshly blooded fawn had gotten there.

It was bait planted by Wolf Who Hunts Smiling and Swift Canoe. Bait intended to lure his executioner.

His anger was tempered by his private amusement as Touch the Sky grasped the situation. For the first time in his memory, Wolf Who Hunts Smiling had lost his arrogant, wily sneer. Why not enjoy this rare turn of events?

"You say you only wanted to kill me in a fair fight. Then tell me, Cheyenne buck. Would *you* face a silvertip bear and call it a fair fight?"

Wolf Who Hunts Smiling was shamed into silence.

"And speak of this thing, great warrior. The night, at the white dogs' camp on the Yellowstone, when you threw rocks to alert the paleface sentry? You ran away and left me to die. Was this another time when you wanted me to die in a 'fair fight'?"

"These—these things were wrong," admitted Wolf Who Hunts Smiling. "But River of Winds has recently sworn that he saw you making medicine with Bluecoats! And that time with the sentry, I was still angry after our fight which caused

Black Elk to turn against me.

"But you were *not* killed as the result of anything I did, each time I left you a fighting chance. This is not the same as murder!"

"A long, thin creature that slides on the ground and bites me with poison is the same as a snake to me," said Touch the Sky. "Call it whatever else you will. When you speak this way, you mangle words. Just like the white men who write talking papers and then steal our land with them. They call a white rock black when it suits their purpose, just as you now honey-coat your treachery."

"Kill me if you will," said Wolf Who Hunts Smiling. "Show me the Wendigo's face and turn me to frozen stone. But do not say I am anything like the white devils who slaughtered my father!"

"I say it again! Evil was not invented by the white man—I have seen red men who would make the white devil Satan proud indeed."

Wolf Who Hunts Smiling looked at the ground, knowing full well who he meant.

"What?" said Touch the Sky. "The child sulks! Will you now threaten to kill me again? It was your favorite sport while I walked the earth."

"I have ears for this," said Wolf Who Hunts Smiling. "You are right to mock me now. I spoke of it too much. Women fight with their words, men let their battle lances speak for them."

Touch the Sky permitted his lips to widen in a wry smile.

"Are you telling me, then, that now you wish you would have killed me quickly and been done with it long ago?"

Wolf Who Hunts Smiling looked like a fox caught in a blind trap. He hadn't meant to reveal so much of his true thoughts. Yet, it was foolish to lie to a ghost—it was said by the elders they could read the human heart the way living Indians could read a game trail.

Fear drained even the wily gleam from Wolf Who Hunts Smiling's eyes. But courageously, he nodded. "I wish now that *I* had sent you under, not Pawnee."

Touch the Sky could not help admiring his enemy's audacious courage even as he loathed him for his petty hatred and jealousy and ambition. Abruptly, he reached down, picked up a handful of dirt, and let it scatter in the wind.

"Tell me, Panther Clan!" he said to Wolf Who Hunts Smiling, each word laced with scorn. "How can a thing of smoke move the dirt—let alone harm a brave warrior such as yourself?"

It took Wolf Who Hunts Smiling many heartbeats to understand his mistake. When he realized, blood rushed into his face. Humiliation vied with rage and relief. Reflexively, he raised the Colt and aimed it at Touch the Sky. For a long moment the two Cheyenne stared at each other, faces carved from stone, eyes unwavering.

Then Wolf Who Hunts Smiling lowered the Colt. "Enjoy your white man's joke. What happened here this day," he said coldly, pointing out toward the battlefield where dead ponies and dead Pawnee still lay, "showed once again your great courage. You know I hate you, yet you saved me."

"I saved a Cheyenne," Touch the Sky corrected him.

"As you say. I *still* believe you secretly play the dog for whites. But I see now that I was wrong about your loyalty to the tribe. A Cheyenne who risks his life for a tribe member he hates will surely stand and cover himself with glory for those he loves.

"Even so, I feel it in my bones, the day comes when we will tip our lances at each other. And I *will* kill you—honorably or otherwise—if I obtain proof with my own eyes that you serve the Long Knives against us. Until such a day arrives, I swear this thing on my medicine bag: Never again will I sully the Arrows by deliberately endangering you in secret as I have done in the past."

"I play the dog for no one," said Touch the Sky. "But I have placed your words in my sash. I fear they are as close to a truce as we will ever come." Touch the Sky recalled his medicine dream at the lake and added, "I too feel we will one day meet in combat. One of us will sully the Arrows by killing a Cheyenne."

Wolf Who Hunts Smiling nodded. "I will wait here with Swift Canoe. Will you tell them back at camp where to find us?"

Touch the Sky nodded. "And I will mark the trail clearly with sign so they will be quick getting here."

Touch the Sky had taken several steps back toward his hidden pony when the other Cheyenne called his name. He turned around.

Wolf Who Hunts Smiling brandished the Colt rifle.

"You have long wanted your weapon back. I offer it freely now."

Touch the Sky debated. Black Elk had already taken the percussion-action Sharps rifle his white father had given him. He couldn't be trusted with it, Black Elk explained, after the report from River of Winds. Why, thought Touch the Sky now, give Black Elk a second weapon to steal? He was riding back to enough trouble and hostility as it was. Approaching camp now with a long arm might even get him killed.

"You turned it into a true firestick this day," Touch the Sky finally said. "I quit claim to it. The rifle is yours."

"I accept it gladly!" Wolf Who Hunts Smiling called to his retreating back. "Just carry my warning close to your heart. I respect you, yes. But I respect *any* enemy who is worth the effort of killing!"

Chapter Eighteen

When he arrived at the rim of the fertile Powder River valley, Touch the Sky halted his pony.

The day was late, and the sun burned low on the western horizon. Far below he could see the Cheyenne camp. The tipis were arranged by clan circle with a huge clearing left open in the center. It was dominated by the largest structure, the hide-covered council lodge. Naked children played at war, riding stick ponies into battle and carrying willow-branch shields. Squaws bent over their cooking tripods to prepare the late meal.

Touch the Sky knew that sentries were posted beyond this point, covering the approach to camp. But something else had begun troubling him as he neared the valley: What if there was now an order to kill him on sight?

After all, he had left camp with most believing he was a spy for the Long Knives. True, Arrow Keeper's power as acting chief was enough to permit his departure. But even Arrow Keeper had warned him to leave right away, during the night—as if afraid the tribe might override him. A chief was bound by the collective will of the tribe. Anything might have happened since he left.

Since his epic vision at Medicine Lake, Touch the Sky wanted more than ever to belong to the tribe, to be accepted. The prospect of being killed on sight did not trouble him because he was afraid, or because the thought of death held a sting for him as for all men. Rather, he did not want to die alone. He did not want to pass through this life on earth belonging nowhere, treated like a rabid cur by white and red men alike.

To belong just once before he died! And for this he had decided once and for all to make his stand in life as a Cheyenne, the blood of his birthright and as good a birthright as any man's. Several sleeps earlier, he would gladly have ridden into a sentry's arrow and ended this eternal fight just to survive.

Now, however, he decided he wanted to live, to explore the full length of his tether before he crossed over to the Land of Ghosts. So he would wait until his sister the sun went to her rest. Then he would slip past the sentries and simply throw himself on Arrow Keeper's mercy.

While he waited, watching the valley slide further into shadows, he picked out Black Elk's tipi. This was simple, for it was easily the finest and newest in the entire camp, and the meat racks behind overflowing. But the entrance flap remained closed. He failed to catch even a glimpse of Honey Eater.

Angry at himself, he forced his eyes away. Yes, he would make his stand with the Cheyenne, if he could. But Honey Eater was smoke behind him now, part of a world that was dead to him. She belonged to a time when hopes for love still lived in his heart. That time was gone. She was married now, another man's wife.

Chief Yellow Bear's words from the recent vision came back to him, a memory echo that pimpled his skin with gooseflesh:

I have seen you bounce your son on your knee, just as I have seen you shed blood for that son and his mother.

But who would his bride be, then? He had no room in his heart for any woman but Honey Eater.

While he thought these things, the sun slid lower and the first stars began to wink high in the night sky. Touch the Sky waited until the valley was shrouded in a cloak of black velvet darkness. Then, leading the gray by her hackamore, he carefully descended into the valley.

He was forced to swing wide, at one point, to avoid a sentry camped on a ridge above the eastern entrance to the Cheyenne village. And Touch the Sky worried, as he reached the edge of the camp clearing, about setting the dogs off: The Cheyenne kept many dogs around, training them to hate the smell of their enemies. But they could also go into a barking frenzy at the arrival of a Cheyenne.

But they ignored him as he slipped out of the trees. Touch the Sky skirted the tipis and the light from the huge fires in front of the lodges of the clans and military societies. First he turned his pony loose in the huge rope corral beside the river. Then, heart hammering against his ribs, he made his way toward Arrow Keeper's tipi.

It stood on a lone hummock between the river and the clan circles. The flap was up, a small fire burned within. The hide tipi cover had stretched so thin that the firelight inside turned it a soft orange-yellow color that glowed like burning punk. The old shaman's hatchet-sharp profile stood out clearly in silhouette.

Touch the Sky glanced inside. Arrow Keeper sat with his back to the entrance, silver-streaked hair spilling over his blanket-draped shoulders.

Touch the Sky looked closer, and a reverent awe filled him: Arrow Keeper held one of the sacred Cheyenne Medicine Arrows. Carefully, lovingly, he brushed its entire blue-and-yellow-striped length with a soft piece of chamois.

Touch the Sky was about to announce his presence. Suddenly, his back still turned, Arrow Keeper's gravelly voice said, "Welcome, Touch the Sky. Step inside and visit with your chief."

The old shaman turned around now. His nut-brown face was sere and wrinkled. But his eyes blazed with the intensity of the spirit flame that stays strong even when the body sickens and ages.

"I knew you were coming," he said as the youth stepped inside. "A great eagle circled camp this morning. It dropped this in front of my tipi."

The medicine man held up the tail feather of an eagle.

Touch the Sky felt his blood singing as he stared at the feather.

"I have one just like it, Father."

The shaman nodded. He slipped the Medicine Arrow back into the coyote fur pouch which held the other three Arrows. Arrow Keeper slid the pouch under his sleeping robes.

"Tell me, little brother," he said. "Did you find the vision you sought?"

Touch the Sky nodded. "It was as you said. Much was not clear, and already I have forgotten some things. But Father, this I know, my place is here with the tribe. Will they accept me?"

Arrow Keeper was silent for many heartbeats.

"I cannot speak the will of the tribe," he finally answered. "I cannot assure you they will accept you, not quickly. River of Winds' report has branded you a spy, or at least a traitor, in the eyes of many. But I *can* assure you they will tolerate your presence. And then perhaps, with time, acceptance will come if you earn it."

"How can you assure this thing?"

"I have long considered something. Twice now you have experienced a medicine dream, this time at Medicine Lake and earlier, before you rode against the paleface merchants of strong water."

Touch the Sky said, "There were two others during my journey. Smaller visions."

Arrow Keeper nodded. "I have reached a decision."

Grunting with the effort, stiff kneecaps popping, Arrow Keeper rose and stepped outside into the night. Touch the Sky was curious when he heard the acting chief call a young boy over. Arrow Keeper said something and the boy raced off.

Shortly after, to Touch the Sky's astonishment,

Black Elk stepped into the tipi.

"You sent for me, Father?" he was saying as he entered. Then he spotted Touch the Sky, and his jaw slacked open.

"You!" He spoke before he could stop himself.

Arrow Keeper was enjoying himself immensely but kept his smile turned inward.

"Black Elk seems surprised," said Arrow Keeper. "Almost as though he were staring at a ghost."

Black Elk had recovered somewhat and regained his fierce aspect. His dark eyes snapped sparks in the soft light of the tipi. In spite of himself, Touch the Sky again found himself staring at Black Elk's dead lump of ear. The warrior himself had sewn it back onto his head with buckskin thread after a Bluecoat saber severed it.

"Not a ghost, Father," he said, "a turncoat spy who licks the hand of his white masters, then sniffs at our Cheyenne women!"

"So you say." Arrow Keeper looked at Touch the Sky. "Have you seen Wolf Who Hunts Smiling and Swift Canoe?" he asked with exaggerated innocence. "They have been gone ever since you left. No doubt our war chief must wonder where his best bucks are hiding."

Black Elk's discomfort was obvious. Now Touch the Sky understood—Black Elk had ordered his death.

"I have seen them," Touch the Sky replied. Briefly, withholding most of the details, he explained that Swift Canoe was hurt and where they could be found.

"Tell me this also," said Arrow Keeper, his sharp old eyes fastened on Black Elk. "Did they attempt to kill you?"

Vision Quest

The silence inside the tipi grew tense. By Cheyenne law, what Black Elk had done—ordering the assassination of a fellow tribe member without decree of the Headmen—was a serious crime. Black Elk could be stripped of his coup feathers and his possessions, lose his position as war leader.

And thus, thought Touch the Sky, plunge Honey Eater into a destitute marriage. He could not do that.

Touch the Sky met Black Elk's eyes as he spoke. He recalled Wolf Who Hunts Smiling's careful distinction between murder and placing a life in danger.

"They did not lift a finger against me," he replied truthfully enough. "Their bloody battle was with the Pawnee."

Relief washed over Black Elk's face. Arrow Keeper studied Touch the Sky for a long time, then nodded. He understood this gesture: The youth was extending an offer of peace to Black Elk, and Arrow Keeper approved this.

But in his secret heart of hearts, Black Elk was implacable in his jealous hatred. This stinking dog had met secretly with his squaw—perhaps he even lifted her dress and bulled her! He could not speak this shame to the others, but neither could he let this outsider return so Honey Eater would see him. Her heart was already filled with thoughts of him as it was.

Arrow Keeper seemed to read much of this in his war chief's face. Now, his voice all authority and business, he said, "The Councillors meet soon. You will make the following announcement. As of this day, Touch the Sky has become my apprentice.

He is blessed with the gift of vision-seeking. Therefore I will teach him the arts of the medicine man."

Both Black Elk and Touch the Sky were stunned by this proclamation. Arrow Keeper was not only acting chief but the tribe's permanent medicine man. This double authority gave his decision the force of law. Touch the Sky's acceptance or rejection by the tribe meant little now—with this important decision, Arrow Keeper had ended all talk of banishment or execution.

"Your training will be hard," he said to Touch the Sky. "And long. There is much to learn, and a young man can quickly grow bored with it. But I am convinced Maiyun has marked you out for a shaman."

Touch the Sky nodded. He was still surprised but submitted humbly. Black Elk, however, started to protest.

"Father! Think on this thing. River of Winds—"

"River of Winds," Arrow Keeper interrupted him, "is a good, honest brave. But he has been deceived by appearances. This buck before you is straight-arrow Cheyenne!"

"But he—"

"Now my old ears can hear no more," said Arrow Keeper. "Your chief has spoken. Now leave, both of you, and let an old man smile in his dreams."

Touch the Sky left his possessions in his tipi. Most of the activity in camp was now centered around the various lodges and the common square, where the young men were gathering for the pony races. He avoided those places, walking down to the river to bathe.

By chance Little Horse had just returned to camp from a word-bringing mission. Arrow Keeper had sent him to Sun Dance's Lakota village to inform the Sioux of the place and time for the upcoming chief-renewal. Little Horse had led his pony to the river to drink. Touch the Sky spotted him and the two friends had joyously embraced.

Touch the Sky was still recounting the events of his remarkable journey to Medicine Lake as the two friends headed back toward Touch the Sky's tipi. Abruptly, Little Horse laid a hand on his friend's arm.

"Hold, brother," he said in a whisper.

He pointed toward Touch the Sky's tipi. Because he had no clan affiliation in this Northern Cheyenne band, Touch the Sky's tipi, like the chief's, stood by itself.

In a slanting shaft of pale silver moonlight directly in front of the tipi knelt Honey Eater. Touch the Sky felt his pulse quicken at this unexpected glimpse of her frail beauty.

Every evening when Touch the Sky was away from camp, Honey Eater added another ritual to her nightly habit of picking fresh columbine for her hair: She would also stop in front of his tipi to verify that the stone was still there—the stone which he had placed there as a symbol of his eternal love. When it melted, he had sworn to her, so too would his love for her.

Tonight, again, it was still there. Honey Eater knelt, picked up the smooth round piece of white marble. For a moment she pressed it to the chamois-soft skin over her heart. An involuntary sob hitched in her chest, escaped in a choking gasp. Teardrops formed on her eyelids, and she placed the stone back down, hurrying away.

Touch the Sky was left speechless for a long time, doubting what he had seen. Then, when he could deny it no longer, he looked at his friend.

"Did my eyes alone just see Honey Eater?"

Little Horse shook his head. "Brother, *this* was no vision! You are a true warrior and can read many signs. But you are slow to grasp what any jaybird could tell you. Honey Eater loves you strong and true. What we have just seen, this takes place each night you are gone from camp. She hides it well, but I have seen."

"Each night I am gone," repeated Touch the Sky in a dumb trance of joy. A tight bud of emotion locked deep inside him threatened to blossom.

"Believe it, Bear Caller! Have I ever talked more than one way to you? Brother, Honey Eater has placed herself at great risk to learn about you. She cries for you and starts up, hope burning in her eyes, every time a rider approaches camp."

These words were soothing balsam for the aching wound in his heart. Touch the Sky's throat swelled tight with emotion.

"Brother," said Little Horse, "perhaps it is wrong to fan your hopes now that Honey Eater wears the bride-shawl. But she loves you, not Black Elk! I am no gossip like the women who buzz around the sewing lodge. But I have heard a thing."

"If you are no gossiping woman, then do not play the coy one either. Speak of this thing."

"You know that my cousin, Long Sash, is a Bowstring?"

Touch the Sky nodded. The Bowstrings were one of the six Cheyenne military societies, open to warriors of any clan. Black Elk too was a Bowstring.

"Long Sash was visiting at their dance lodge when Black Elk showed up with blood in his eye. You know that Black Elk despises all talk of feelings. But Long Sash says Black Elk had been drinking corn beer with the Lakota. He spoke of cutting off Honey Eater's braids to shame her into doing her duty as his wife. He swore by the four directions that she *would* give him a son whether she chose to or not.

"Brother, is it not as plain as tracks in fresh mud? Honey Eater is not lying with her own husband. Do you think any woman can treat Black Elk this way and not suffer for it? Her heart is for you, buck!"

First Arrow Keeper, now Little Horse—both assuring him Honey Eater's heart belonged to him despite everything. And now Touch the Sky had seen the proof with his eyes. A woman in love with her husband would not be crying in front of another man's tipi!

Honey Eater loved him. Now he had the best reason of all for staying. Never mind that she was married to Black Elk. It was marriage in name only. Clearly, Black Elk's furious jealousy foretold great trouble for both of them. But so long as she loved him—so long as her body ached for his as he did for her—he would never let his hopes face anywhere but east.

"Brother," he said to Little Horse, "I am glad

you are my friend. But your loyalty will soon be sorely tested. This time I stay. I am a Cheyenne. Anyone who plans to drive me off must be ready to kill me or die."

CHEYENNE

DOUBLE EDITION
JUDD COLE

One man's heroic search for a world he can call his own.

Arrow Keeper. A Cheyenne raised among pioneers, Matthew Hanchon has never known anything but distrust. The settlers brand him a savage, and when Matthew realizes that his adopted parents will suffer for his sake, he flees into the wilderness—where he'll need a warrior's courage if he hopes to survive.

And in the same volume...

Death Chant. When Matthew returns to the Cheyenne, he doesn't find the acceptance he seeks. The Cheyenne can't fully trust any who were raised in the ways of the white man. Forced to prove his loyalty, Matthew faces the greatest challenge he has ever known.

___4280-0 $4.99 US/$5.99 CAN

CHEYENNE

JUDD COLE

Don't miss the adventures of Touch the Sky, as he searches for a world he can call his own.

Cheyenne #14: Death Camp. When his tribe is threatened by an outbreak of deadly disease, Touch the Sky must race against time and murderous foes. But soon, he realizes he must either forsake his heritage and trust white man's medicine—or prove his loyalty even as he watches his people die.

_3800-5 $3.99 US/$4.99 CAN

Cheyenne #15: Renegade Nation. When Touch the Sky's enemies join forces against all his people—both Indian and white—they test his warrior and shaman skills to the limit. If the fearless brave isn't strong enough, he will be powerless to stop the utter annihilation of the two worlds he loves.

_3891-9 $3.99 US/$4.99 CAN

CHEYENNE

JUDD COLE

Follow the adventures of Touch the Sky as he searches for a world he can call his own!

#3: Renegade Justice. When his adopted white parents fall victim to a gang of ruthless outlaws, Touch the Sky swears to save them—even if it means losing the trust he has risked his life to win from the Cheyenne.
_3385-2 $3.50 US/$4.50 CAN

#4: Vision Quest. While seeking a mystical sign from the Great Spirit, Touch the Sky is relentlessly pursued by his enemies. But the young brave will battle any peril that stands between him and the vision of his destiny.
_3411-5 $3.50 US/$4.50 CAN

Dorchester Publishing Co., Inc.
P.O. Box 6613
Edison, NJ 08818-6613

Please add $1.75 for shipping and handling for the first book and $.50 for each book thereafter. NY, NYC, PA and CT residents, please add appropriate sales tax. No cash, stamps, or C.O.D.s. All orders shipped within 6 weeks via postal service book rate. Canadian orders require $2.00 extra postage and must be paid in U.S. dollars through a U.S. banking facility.

Name_____
Address_____
City _____ State_____ Zip_____
I have enclosed $_____in payment for the checked book(s).
Payment <u>must</u> accompany all orders.☐ Please send a free catalog.

CHEYENNE
JUDD COLE

Born Indian, raised white, he swore he'd die a free man.

#10: *Buffalo Hiders*. When white hunters appear with powerful Hawken rifles to slaughter the mighty buffalo, Touch the Sky swears to protect the animals. Trouble is, Cheyenne lands are about to be invaded by two hundred mountain men and Indian killers bent on wiping out the remaining buffalo. Touch the Sky thinks it will be a fair fight, until he discovers the hiders have an ally—the U.S. Cavalry.
__3623-1 $3.99 US/$4.99 CAN

#11: *Spirit Path*. Trained as a shaman, Touch the Sky uses strong magic time and again to save the tribe. Still, the warrior is feared and distrusted as a spy for the white men who raised him. Then a rival accuses Touch the Sky of bad medicine, and if he can't prove the claim false, he'll come to a brutal end—and the Cheyenne will face utter destruction.
__3656-8 $3.99 US/$4.99 CAN

#12: *Mankiller*. A mighty warrior, Touch the Sky can outlast any enemy. Yet a brave named Mankiller proves a challenge like none other. The fierce Cherokee is determined to count coup on Touch the Sky—then send him to the spirit world with a tomahawk through his heart.
__3698-3 $3.99 US/$4.99 CAN

Dorchester Publishing Co., Inc.
P.O. Box 6613
Edison, NJ 08818-6613

Please add $1.75 for shipping and handling for the first book and $.50 for each book thereafter. NY, NYC, PA and CT residents, please add appropriate sales tax. No cash, stamps, or C.O.D.s. All orders shipped within 6 weeks via postal service book rate. Canadian orders require $2.00 extra postage and must be paid in U.S. dollars through a U.S. banking facility.

Name _____
Address _____
City _____ State _____ Zip _____
I have enclosed $_____in payment for the checked book(s).
Payment <u>must</u> accompany all orders.☐ Please send a free catalog.

DOUBLE EDITION
The West is Taggart's land—his gun his only friend!
JAKE McMASTERS

Bloodbath. They are a ragtag bunch of misfits when Taggart finds them, a defeated band of Apaches—but he turns them into the fiercest fighters in the Southwest. And then, on a bloody raid into Mexico, some of his men rebel, and Taggart has to battle for his life while trying to reform his warriors into a wolf pack capable of slaughtering anyone who crosses their path.

And in the same action-packed volume...

Blood Treachery. From the Arizona Territory to the mountains of Mexico, Taggart and his wild Apaches ride roughshod over the land. Settlers, soldiers, and Indians alike have tried to kill White Apache, but it'll take cold cunning and ruthless deception. And when a rival chieftain sets out to betray Taggart's fierce band, they learn that the face of a friend can hide the heart of an enemy.

___4271-1 $4.99 US/$5.99 CAN